Praise for **I'm Frankie Sterne** by Dave Margoshes

"[Margoshes] has created a lively and often lyrical portrait of an uncertain but open-minded young man trying to find his place and some meaning in the world."

—*The Winnipeg Free Press*

"Margoshes observes well the details of the era . . ."

—*The Edmonton Journal*

"This whimsical novel is a delight to read. Margoshes peels away the personas of his character like you'd peel an onion, but in the end it is still left to us to decide whether or not Frankie's search is rewarded."

—*The Star Phoenix*

"Frankie Sterne does more one-night stands, dons and discards more outer layers than Gypsy Rose Lee. I can't think of a livelier way to revisit the sixties than to follow Frankie around the continent. This debut novel should travel nicely."

—Dave Carpenter

Drowning
MAN

Dave Margoshes

NEWEST
PRESS

National Library of Canada Cataloguing in Publication Data
Margoshes, Dave, 1941-
Drowning man / Dave Margoshes.

ISBN 1-896300-57-X

I. Title.
PS8576.A647D76 2003   C813'.54   C2002-911461-6
PR9199.3.M354D76 2003

Editor for the Press: Lynne Van Luven
Cover and interior design: Ruth Linka
Cover image: Mike Reichert Steinhauer
Author photo: Bryan Schlosser

Canadian   Patrimoine
Heritage   canadien

NeWest Press acknowledges the support of the Canada Council for the Arts, the Alberta Foundation for the Arts and the Edmonton Arts Council for our publishing program. We also acknowledge the financial support of the Government of Canada through the Book Publishing Industry Development Program (BPIDP) for our publishing activities.

NeWest Press
201–8540–109 Street
Edmonton, Alberta
T6G 1E6
(780) 432-9427
www.newestpress.com

1 2 3 4 5 07 06 05 04 03

PRINTED AND BOUND IN CANADA

This book is dedicated

to the memory of my father,

Harry Margoshes,

and to that of Herman Morgenstern

What is life? It is a flash of a firefly in the night.
It is a breath of a buffalo in the winter time.
It is as the little shadow that runs across the grass
and loses itself in the sunset.

—Crowfoot

"Remember this in the future—if I order a limousine, I want that kind of car. And the fastest midget racer you ever saw wouldn't do. Now"—He looked around. "—shall we go any farther?"

—Monroe Stahr in Scott Fitzgerald's *The Last Tycoon*

Plunge in: this is the drowning!

—Johannes Eckhart

I

AFTER ALL THOSE YEARS, THE PLACE THAT SEEMED MOST like home to Sweeny was the morgue, its cool tongue soothing him. In the past few weeks, he'd found himself drawn to the musty, high-ceilinged room by a force he didn't bother to explain to himself but could have; he spent more time there than was necessary, breathing in the dust, letting the communal memory that hovered there seep into his pores, sweat moving backwards. If there was such a thing as learning through osmosis, he believed, this was the place for it—let a Martian loose in a newspaper morgue for a few hours, not rifling through files written in a language it couldn't comprehend but just *sitting*, letting the dust settle, allowing some spark of its own tribal memory to be kindled, and it would come away with, if not knowledge, at least some *sense* of the people it had come to visit.

The morgue took up most of the second floor of the old building, what had once been *his* old newsroom. It was cool here, too, always three degrees cooler than the newsroom in the summer, three degrees warmer in the winter; that's the way it was at other papers he'd worked, too—

something to do with the way paper absorbed moisture. And behind the glass door, the racket of the typewriters and wire machines, the ringing telephones and babble of voices in the attached new building could no longer be heard—it was the only spot in the whole complex where you could hear yourself think. But it was more than that, of course. There was history here, not just abstract particles seeking a place to settle, but Sweeny's own, and what he was doing most of the time when he crept back here was pleasantly resisting the temptation to plunge into it, like a terrier into leaves.

If he dug back far enough—over forty years, back to the days when the morgue was no more than a pile of old papers stacked behind Ezra Highmountain's desk, where the old man would throw a copy every Wednesday after he was through with his scowling inspection—he'd be able to find the first story ever to carry his byline. That was more than history. That was his youth.

Later, the young Sweeny as editor and proprietor himself had assigned the overflowing pile a small room of its own, and, briefly, hired the compositor's wife, a former school teacher, to come in a few hours a week to clip and file, turning the unruly stacks into a true archive where things could actually be found. Now that room had expanded four- or sixfold and the filing evolved into a complicated system with indexes and card catalogues in shiny maple boxes with smoothly sliding drawers. Still, not everything could be found.

"Can I help you, Mr. Sweeny?"

Behind her glasses, the cool brown eyes of the girl were smiling at him—*Here, old-timer, let me give you a hand.* There were three of them working in the morgue, women, really, but Sweeny thought of them as girls, and couldn't remember, couldn't be bothered to remember, which one was which—there was a Nancy, a Lois and, he thought, a Jean or Joan. He didn't like the way they called the place the "library," like some sanitized repository of dusty books that was merely *about* life, rather than artifacts of life itself, nor the way they called him "Mr. Sweeny," as if he himself were some relic, to be treated with respect more for his age than his worth. "Been in this business long as I have and you get to know that any-body who calls you mister is up to no good," Highmountain had told him. It was true.

"No, don't trouble yourself, I'll find it. This is *L* here, right?" He ges-tured toward the open catalogue drawer protruding into his belted mid-section. The girl couldn't see the identifying index card snapped to the front of the drawer but the one directly above had a *K,* so it was obvious.

"Yes. Well, when you find what you want, let me know the number and I'll get it for you." She turned away to hide her frown. Sweeny watched her hips, snug in slacks the colour of new leaves, recede around the corner of the stacks. The morgue girls were possessive. You were supposed to tell them what you were looking for, or, if they were busy, write it down on a sheet of lined paper on a clipboard hanging above the desk near the door, and they'd look it up for you, get it out of the stacks, put it in an out-bas-ket for you to pick up. If you were in a hurry, too damn bad. Deadlines could come and go, the building could burn down, they didn't care. It was more than mere impatience that goaded Sweeny to circumvent this proce-dure, of course—he just liked doing things himself, and he liked being here. In here, with the dust.

He ruffled the index cards with his thumb, frowning with irritation. "Limehouse," "Limeric," "Limhouse, Henry R."—that one caught his eye and he stuck his thumb down to stop the cards and leaned forward squint-ing. Limhouse, that old son of a bitch, was still alive. That was clear because a small black circle would be beside the name if there was an obituary file on him. Not much information on the card, just the name, address, and the succulent piece of news that the subject was owner-manager of Timber Chevrolet. A car salesman, that was a good one. They'd been pals, of sorts, in high school. Well, that wasn't exactly true. They'd known each other, been in the same class. Henry had been too clumsy to learn how to drive, Sweeny remembered *that*; had to give up bicycles after demolishing half a dozen of them, sometimes even had trouble walking without falling on his face. Henry was the guy who always got drunk first, had to be taken home. A car salesman, that was a laugh. He'd have to go out and see old Limy, call him, at least. Or stop by the Chevy place and have the boy take him out for a spin. Limhouse. Maybe that was who he was thinking of. No, he didn't think so. He flipped past—"Liminsky," "Limley," "Limner," "Limpsin." He stopped and flipped the last card back. No "Limousine."

The file drawer slid shut with a rasp and a bang and Sweeny flexed his shoulders, scratched the back of his head where the white hairs were thinnest. "Hmmmm. Limousine. Limousine. Shit." He hated going back to his desk empty-handed, hated to leave the cool dust.

"Find it?" The girl was right behind him, and Sweeny realized he'd been mumbling out loud.

"Nope, couldn't find it. I mean, it's not there. Limousine, Nicolas. These the only master files you've got?"

The girl gave him a bright, patronizing smile. "That's all there is, Mr. Sweeny." She put the eraser end of her pencil to her overly red lips, and Sweeny shook his head to dispel a rude thought.

"Let me think . . . Limousine." The girl frowned, the chocolate eyes darkening slightly behind the lustre of her glasses. "Is he from Timber?"

"Well, I don't know. I just know I know his name, but I don't know from where." He tapped his forehead. "Been a lot of places, got a lot of names floating around up here, along with a lot of other garbage. Sometimes it's hard to pin them down. Let's take a look at the encyclopedia."

The girl led the way, her lime-green hips casting a light for Sweeny to follow. Together they pored over crisp, dry pages.

"Doesn't look like many people use this," Sweeny said. The closest entry in the *Britannica* was Limousin, a region of France and a breed of cattle.

"Nothing here, Mr. Sweeny." The girl had been going through the *Americana* and the *Columbia*. Sweeny took a gamble on *Who's Who*, first the American edition, then the Canadian. The most recent edition they had was 1968, already two years out of date.

He shook his head, the left side of his mouth lifting slightly. "Maybe I was wrong. Thanks for the help."

"That's all right. Maybe it'll come to you." The girl smiled.

Despite his bias against her, she was pretty and seemed nice enough. He felt his irritation evaporate. He wished he knew which one she was. Nancy?

"Most things do." He smiled ruefully. "Most things do."

❦

He had been doing obituaries, an early morning pre-deadline chore he found not at all disagreeable, starting the day by recording the stories of those who had failed to see another one. The obit was the news story in its purest form, Sweeny believed, the drama of life reduced to its bare essentials, life itself, and death, like a biography or a Russian novel. Fires, robberies, murders, elections—they were all good, especially news stories about murders, which were, after all, dressed-up obits—but they didn't have the appeal of a good obituary, its simplicity. As a cub, he'd written plenty of them, but it had been years. The big papers he'd worked on in Toronto and Washington rarely ran them anymore, except for notables, but the little *Chroncle* in provincial Timber maintained the tradition—in death, everyone in the community was equal, more or less. A banker got more column inches than a plumber, sure, but everyone got some kind of story. Sweeny liked that.

The procedure was as simple as the stories' own nature: the mortuaries called in the news of the night, usually with plenty of time to spare. Sweeny sat at his typewriter, drinking coffee from a paper cup and juggling the calls. He'd jot down the information on a printed form, and, as soon as he'd hung up, begin to type.

"Francis Laedeker, 86, a retired member of the Timber fire department, died last night after a long illness." He'd wave for the copy boy, who'd bring him the file on Laedeker from the morgue. In the yellowed clippings, he'd discover that the man had been an original member of the department, way back when it was all volunteers, that he'd been injured once, badly, in the Woodward's fire in 1946, when a whole square block of downtown went up. The funeral director hadn't given him this information, but this was the stuff that made the story worth reading—the same stuff that had made the old fireman's life worth living.

Before the story was finished, the phone would usually ring several more times and Sweeny would accumulate pages of notes. The copy boy hustled back and forth to the morgue, bringing out the files. In a city like Timber, there were few people who hadn't been in the paper at least once—when they'd played hockey with the Senior A league, been promoted or retired or married, elected to office, honoured by the Kinsmen for long service.

The whole process—from first phone call to deadline—took about an hour, and rarely in the two months Sweeny had been doing the chore were there more deaths during the night than one reporter could handle in that time.

One good, fast, thorough reporter.

But today, the Limousine call had been the first and it was preying on his mind as he wrote the other obits, upsetting the routine.

"Sweeny? I got a good one for you this morning." The voice was that of a round, fat man, the kind who played Santa at office parties, but Sweeny knew it belonged to Harold Benno, a tall, lean, sharp-eyed man who officiated at Benno & Benno Funeral Home, a man who seemed to have been made to order for his vocation. "Check this name, will ya? Limousine, Nicolas Limousine."

"I know him," Sweeny said, without hesitation.

"No kidding? You know this guy? Nobody else does. Where from?"

"I mean, I know the name," Sweeny said. He smiled at Benno's use of the word "guy" to describe a corpse. Benno took his work most seriously only in the company of the bereaved. "I don't remember where. An actor?"

"Not with the face this guy has. I can't tell you much, I'm afraid. Don't know if you'll even want to put it in the paper, not for a while, anyway. Died during the night at the Queen's. Nobody with him. Had just checked in. No identification hardly, I understand. Just the name, that's all I know, that and he's a big man, kind of an ugly puss. Wouldn't even guess his age until I examine him, which I haven't done yet, could be anywhere from forty to eighty."

"Limousine," Sweeny said thoughtfully. "Why am I getting this from you, by the way? Sounds like the police reporter should be getting it from the cops."

"Oh, maybe he is, I'm not stopping him. But I don't think they're involved anymore. Natural death, they turned the body over to me. Anyway, this isn't a regular death notice I'm giving you, Sweeny. I'm just *telling* you."

"Well, thanks. I didn't mean to sound like I don't appreciate it. *Limousine*. It'll come to me. Christ, I've interviewed so many people. . . . When I think of it, I'll let you know." His eyes flicked to the clock above the news desk. "Anything else?"

"Two old folks," Benno said flatly, back to business.

Sweeny took them and began to work on the first one, Agatha McLeod, a long-time resident, founding member of the St. James Anglican Church, former president of the Timber Rose Society, former president of the Kootenay Horticultural Society. At home, after a long illness. The phone rang. It was an hour before he was finished with the lot— five stories recounting in brief the lives of five souls who hadn't made it through the night. An average bunch. Agatha and the other old-timer, in his eighties and living in old-age home; a businessman in his forties, ticker wound down; an infant, cold and blue in its crib; and a teenager, his brains and guts blended with motor oil in a viscous puddle at the base of a utility pole on the highway. De Lisso, the police reporter, would have the story of the accident—that the boy was killed, his automobile totalled, how fast he was going, what got in the way, what the policeman on the scene had to say—but it was left to Sweeny to put together the pieces of the dumb bastard's life in a chronological order for the world to see. Not much to say about a seventeen-year-old boy—born, took communion, attended school, played defence for two years on the school hockey team. The paragraph listing survivors was longer than the three biographical ones that came above.

He'd left Limousine for last, then gone to the morgue himself to check the name out.

That had turned out to be a waste of time, although the sight of the brown-eyed librarian's tight green hips swaying in front of him did put an idea into his head, spinning out of particles of dust into a recognizable shape. Four months was too long to go without, even at Sweeny's age. As he made his way back to his desk, he tried to summon up the face, name, *anything* of the woman he'd last been with, but she was a blur, part of the omelet of sensations that had been his final binge in New York. He gave his head a shake, to dispel those ghosts, those tinglings. That was a different life.

On his desk, the Limousine obit form looked up at him like a reproach. Sweeny had scribbled question marks on some of the blanks, but most were empty. He picked up the form and looked it over:

CHRONICLE OBITUARY FORM

Please supply the information asked for below and send to the newspaper office as quickly as possible. Relatives, friends and neighbours of the deceased will appreciate prompt reporting of this news so that they may attend funeral services or send condolences.

Full Name of Deceased: ___ Nicolas (?) Limousine ___

Address: ___ ? died at Queen's ___

Age: _??????? 40 to 80 ??????_

Date of Death: ___ overnight—Wed morning 4/8 ___

Place of Death: _ hotel room ___

Cause of Death: ___ ?????? natural ??????? ___

Time and Date of Funeral: ___ not set ___

Place of Funeral: _____ ???? ___

Place of Burial: ___ ??????? ___

Officiating Clergyman: _____

Place of Birth: _____

Places and Lengths of Residences: _____

_____

Occupation: _____

Public Offices: _____

Maiden Name (if Married Woman): _____

Name, Address of Surviving Wife

(or Husband): _____

_____

Please Turn Over

(Form 48)

On the back were more blanks to be filled in: Marriage, When, To Whom; Surviving Children, Names, Addresses; Surviving Brothers, Sisters, Names, Addresses; Parents (if living), Names, Addresses; Number of Grandchildren (Great, Great-Great etc.); Other Survivors; Organizations, Office Held; Organizations, Member; Additional Information. They were all blank.

He sighed—still more than five minutes till deadline. He swivelled out of his chair and walked three desks down to where De Lisso was banging away at a typewriter, his heavy eyebrows beetled into a frowning shield as effective as a green eyeshade.

"Jim, got anything on a natural death at the Queen's, cat named Limousine?"

"Nope." De Lisso didn't look up. He was attacking the big Remington Standard with single-minded determination, eyes narrowed to protect them from a stream of smoke curling up from the cigarette clenched between his thin lips. He was a mild man, a family man who grew cabbages and prize-winning zucchinis in his back yard, but who affected a ferocious demeanour on the job, as if to hide a part of his life he was ashamed of. In the two months Sweeny had been at the paper, the police reporter had never said hello, just a curt nod of his head in recognition.

"I do. Mind if I check it out?"

"Nope."

This bit of courtesy accomplished, Sweeny went back to his own desk and sat on its edge while he dialled. Four minutes to go.

"Oh, hi, Wilf Sweeny at the *Chronicle*. I'm checking out a report of a natural death at the Queen's Hotel during the night. A male, named Limousine. Got anything?" He listened. "Yeah, I'll hold."

He cradled the receiver in the hollow between his cheek and shoulder and lit a cigarette, one of the Player's he'd happily reacquainted himself with since coming back to Canada, watching the second hand sweep around the clean white face of the clock. He put his hand over the mouthpiece. "Callan, got room for about two inches of public death?" he called.

Across the room, the managing editor lifted his head over a furiously moving pencil, cocked his eye at the clock and nodded sharply, just once, as the voice came back in Sweeny's ear.

"Uh huh, yeah. Yeah. Wait a sec." Sweeny scribbled something on a scrap of notepaper. "Yeah, uh huh. Okay, then . . . oh, wait a sec. How about an autopsy? Uh huh. Inquest? Uh huh. Okay, thanks."

He hung up and slid around the desk to the chair, sandwiched a sheet of carbon paper between two pieces of pulpy copy paper and rolled the package into the typewriter. He had about two minutes. Sweeny smiled, two fingers hovering over the keys. He began to type:

death

Sweeny

4/8

Police are investigating the death overnight of a guest at the Queen's Hotel, apparently of natural causes.

The man, tentatively identified as Nicolas Limousine, no known address, was carrying little in the way of identification, causing difficulty for police in notifying next of kin.

No foul play is indicated, a police spokesman said this morning, but an autopsy to determine the exact cause of death is likely. No decision has been reached on holding an inquest.

-30-

II

INSTEAD OF TAKING HIS LUNCH AT THE COFFEE POT, AS he'd been doing the past few weeks, Sweeny strolled the two blocks over to the Queen's Hotel. The Queen's was on a slight hill and, before plunging into its dark, barn-like tavern, he paused to admire the panoramic mountain view, the Purcells to the east, Selkirks both north and south, the Monashees to the west, beyond the twisting river. An unusually early spring had chased the last of the snow from Timber's streets, but there was still plenty in the mountains and would be for quite a while.

He had the special—hot roast beef sandwich, mashed potatoes and gravy, tiny green salad—and washed it down with a Kokanee, first drink he'd had since coming home. *Home*. He rolled the unfamiliar word around on his tongue along with the mashed potatoes, then swallowed it with another blessed mouthful of beer. He had sworn never again, well, he had sworn to *try*, but he didn't see how one with lunch could hurt, and it didn't, not that he could notice anyway.

He enjoyed the smell and sound of the tavern, a place where you could put your face to the wall and block out everything else. The feel of the place, Sweeny believed, put him into context with himself.

At the next table, a loud man was attempting to fend off a shrill woman. Sweeny eyed them casually, wrinkling his nose without thought. The man was the same size, shape, and age as Sweeny himself—tall, broad-shouldered, thick in the middle, with thinning, grey-specked hair, the kind of man they'd get Robert Mitchum to play in the movies. Or John Wayne, whose teary-eyed face was on Page 1 of the *Chronicle* winning an Oscar last night. That over-the-hill marshal in *True Grit*, a movie Sweeny had liked. This man was over the hill, all right, but he was no Wayne—his mug was battered, red and flat except for a heavily veined nose; his eyes were dark and sunk deep in their sockets, fish in underground pools. His suit was wrinkled and greasy, covered with flecks of lint like points of interest on a roadmap that was wearing thin along the fold lines. The woman was younger, fat, coarse-skinned, with dyed henna hair and reddish shadows above her eyes. She was the kind of woman, Sweeny thought, you never see anywhere but in a tavern, as if they came with the place, along with the chandeliers, the coolers, and the beer taps. If you kissed a woman like that, you could suffocate in her beery breath; if you took her to bed, it would be like sliding into a tight brewery. Sweeny turned away with familiar distaste.

Their conversation had been buzzing at the outer edge of his hearing. Without actually being able to make out any words, he knew the sense of what they were saying: the man had promised something, now he was denying it, she was insisting. She underlined her demands with pokes in his ribs from a pointed finger wielded like a policeman's stick. Suddenly, the voices rose, pulling Sweeny into their orbit.

"Gee-zuzz, didja ever see such a woman?"

Sweeny raised his head to look at the man, who gazed back with drunken calm, mouth twisted into a crooked smile, hands lifted in mock despair. He had contorted himself in his chair, arched back, so his knees were still facing into the table but his trunk was turned toward Sweeny. The woman was motionless, one sharp-fingered hand extended toward her companion's back, an expression of expectation on her moon face.

"Eh, didja?" the man asked. He nodded his head to make it clear he was talking to Sweeny, not himself. "Didja ever *see* such a *woman*?"

"Yeah, I have." A kaleidoscope of faces flashed through Sweeny's mind.

"Where?" The man's tone had coloured slightly, edging sideways from good humour to belligerence.

"Here, a million other dives just like it." A sooty window floated into his line of vision, behind it luminescent winter night frosted with stars, the cold thick as cream, and the ache returned to his shoulders, the feeling of the hard, bare floor beneath them. In his stomach, a fist opened, closed, opened again. He shook his head.

"Hah." The man sputtered with laughter, banging his fist against the table and upsetting a glass of beer. The woman, too, began to quake, the flesh on her arms jiggling.

Sweeny's chair made a sharp scraping noise as he got up.

"Hey, where ya goin', buddy? Siddown, siddown, have a beer with us."

"No, thanks, I'm meeting someone." He pointed to the door to the lobby.

"Who's that?" The belligerence in the man's voice, sweeping back without warning, caused Sweeny to stop.

"Cat named Limousine, Nick Limousine. You oughta know him, used to hang around in here quite a bit in the old days, eh?"

"Nope, don't know 'im." The drunk rolled his shoulders, borrowing dignity. "I don't hang around this crummy place much." He gave Sweeny his back.

"How about you?" Sweeny turned to the woman, talking over her friend's shoulder. "Limousine? Big pug-ugly guy. Know him?"

"Lim-o-zeen." She rolled the name on her tongue like candy, sucking at the vowels. "I rode in one, oncet. Me an' the showfer, we went in the back seat . . . " The sentence exploded into a fit of giggling as she tipped forward, bumping her head against the man's. In another minute, Sweeny knew, neither of them would be able to remember what they were laughing at and their quarrel would continue.

For a moment, as he hesitated beside their table, he was pierced by a sliver of loneliness sharp as any he had felt since leaving New York, and a fierce thirst seized him. It would be so easy to sit down, to down another beer, to insinuate his way into the drunken couple's conversation, to loosen his tie, unbutton his collar, forget about work for the day, to forget about his life, to let go, let go. So easy. All he had to do was sit down. Sweeny shook his head. Uh uh, damned if he would *let* it be that easy.

On his way out, he stopped in the lobby, where Charlie Cook, the assistant manager, was standing behind the broad oak counter, nose buried inside the *Chronicle*. "You won't find it there, Charlie," Sweeny said. "It didn't run."

Cook looked up, the bulging nose followed by the disappointing rest of his face. "Sweeny. I didn't think they would, and just as glad, too. The last thing we need is stories about stiffs in our rooms. Christ, what a strange one."

"Don't thank me. I did a story, but it didn't make it in. Too much going on in the world. What'd he die of? Anybody know yet?" He put a Player's in his mouth and leaned toward the small flame of the lighter Cook offered. He was a small man with a wolfish mouth and a weakness for plaid sports jackets. Today's model was red and green, giving him a slightly comical Christmasy look. Sweeny had known him when he was a bellhop and was amazed, meeting him again, at how little he'd changed.

"Damn if I know. Somebody heard a noise about 2 AM and called Bill Weaver, the night clerk. It was just a nervous neighbour, but Bill's a real nervous fellow himself, so he went up to take a look-see. Knocks on the door, no answer. So he lets himself in with the house key. Sure enough, the party's dead, on the floor, rolled out of bed, that's what made the noise. A big man, well over two hundred pounds, I'd say. Good thing for the nervous neighbour, or the maid would've found him when she went in to make the bed. Then there *would* have been hysterics."

Sweeny smiled. "And not much ID, I hear."

"That's the really funny thing. None. A bulging wallet, but all we got out of it was his name, Nicolas Limousine. Ain't that something? Credit cards, that's all there was. The works, too. Chargex, Mastercard, Diner's Club, American Express, BankAmerica, all the oil companies, Carte Blanche, that's a good card, by the way. We don't accept it here, but a lot of hotels do."

"American Express's the only one I've ever had," Sweeny said. "You really need it to get along in Europe. Nothing else?"

"Not a thing. Just all those credit cards. No Social Insurance, no driver's licence, not even a library card. And no money, either. He paid with American Express, or said he would. Hadn't actually paid the bill yet, said he might want to make some long distance calls. I'm stuck with his bill, top of everything else."

"You didn't get an imprint off his card?"

"Naw, we don't bother with that, wait till they check out."

Sweeny's tongue clucked in sympathy. "No pictures in the wallet?"

"No pictures, no scraps of paper like we all have in our wallets. Nothin'."

"No driver's licence. Huh. How'd he arrive?"

"Beats me. Cab, I guess, from the airport. Just came walking in yesterday afternoon, no reservation, asked for a room for the night. Had a suitcase. You know, as long as they have luggage, we don't ask any questions. It's funny, though, you know? Seems almost like he came here to die."

"Yeah, it's funny." Sweeny was wishing mightily he hadn't had the beer with lunch, or that he could have another. "What about the suitcase? And, hey, *did* he make any calls?"

"I've got the suitcase in my office. Don't know about the calls. Wait, I'll check with the switchboard girl. Kind of like to know that myself."

Sweeny propped his elbows on the counter and glanced through the paper. Considering some of the junk they'd used, he wondered why his mystery death hadn't run. For some reason, it seemed important. The obits took up a good chunk of page two, sharing the space above the ads with the minor crime stuff, some regional wire news from Kamloops and Kelowna, and the weather. Two nickel-and-dime break-ins from De Lisso could have been bumped easy.

He shook his head, glancing at the weather story. He'd been awoken during the night by thunder, unusual for so early in spring, and then, to his surprise, a single wave of sheet lightning that illuminated the moonless night sky longer than he would have thought possible. Then, as he lay back and sought sleep again, a fierce but brief downpour had melted away the last orphan patches of snow and left the city smelling newborn in the morning. But there was no mention of any of that in the wire story from Kamloops, just the routine: continued unseasonably mild, chance of evening showers, chance of rain Thursday.

He flipped the paper over to where a dark-jowled Nixon flashed his death-head grin from Page 3, but, before he could read the caption, he felt eyes on him and looked up to catch a slim girl with blonde hair like a hay-mow turning away behind the counter. He smiled but she kept her lovely back to him. That reminded him of something, which, in turn, made his thirst stronger.

"Son of a bitch," Cook said, coming through a doorway. He was frowning, beads of perspiration standing out on his forehead. "Son of a bitch made almost a hundred dollars worth of calls last night—Los Angeles, New York, Miami, London . . . London, *England* . . ." He glanced at the piece of paper in his hand. "And some place called King of Prussia, Pennsylvania."

"King of Prussia, that's near Blue Balls," Sweeny said, brightening. "Coal mining country, something like around here. Pennsylvania Dutch, hexes, all that."

"Blue Balls, my ass. *Son* of a bitch. Not only a stiff in a room, but stiffed for a hundred-dollar phone bill. And he had a meal sent up to his room, too. Steak. The New York cut. *Shit.*"

Behind Cook, the blonde girl was answering the phone, shaking her mane like a horse flicking away flies.

"Get hold of one of these credit cards, Charlie. That ought to square it." Sweeny went back to the tavern and had a beer. Halfway through it, he ordered a shot of rye and gulped it down. One wouldn't hurt, he was sure of that—*but that's all, goddamn it, that is all.*

It was a nice day for walking, the kind of April day when you get the feeling everything bad is coming to an end and good things will be falling with the next shower. Sweeny's car was in the *Chronicle* lot, which suited him fine. It was a rusted-out clunker, a '55 bottom-of-the-line Plymouth, the cheapest thing he could find when he got to town. It would have to last until he was sure he was staying and could feel free to buy something better. The less it was used, the better he liked it.

He headed north on Mountain Avenue, the snowy peaks of the Selkirks looming over the cityscape. Walking the streets of the town he'd been born and raised in was still a strange experience, even after two months. Once he had known everyone in town, if not by name at least by face. Now, thirty-five years after he had said goodbye for what he thought was the last time, Timber had mushroomed from the lumber-company town it had been into a small city with a variety of economic interests, and there were too many people for anybody to know. Most of those he had known were either dead or gone, Sweeny was finding out, which was why he'd been so tickled to run across Limhouse's name.

There were some, of course, who gave him points of reference, old friends, classmates, neighbours—they kept popping up, unexpectedly, like old Limy, the Chevy dealer, in strange places, sometimes even on the street. "Hey, aren't you Sweeny? Wilf Sweeny? Remember me?" And there were sons and daughters of people he'd known. He'd see their names in the paper, or find himself doing business with them. "I knew your father, we grew up together," he'd say. Usually, the response was colder than he would have expected, suspicious. "Well, isn't that something? Mom and Dad live in Phoenix now, for the climate. How about that?" Then they'd move on, nervous, speechless in the face of the unexpected connection to their own lives. So much for western hospitality. A small town becomes a city too quickly. Thirty-five years—is that one generation or two? How do you measure things like generations? His was supposed to have been the lost one, or did you have to have lived in Paris to qualify for that? During the war, he'd been there, and afterward he'd drunk at all those bars where Hemingway and Callaghan had gone. Hadn't made him feel much different, no more nor less a man. The whisky had been good, though.

Sweeny paused at the bank corner, Mountain and Main—Bank of Montreal kitty-corner from the Royal, Nova Scotia from the Timber Credit Union. The old-fashioned round clock on the Montreal showed 1:15; the credit union's red neon said 1:20. He was supposed to go down to the sewer plant that afternoon for a feature. They were using a new treatment system or something—Callan had given him a note he hadn't carefully read yet. Like obituaries, sewer stories were second nature to Sweeny. Everywhere you go, there are sewers, and the refuse of a city flows into them, no matter what the city is or where it is, regardless of politics, economy, or colour, drought or famine, and they always make news. Not very good reading, unless a dead body pops up in one, as Sweeny had sometimes seen, but news nonetheless. The taxpayers supported them, and that made them news. In a deeper way, they were thick with the secrets people flushed away, and *that* made them news. Sweeny shook his head, grimacing at his metaphors. He had forty minutes or more until his appointment and he didn't think there was anything in the newsroom that needed him. He had to watch his step—almost sixty-three fucking years old, more than forty-five years in the racket and he was on probation. That was a laugh, especially on the paper where he'd started out, had once owned. Still, the job was a small miracle and he didn't want to sour it. But this Limousine thing had him by the balls and he knew what would happen if he didn't shake it loose. Maybe there'd be a story in it, anyway.

He crossed the street and went two blocks west on Main till he came to an imposing building of spotless white stucco adorned with pretentious faux-Greek arches and pillars, the name Benno & Benno incised into stone above the door in the fashion of a headstone. Although the word "mortuary" didn't appear anywhere on the building, its purpose was self-evident. Sweeny opened the heavy oak door and stepped into a modest lobby carefully decorated to give the appearance of the entranceway to the private home of someone well off but not ostentatious. Beyond the lobby, he knew, the draped chapels and sitting rooms, in various shades of mauve and grey, continued the theme, as did Harold Benno's sparsely furnished office beyond the open door to which Sweeny headed. The pictures on the wall were neutral—Currier and Ives, neither cheery nor depressing—and the decor was easy on the eyes, easy on the seat of the pants. Sweeny slumped into the black leather armchair Benno pointed to and sighed. "Getting warm out, Hal, feels like a good rain coming on."

"I don't like April weather," Benno said. "Too changeable. Cold one day, hot the next, and you can never count on rain. May is dependable. Of course, weather doesn't stop us but it can get us wet." The leathery face cracked into a smile, as if the movement of muscle was an effort. Benno, in his early fifties, looked like somebody's father, although he was, in fact, childless, widowed in middle age with no inclination to seek a second wife, meaning there would be no heir to carry on the family business. Sweeny had known his father in the old days, when the mortuary was called just Benno's, had known Harold too when the lean, antiseptic-smelling man sitting across an uncluttered desk from him was just a kid running errands for his dad. Even then, the younger Benno had looked grown up, with the face of someone's father, as if all that inhalation of death and its fumes had smoked him like a ham. It was remarkable how little either the man or his business had changed. Benno offered Sweeny a cigar.

"Thanks, but I can't. Doctor's orders. Shouldn't be smoking these, either." Sweeny lit a cigarette and placed the spent match in a spotless ashtray.

"Think of who Limousine is yet?" Benno had a flat, even voice, with none of the highs and lows that can get in the way of meaning. Sweeny shook his head. "Well, I can't tell you much more than I did this morning. The coroner was here—you know Lloyd Kramer? No, I guess not, he hasn't been here all that long. Nice young fellow. Get this, though, Kramer doesn't *know* what he died of."

"Doesn't know?" Sweeny sat forward.

"I thought it was probably a heart attack. That's what these things usually are, the sudden, middle-of-the-night sort or thing. But Lloyd doesn't think it was a heart *attack*, a coronary disease sort of thing. Doesn't know, in other words, what made the heart stop working."

"You mean something caused the ticker to quit even though it was healthy?"

Benno looked at him coolly over the smouldering end of his cigar. "Something like that. It's not all that common but not that rare, either. A sudden scare could do it. Or a clot somewhere, but Lloyd doesn't think it was a clot. Tension can do it too. People know all about how tension can give you ulcers but they don't know that tension can kill you too. Of course, an autopsy would probably tell quick enough, but Lloyd isn't going to do one." Benno raised his cigar to cut off Sweeny's question. "Doesn't think it would be worth it. Probably right too."

"So what you're saying," Sweeny said, leaning forward to tap his cigarette against the glass tray, "is that this cat Limousine died of something that can't be pinned down."

"That's what *I* think. I think Lloyd does too. Charlie Cook, over at the hotel, thinks this fellow *came* here to die. Kind of spooky, eh?" Benno tilted his eyebrows like cartoon caterpillars.

Sweeny laughed. "Yeah, I talked to Charlie Cook. But I didn't think morticians ever got spooked."

"Why not? Sure, death doesn't move us very much, we're used to it. I could tell you some stories that would turn even your stomach, Wilf, make chills run up and down your spine too. But, hell, we're human, just like the next fella. When I'm working on someone, I like to at least know who he is. And, far as spooky goes, I'll tell you this. You get to know a lot about the human body in this business, even if you aren't a physician. You get to know a lot about the body in death, and from that you can infer a lot about the body in life. I think people do know, some of them, that they're going to die. So the idea of someone going some place special to die isn't superstition, it's just psychology. The question that puzzles me is, why come *here*?"

"That's what I'd like to know," Sweeny said, rising to leave. "Thanks for the medical lesson."

❧

In his dream, Sweeny is a boy again, getting out of his Uncle Tomas's car in front of the weather-beaten farmhouse, and a woman—is it Greta, or his mother?—is rolling down the porch steps toward him like a cloud, drawing him to her pillow breast smelling of flour and eggs and warm milk, smothering him. "Poor baby, poor baby," she is saying, though whether she is speaking in Swedish or English isn't clear. Uncle Tomas and the car are gone, and the woman is whispering: "Come, Grampa is waiting." Grey paint is chipped from the steps, a pebble sits like a forlorn island in a vast sea on one tread, and there are muddy paw prints leading up, taking the boy's eyes with them to where the old man sits stiff in the rocker above them, staring out at the road as if expecting someone further, not really looking at *them* at all, not looking at *him*.

The boy stands on the porch, on the next-to-the-top step, eyes level with those of the old man, cramped by pain, face dried to a fist. The old man's immobile eyes are two small wounded bluebirds locked in cages of bone and weathered skin. "I've come to live with you, Grampa, is that okay?" the boy says finally.

The old man's eyes blink slowly and his face contorts as he lifts his arms, his head rocking on his thin shoulders like a toy mouse dimly remembered from the boy's childhood. "Ya, boy, ya, come, come here," the old man says. There is darkness, he is alone, adrift in darkness, lost, falling, spinning, floating, then he can feel the hard floor beneath his shoulder blades, hear the dry rasp of a match striking flint, his nostrils filling with the acrid stink of sulfur, a light, above him a window, dark starless night beyond, shivering with cold. "Ya, boy, ya, come, come here." Then he is engulfed by smells, wood and smoke and sweat, and something stronger, something that disturbs Sweeny's sleep now, rolling his body and opening his mouth to a small injured sound at the smell he can never identify, has never smelled again except in his dreams, his chin in the brown hollow of the old man's collarbone, the thick, twisted old hands gripping his shoulder blades, the rocker swaying, creaking. "It be okay now, boy," the old man says in a voice thick and rough, and for reasons the boy cannot hope to understand, he believes him.

III

Thursday

A NEW FORM OF DEHYDRATED FOOD WAS GOING TO BE tested by NASA on the Apollo 13 flight. There were to be no crumbs. On previous flights, they had proven to be a hazard, floating about in the weightlessness of the space capsule. The experimental food had been developed at a cost of $40,000. Computed at three meals a day, for the three astronauts, for the expected eleven days of the flight—ninety-nine meals in all—that came to $404.04 per meal.

Sweeny let out a low whistle and quickly calculated how many dinners at the hotel that would buy him—if each was $4, that would be 101 meals; if only $2, that would be 202; they were, in fact, around $2.50; throw in the tip and whatever, let's say $3, on average, so that would be about 135 meals.

"Holy shit, I could eat over a hundred good meals for what it costs to feed one of these jokers one lousy no-crumb breakfast," he said out loud. "I could eat for four months while that astrofart starves to death after his first and last no-crumb ham on rye." He looked up from his crumpled copy of yesterday's *Chronicle* as if expecting a reply, but there was no one nearby to hear him.

Across the almost empty newsroom, the bleary-eyed morning shift on the copy desk struggled with headlines for stories filed during the night from the bureaus and the wire service morning leads on yesterday's big stories—a major battle in Vietnam and an Israeli air raid in Egypt with many children killed, meaning the headlines on both would be filled with bodycounts. There was also the countdown to Saturday's Apollo launch. One of the astronauts had the measles, and they were giving a replacement crash training to get him ready in time. Peterson, in the slot, McDowell, Carney and Coleman draped around the rim, each with his head lowered over a typewriter, each with an identical puzzled expression flitting about his eyes and lips as if all had been asked the same insoluble question. Sad-eyed Carney, Sweeny noticed, was actually moving his lips, trying out the sound of the words. Perspiration broke out on the back of Sweeny's neck and he frowned at the thought of his own lips yammering away, talking to himself.

To the right of the copy desk was the news desk, a belly button on the bloated rim's tummy, with Callan slouched behind it, a galley proof in one hand, the other hand dialling the phone, the receiver hooked on his shoulder, a pencil in his mouth. Intense, that's what that man is, Sweeny thought. He was half Sweeny's age, but had older eyes and less hair. Not a bad man to work for, though—Sweeny had worked for a bunch, and Callan was okay. He'd been giving Sweeny room, time, and respect—what more could he ask?

Beyond the cluster of editors, Jim De Lisso sat comfortably in the hive of desks that made up the sports department, looking lonely but content, his feet propped up on one typewriter while he pecked casually, one-handed, at another, a phone cradled in the nest formed between his neck and right shoulder. There wasn't any necessity for De Lisso to be over in sports—his own desk sat abandoned in the wide, deserted cityside that took up half the newsroom—he just liked it there.

Where Sweeny himself sat, watching all this, was in the leather swivel chair of the women's editor, a smoothly tailored blonde of indeterminate age to whom Sweeny had taken an immediate dislike, although he coveted her chair. She and her staff—an elderly woman with arms thin as bird legs and a girl still damp with journalism-school dew—wouldn't be in for another hour or two, when work on today's paper would have ended and the daily dislocation of time began again. The word "today" in all copy would mean tomorrow, and "yesterday" would mean today.

For Sweeny, "today" also meant "yesterday." A long time before—he wasn't sure just when but he supposed it was about the same time the drinking had started to get out of hand, whenever *that* was—he had stopped reading the day's paper and turned instead to the previous day's. Nothing as dead as yesterday's news, the saying went, and damn right, Sweeny liked to think, the deader it was, the better he liked it. Today's news was too close; yesterday's couldn't hurt you, not so much, at least.

He turned back to the *Chronicle*, shaking his head again over the astronauts' crumbs, and skimmed past a Vietnam headline. That was a story he didn't like to read any day, day-old or not. He hadn't covered that war, but he'd been to a few others and had seen his fill. There was that photo of Nixon on Page 3 again, looking like death warmed over, railing against the Senate for shooting down a Supreme Court appointment. He turned to the sports pages, shaking his head. The Stanley Cup quarter-finals had started and there wasn't a single Canadian team in the mix.

The phone rang, startling him. He picked it up in the middle of the second ring. "*Chronicle*, Sweeny," he said, reaching for an obit pad and a pencil. A few minutes later, he was typing, his day begun.

"Funeral arrangements are pending at Malloy & Sons Mortuary for Mrs. Clarence (Flo) Reilly, 79, of 247 West Benton St., who died quietly last night following a long illness. . . ." The keys clicked rhythmically, without any apparent effort on Sweeny's part, the information scrawled in his erratic shorthand on the obit form transformed into the clipped, expected sentences that flowed down his spine into his shoulders, arms, hands, fingers, and onto the keys with an electric leap, the words appearing on paper as if by magic. It was so automatic it seemed to have very little to do with him, as if he were no more than an instrument. He hardly paid any attention to what he was doing, stopping in the middle of a sentence to answer the phone and grab his pencil.

"Luck & Luck . . . Mrs. William (Janet) Beard . . . 68 . . ."

Damn, he wished Benno would call.

❧

The day shift begins at 5 AM when Gene, the copy boy, comes in and starts to tear the long, rolled accumulation of the night's news off the wire machines, where they've been piling up since midnight, when the night editor goes home. Peterson, the thick-handed news editor, comes in at 5:45 and sits frowning over a steaming cup of coffee at the morning Canadian Press budget, which Gene has laid on his desk. At six, the rim men come in and get to work on the wire news and last night's leftovers. All they have to fill is page one and half of page two, where the obits go, and the local split page. At 6:30, De Lisso comes in to start running down the police and fire stations, and at 7 AM the on-call reporter, who has been Sweeny since his return to the *Chronicle* two months ago, arrives to help out, and wait on the obits.

At 8 AM, or just a little after, Benno called.

"*Chronicle*, Sweeny."

"Benno & Benno. Have a couple for you this morning. The family called, by the way. That Limousine guy."

"The family?" Sweeny snapped forward, dropping his pencil on the desk and reaching for a cigarette.

"Well, I shouldn't say *family*, maybe," Benno's flat voice droned, "but somebody called. Family is a word we use. From Arlington, Virginia, and said to arrange for a funeral Saturday and . . ."

"Saturday?" Sweeny cut in.

"Yes, this isn't confirmed yet but it'll probably be 3 PM at Memorial, with services here first at 2, no clergy, just a gathering of . . . well, I *guess* the family, and friends. He said quite a few people would be arriving, that I should have a limousine meet all the buses and planes . . ." Benno sounded impressed.

"A limousine?" Sweeny snapped a match against the flint of a crumpled book and drew smoke into his lungs.

"Yeah, sure, a lim . . . oh, I get it, ha ha, very funny. That *is* what the cars are called, Sweeny, and I'm sure there's nothing mysterious about it."

"Didn't say there was. Go on. Who was it who called?"

"Let me see, I've got it written down here . . . a Mr. Harriman, Ormand Harriman, said he was very close to the deceased but didn't actually say he was a relative. I had the impression he was more of a close family friend, that sort of thing."

"Uh huh."

"Very first-class sort of person." Benno's impressed tone had crept back. "Didn't even inquire about the cost, just said he'd take care of everything. Simple but with dignity, plain casket, closed . . ."

"Closed?"

"That's not all that uncommon, especially after an autopsy."

"Autopsy? I thought you said whatshisname, the coroner, wasn't doing one?"

The young redhead who worked in the women's section swished past him, trailing perfume like a cloud of bees. Karen or Barbara. There was a girl on cityside about the same age and build and colouring and Sweeny couldn't keep them straight. "Good morning, Mr. Sweeny," she said, turning past his desk. Sweeny's eyes focused on her hips unconsciously.

"Kramer," Benno was saying. "Seems he got a phone call from Mr. Farr requesting that one be done."

"Farr?"

"The chief Crown prosecutor."

"Oh, yeah, Frank Farr. His dad was the best lawyer this town ever had."

"Oh, I don't know. Bill Trebler beat him out in my book. Bill had a voice like an angel, could convince a jury Pontius wasn't even in *town* when Jesus . . ."

"Anything else on Limousine?" Sweeny interrupted. His eyes were on the wall clock now. The copy boy had just deposited two yellowed envelopes from the morgue on his desk, and the obits were calling to him.

"No, that's all," Benno said. His voice sounded smaller, thinner, as if he had been offended. "I've got a couple for you, though."

By the time he was finished writing, it was 8:40, just five minutes till deadline, and Callan was yelling. Sweeny checked with De Lisso, who still didn't have anything from the cops about the Limousine case, then went out for coffee. He came back a little after nine, pulled out the phone book and dialled the court house.

"Mr. Farr, please," he told the cheerful voice which answered.

"Just a moment, sir, I'll connect you."

Another cheerful voice. "Mr. Farr's office. May I help you?"

"Mr. Farr, please. Wilf Sweeny at the *Chronicle* calling."

"Mr. Farr's in court this morning. Can I take a message?"

Sweeny looked at the clock. "No, I'll find him. Which courtroom?"

On his way out of the newsroom, raincoat over his shoulder, he stopped by the desk of the girl in Women's, determined to break out of the isolation he'd put himself into. He'd checked her byline in yesterday's paper.

"Hey, Karen, how you doing?"

The girl looked up from her typewriter with an amused expression and Sweeny noticed a smear of lipstick on her upper teeth as she smiled, like the soft suggestion of colour along the tight ridges of her pale cheeks.

"I'm fine, Mr. Sweeny. How are *you?*"

"Me? I'm great, never better. But, please, call me Wilf, okay? It's awful, but better than *Mr.* Sweeny. That was my uncle's name, and even *he* didn't like it much."

The girl laughed, shaking her orange hair, which hung shoulder length. Her face was dotted with freckles and she seemed hardly old enough for her job. "Why your uncle? People usually say that about their fathers, don't they?"

"Yeah, well." He shrugged. "My father was *Dr.* Sweeny. But I barely knew him anyway. He died when I was little."

Karen's eyes shifted slightly out of focus, as if trying to adjust to the notion of the big man with white hair and battered face slumped in front of her ever being a child. "Oh, I'm sorry," she said, her voice colouring with conviction, as if consoling someone with a loss still fresh.

"Hey, that was three hundred years ago," Sweeny said. "I'm over it."

"Oh, I know." The girl's cheeks reddened and she laughed with embarrassment. "I just, you know . . ." They fell into awkward silence, and the gulf between them seemed to stretch out like the limitless space astronauts hurtle through. It was more than age, Sweeny knew, a kind of gulf that people of different languages, different cultures, men from different planets must cross. His hand rose, as if to bridge the space between them and gently rub the lipstick from the girl's teeth, and wound up running through his thatch of hair as he shrugged, shifting the raincoat from one shoulder to the other. "Hey, I gotta run," he said. "See you later, eh?"

His eyes were on the floor's linoleum squares and he narrowly avoided banging into Gene at the newsroom door, the first copies of the paper, ink still wet, in his hand. "Hey, better watch that Sweeny," the copy boy said, his acne-scarred face alight as he gazed over Sweeny's shoulder.

"Oh, sorry, kid, I was thinking about something . . ."

"Not me, man, the chick, the *chick*."

❖

Nine PM finds Sweeny ruminating, alone in the bathroom of his newly occupied, anciently furnished apartment, shaving. Too long on the night shift has left him with the annoying tendency to be uncomfortable with the itch of growing hair on his face after sunset, and for many years he shaved in mid-afternoon, just prior to going to work. Now that he's day people again, he's fallen into the habit of shaving twice a day—once in the morning, before work, and a second time in the evening, whenever the spirit moves him or his cheeks begin to twitch.

Whenever nature calls—and it can be almost any given time after 3:30 PM, when his official working day at the *Chronicle* ends—Sweeny is usually available. There is not very much to do in *Chronicle*land, regardless of the weather, for a man in his sixties who, despite all the people he knows, has no friends.

The conversations he's had in the past few weeks, with one or two notable exceptions, have been of the awkward, go-nowhere kind he'd had with the girl in the newsroom, or the kind that morning with Benno—someone who might be described as an old friend, for no better reason than that they'd known each other thirty-five years before—or that afternoon with Farr, the well-oiled Crown prosecutor: short, polite, businesslike for the most part, with just a touch of good humour and nostalgia for what people persisted in calling "the good old days."

"What was so fucking good about them?" Sweeny says aloud. He sloshes water on his face, melting neglected patches of suds first into isolated bubbles, then into a thin sheen, slick and smooth beneath his fingertips as he pats the skin dry. But he has to smile, too, first absently, then broadly at the face he catches in the mirror, smiling absently, then broadly—yeah, all right, some of them had been okay, there *had* been some good times, like those years in Toronto and Washington and New York, those footloose years in Europe after the war. Fucking A, and he knew it.

This Farr, though, he was the kind of bureaucrat Sweeny could remember fucking up good times, worsening bad times the world over since the Year One. What was it Benno had said about that other lawyer he was singing the praises of, the one who wasn't Frank Farr's dad? That he could persuade a jury Pontius Pilate was out of town? Not if *this* guy was the prosecutor, he couldn't. No, this guy was the kind who would make the jurors want to help spring the trap door—but at the same time you knew damn well he didn't see anything wrong with condemning Jesus anyway.

"Mr. Farr? Wilf Sweeny, from the *Chronicle*. Got a minute?"

They were standing in a corridor on the third floor of the courthouse, Sweeny blocking the path of the neat, roundish man like a polar bear in the path of a penguin on an ice floe. Sure, you could go around him, if you didn't mind getting wet.

Farr smiled neatly. "Surely, Mr. Sweeny. If you're the Mr. Sweeny I think you are, then I've heard my father speak of you."

"Judiciously, I hope."

Sweeny had sat through the better part of a dope trafficking preliminary hearing waiting to see Farr, and his mouth was dry, the palms of his hands wet.

"Oh, yes, very good, very good. What can I do for you?" The prosecutor spoke with a toneless precision, like a recorded telephone message.

"I understand you've ordered an autopsy on this Limousine fella."

"Beg pardon? Lim . . ."

"The man who died at the Queen's Hotel the other night."

"Oh, yes. Was that his name? Well, you understand not exactly right. There will be an autopsy performed, but I didn't order it."

"I understood that you had."

Farr smiled sweetly. "You've been in the States, I gather, where they do these sorts of things somewhat more dramatically than we do here." He raised his hand to scratch his forehead just below the hairline with his thumbnail, and glance at his watch. A well-dressed, lean man, another lawyer, strolled by, touching Farr lightly on the shoulder. "Frank." Farr nodded, smiling. He absently turned his face back to Sweeny. "Autopsies are performed as a matter of course in this province, in any instance of unusual or unexpected death that occurs outside the home or where a doctor's care is part of the pre-death procedure."

Jesus, Sweeny says aloud now, *the man talks like a fucking manual.*

"So any hesitancy as to performing an autopsy in this instance was based not so much on procedure as on interpretation." Farr's mouth formed another neat smile, the kind reserved for the end of a conversation.

"Interpretation?"

"Was the death unusual," Farr said flatly. "Dr. Kramer, the coroner, was unsure at first whether this particular death would fit into that definition and he asked my advice. I told him I thought it would."

Sweeny allowed himself to smile. "I get it. And why might the coroner have any doubts as to the unusualness of a death that occurred in the middle of the night in a hotel room to a man with a minimal amount of identification on him?"

This time Farr let impatience seep around the smile, and he glanced openly at his watch. "That would be a medical question, I suppose, or at least one that would be best put to Dr. Kramer. Why don't you ask him?"

"I will." Sweeny put the unused notepad and pencil back in his pocket.

"May I give your regards to my father?" Farr asked as he began to glide down the corridor.

"Please do. He doesn't still live in town, does he?"

"No. He and Mother have a cottage on Vancouver Island, but I speak to him regularly. I'm sure he'll be interested to hear that you've returned to your old stomping grounds."

There was a chilly tinge to Farr's voice, and Sweeny couldn't tell if there was sarcasm there as well. Did he know? How much did anyone know about him?

Sweeny laughed. "I buttonholed him a few times in this same corridor."

"Surely," Farr said.

❖

The apartment Sweeny lives in, in a block of suites on a quiet street filled with similar buildings, is not substantially bigger or significantly different from his first place almost forty-five years before, above a hardware store in the Heights area, not too far from his Uncle Tomas's feed and grain business. There is a small bedroom, a tiny bathroom, and a combination living room-kitchen. The kitchen part of the big room is cluttered with unwashed dishes and the living room part, where Sweeny sits now, a little after nine, slouched in the frayed grey chesterfield, its yellow spread bunching beneath his heavy legs, is little better. Light glows from the cracked yellow shade on the brass floor lamp beside him, illuminating the crammed bookshelves along the wall and the newspapers piled on the plastic-topped desk in the corner, a month's worth of *Chronicles*, all still neatly folded, the copy he puts under his arm when he leaves the office every afternoon to show he's interested. He flicks an ash into an overflowing ashtray with the words Queen's Hotel embossed along the rim and stares absently at a pile of magazines on the floor by the shelves. In the back of his mind, amidst all the clutter *there*, he searches for Limousine.

"Shit."

After seeing Farr, Sweeny had gone back to the office and telephoned the coroner, whose secretary said Dr. Kramer was out, and, before quitting time, wrote three stories for tomorrow's paper: the price of haircuts has gone up twenty-five cents, for the third time in as many years (this based on a interview with two local barbers); the Parks and Recreation Commission will listen to objections to the development of a new playground in the southwest section of the city on Wednesday (this based on a call to the secretary of the commission, at the request of the city hall reporter, snowed under with another story); and Staff Sgt. Louis Holly, US Army, a Canadian citizen living in the States with his father since he was twelve, wounded three times in action, will return to Vietnam "rarin' to go" at the end of his thirty-day leave, part of which he has been spending with his mother, who lives here. This last story was based on an interview Sweeny had done two days earlier, in the home of the soldier's mother, a silent, bitter-mouthed woman who chewed on her lower lip as she sat listening to the two men talking. The disappointed look in her pale eyes was like those Sweeny had seen in the dark, thin faces of German and Italian women after the war as they waited for men they knew would never return. He'd written good stuff in those days, real stories. The stories he was doing for the *Chron* weren't a patch on some of them, but he was glad to have them.

During the course of the afternoon, he also made a number of telephone calls, starting with the Pacific Western ticket agent: "Hi, Wilf Sweeny here, can you do me a favour? I'm a little worried about a pal of mine, fella named Nick Limousine. He was going to be in town Tuesday on a business trip, said he'd phone me, but I haven't heard anything. Could you check if he was on one of your flights?"

"We're not allowed to give out the names of our passengers, sir, " the voice on the other end of the line said, certain but not *too* certain. It was the voice of a young man not yet entirely spoiled by success.

"Well, sure, but I don't want you to give *me* a name, just see if the name I give *you* is there. That wouldn't break the rules, now, would it?"

"I guess I could do that for you, sir, if you promise not to tell my boss."

"Sure, sure, but, hey, I thought *you* were the boss."

"What was the name again?" During the long silence, Sweeny lit a cigarette and gnawed at the rough edge of a fingernail. "No, I'm sorry, sir," the cheerful voice came back on. "No one of that name on any of our flights Tuesday, or Monday, or Wednesday either. I took the liberty of checking all three days, just to be sure."

Sweeny put the phone down and stared at it. For some reason he wasn't surprised, hadn't expected Limousine to have arrived by plane—no, that wasn't it, he hadn't expected it to be easy to find out—but he was troubled just the same. The only alternatives were Greyhound or a rented car, but a bus seemed like an unlikely way for a heavy man to travel, especially a heavy man laden with credit cards; no driver's licence seemed to make a rented car out of the question. Just the same, he called the three agencies in town, with no luck. No luck either with the dispatchers at the two cab companies, who said they'd ask around among the drivers. When Sweeny phoned back, it was as he'd expected: nobody remembered taking a big man to the Queen's Tuesday night or picking up a man of that description at the bus station to be taken to any hotel, any destination at all.

Between those calls and the stories he wrote, he tried Kramer's office three more times; Kramer was always out. "A very busy man, your boss," Sweeny said to the secretary. "Do you have to die to get an appointment to see him?"

He took his lunch at the Coffee Pot, an affable little restaurant just around the corner and only a block away from the building where the television station and one of the two radio stations were housed, a place with a reputation, therefore, as a hangout for celebrities of various sorts, from disk jockeys to reporters. That suited Bill Delancy, the owner and manager, a man who liked knowing people, especially those who knew many others themselves, and who took special delight in knowing that Sweeny had walked on a street in New York City that shared his name.

Sweeny and Delancy had been friends since they were boys. Forty-five years ago, when Sweeny was still what in those days they called a "cub" on the *Chronicle*, Delancy was a delivery boy in his father's grocery store, which stood at the same spot, corner of Mountain and Burrard, where this afternoon Sweeny consumed a ham sandwich on rye, pickles on the side, and a cup of coffee, black, no sugar. By the time Sweeny *owned* the paper, Delancy's father had died and the young man had already turned the store into a restaurant, changed the name from Delancy's ("That makes it sound like a tavern in Montana") to the Coffee Pot, and was already showing signs of a tendency toward both success and corpulence. Sweeny drank a cup of coffee there the day he left town, supposedly never to return, before picking up his carpetbag and Royal portable and heading down to the train station to catch the Great Northern. Except for the ticket-seller, Delancy was the last person he said goodbye to. Now, thirty-five years later, the *Chronicle* building and the Coffee Pot were both still in the same spots, but both had been rebuilt and expanded, and both now turned out smoother, slicker, more expensive products, probably each equally unpalatable, and even unhealthy, considering all the cholesterol in Delancy's baked bean salad, a specialty of the house, and all the news of war and sewage in the *Chron*.

Sweeny and Delancy had both put on weight—Delancy was actually fat, and Sweeny's flesh wore down on him with a weight more than its own—and both were older, of course. There were other changes as well: Delancy had been married and had three children, but his wife was dead and his children grown and gone; Sweeny had been married and divorced twice, and was childless. Delancy still owned his piece of real estate, though, while Sweeny came back to town with no more than what he'd left with, even the same battered typewriter, which had been with him now halfway round the world and back.

Right from the bus station, even before finding a hotel room, Sweeny had sought out the Coffee Pot, certain it would still be there. When he went through the heavy glass door, amazed by the change the restaurant had undergone—although, in fact, it was no different from hundreds of others Sweeny had been in—Delancy was standing at the cash register, counting out change for someone in a hurry. He looked up, a smile creasing his round, smooth face: "Sweeny," he said.

"Jesus," Sweeny had replied, "have I really changed that little?"

"Limousine," Sweeny said now. "Nicolas Limousine. Name mean anything to you? Big man, heavy set, ugly face, late middle age."

"You sure you're not talking about me?" When Delancy laughed, his belly sent vibrations skittering across the apron tied around his middle. He was a working manager, grease-stained and damp-handed.

"No, this actor is dead. You still seem to be breathing." Sweeny wiped a trace of mayonnaise from his lips with a napkin.

Delancy looked around the sparsely populated restaurant, as if searching for the man Sweeny had described among the trickle of late lunch customers. "He's an actor?" A grin cracked the wrinkles of his turnip face.

"No, that's just an expression."

"Oh, from the way you described him, I was thinking maybe of Walter Slezak. Saw him on the late movie the other night, a fine actor but kind of ugly."

Sweeny finished his coffee and checked the clock above the counter. He wanted to try Kramer again. "No, this actor should be local. Someone we both know, maybe from way back."

"Limousine?" Delancy shook his head. "You don't mean Limhouse?"

"I already thought of him. No."

"He's a big Chrysler dealer now, you know."

"Chevy."

"Same difference. Lives over in Highview. He's on his *third* wife."

"So might I be," Sweeny said, "if they'd let the poor girl out of the asylum."

Delancy lifted Sweeny's dishes and wiped the counter expertly with a damp cloth. "You won't give me any more clues, right?"

"Right. I don't even know much more about the cat now to give you as clues, but anyway, I don't want to confuse you. It's not *now* I'm worried about. What I want to know is about him *then*, way back. Think on it."

"Broderick Crawford," Delancy said. "Another big, ugly actor."

"And while you've got your thinking cap on, tell me this, Mr. Delancy, sir," Sweeny said, pushing himself up from the counter. "How the hell do you get to this town if you don't fly, drive, or take the bus?"

"Walk," Delancy shrugged. "Or ride a horse, though that leaves a bit of a trail, don't it now. Or flap your arms and make like an angel."

"Thanks a lot, you're a great help."

"You're saying your Nicolas Limousine friend didn't travel in any of those orthodox ways? You know that for a fact?"

"Not a fact," Sweeny said, "but he sure didn't leave any trail. No horse shit and nothin' else."

Delancy shook his head like a schoolmaster with a dull student. "Well, I guess this sort of thing wouldn't occur to a globe-trotter such as your-self, but it's no mystery to a man such as myself, who doesn't *own* a car, because I hardly ever go anywhere, and doesn't fly because I don't trust the damn things. I get my son or my nephew to drive me. My nephew Jimmy has a Chrysler, real fancy thing, air conditioning and all."

"Your nephew, fine," Sweeny said, blowing smoke.

"Son, nephew, that's not the point. The point is, somebody gives you a lift, that don't leave any trail at all, does it now?"

Sweeny crushes his cigarette and heaves himself to his feet, swallowing away the dryness in his mouth, heading straight across the room like a bird dog to the pile of magazines he's been staring at, *Time, Newsweek,* and *Maclean's*—a photo of Gordie Howe on the cover—and *Playboy, Cavalier,* and a batch of cheaper versions of the same form, all mixed in together. He has been amusing himself reading stories in the men's magazines lately, giv-ing some thought to trying his hand at writing one. They seem easy enough, a straightforward, simple-to-hold plot with a little sex thrown in and a twist ending if possible, for good measure. One of these days, he's going to sit down, write one, try to sell it. If nothing happens, well, nothing much lost. If it sells, he'll start writing them in earnest. Maybe he could get out of this lousy racket once and for all. It wouldn't be a bad life—he could get a cabin in the mountains outside of town, someplace where there wouldn't be much distraction and he could live cheaply, and he'd spend his days at the typewriter, his nights in front of the fire, dreaming lightly.

He thumbs through one of the magazines, not looking for anything in particular, until a picture of a girl catches his eye. She is naked except for a pair of gauze panties, down on her knees with her ass wiggling toward the camera, her face beaming over her shoulder with a come-on-and-fuck-me grin plastered over it. Sweat suddenly breaks out on Sweeny's forehead and his legs tremble, tipping him toward the bookcase, as memory courses through him like electricity through coiled copper strands. He was in the grimy office above the print shop of the old *Chronicle* building, where the morgue is now, his pants down around his ankles, legs trembling as he surged back and forth against the girl, pumping, his skin on fire against the cool, expressionless pock-marked face, her bored eyes. He'd brought the girl, a Métis whore who hung out at the Queen's tavern, back to his jumbled office. She shook her head at the rough wood floor and he was in too much of a hurry to clear his desk so they wound up standing there, legs spread, her skirt lifted and her naked ass against the cold glass of the door leading to the stairs and the darkened print shop below, shivering a little as she guided him into her and he shoved—"Easy, don't break the fuckin' glass," she said, but he was already coming and couldn't control the violent shakes rattling the door. When he had his breath back, he moved away from her, almost tripping on his bunched pants, his shirt tucked up under itself, his forehead bathed in sweat. It was his first time and the girl had bad teeth, a black, decaying mouth flashing like reversed stars across the years when she smiled. "Geez, that was fuckin' cold," she said, rubbing her ass.

Sweeny shakes his head and throws the magazine back on the pile, sighing. He picks up another and thumbs through it, but memory has a hold on him now and won't let go. He'd gotten a cot for the office so he'd never have to force a young lady to freeze her ass again—the nearby rooming house where he actually lived was not the place to take a woman—and he'd gotten his money's worth out of it. He'd even fallen in love, with a girl at the bank, and actually courted her some, took her out walking and to the movies and to dinner at Chin Li's Chinese and Western Cuisine on Burrard Avenue, until she got tired of his being busy so much of the time and his irregular hours and some of the language he used and wouldn't quit using, even for her. Before he knew it, she'd gotten herself engaged to the chief cashier, a man who wore garters on his sleeves. More than thirty-five years later, Sweeny can remember the winning man's sleeves better than the face of the girl.

"Ah, hell," Sweeny says. There is a rumble of thunder and he goes to the window and gazes down at the dark street, then up at the dense sky. After a few moments, it is illuminated for an impossibly long second by a broad stroke of sheet lightning that thrills him. A car creeps to the corner, hesitates, then roars through. The street is empty again, dark, but Sweeny stays by the window looking out at nothing in particular. Over the years, he thinks, he's written all kinds of things but it was a long time since he'd written any fiction other than press releases, or even tried to. He smiles at his ghostly reflection in the window. He'd written a novel, right about the time the girl he loved was marrying the man with the garters, working on it in the same office where he'd screwed the girl with the bad teeth. It all seemed to be connected now, as if the two women had been muses coaxing him into something he hadn't wanted to do. But it was so long ago, not just a distance measured in years but a whole different life. He had written late at night, snatching time when he could after he'd drained himself and couldn't do one more thing for that goddamn leech, that "bitch worse than a wife" he liked to call the *Chronicle*. He would write a page or two, his back arched like a comma, shoulders hunched, head down, cigarette smoke drifting into his eyes, one bare bulb shining above him, fingers going so fast over the keyboard the clatter they made melded into a constant hum rather than an orchestration of individual notes. When the novel was done, he read it over, decided it wasn't any good and destroyed it, just as he'd always done with the stories he'd written as a boy. That was that. Later, in Europe, he started half a dozen other novels, Hemingwayesque war stories that went nowhere. A few chapters and he'd lose interest or run out of steam.

Something flickers through his mind, swift as a bat in a cave, and Sweeny starts, raising his hand to his mouth as if to help his lips form the words he needs to hear, but whatever had stirred is already gone. Outside, the sky is clearing quickly—he can actually see, in the light of a remarkably bright moon, the clouds racing across, as if in flight. The moon is full, preternaturally large and dark, almost orange, more a hunter's moon of fall than of spring. He gazes at it for a minute, the pattern on its face wavering into one almost-discernible shape, then another. Funny, he's sure there was no moon the night before, that it was on the wane all last week. Memory playing tricks with him again. He shrugs and turns away, shaking his head with disgust at the disorder of the room, from the television set on the floor to the overflowing ashtrays on the table. He's been here two months but the suite has the look of a place that has been lived in forever. Maybe this weekend he'll get to it, after the fucking funeral, or Sunday.

He slumps down on the chesterfield and switches on the radio on the small table beside it. Familiar music blares out loudly—"Let it Be," the Beatles song that's been everywhere for weeks and he's sick of it—and he lowers the volume, then clicks it off entirely. He rises, flicks on the television and goes back to the chesterfield, stretching out, swallowing away dryness. A picture flickers into view, but the sound is inaudible. *God, he could use a drink.* He shakes his head, dispelling that ghost, sending it skittering across the room, just out of reach but not out of sight, like an ant determined to crawl up your leg. "That fucking funeral," he says to the mute TV screen.

Why the hell was he going to it, anyway? Funerals were bad enough when you had to go, when it was someone you knew or loved who had died. He'd covered a few, too—a dandy one, once, when he was working in New York, for a gangster, out at the Jersey Shore somewhere, the biggest, grandest funeral he'd ever seen, with hundreds of mourners, almost half of them cops or feds of one sort or another, taking notes on the half who *weren't* cops or feds, but all showing remorse, all with tremendous dignity, a funeral that was an event. And he'd covered one, too, down in Florida, for the chief of a motorcycle gang who'd been killed in a rumble, beaten to death with a chain, hundreds of blank-faced men in black leather on glistening chrome bikes, white arm bands fluttering on their sleeves, one naked girl with a shaved head, face painted with circus-clown make-up to resemble a skull. She was perched on the big, black leather saddle of a motorcycle wheeled by two stiff-backed men up to the open grave. As they passed the spot where Sweeny and a photographer were standing, the girl stuck out her tongue, a tiny pink bird fluttering its wings against the white cage of teeth, and batted her eyelids, dark as death with mascara. Through the moment of silence that followed the eulogy, delivered by another biker chieftain in full regalia, and surprisingly eloquent he was too, the only sound in the leafy stillness of the cemetery was the rhythmical snapping of the naked girl's gum.

There wasn't likely to be any such theatrics Saturday, at the last ceremony for Nicolas Limousine, whoever the fuck he was. Sweeny wasn't even assigned to go. He would be doing it on his own, throwing away a perfectly good day off for some perverse sense of curiosity that had, for some reason, gotten the better of him. Well, there was something funny going on—something more than just the name, more than just who he was. *Limousine, Nicolas Limousine.* Maybe a drink would help, ease off the cork stuck in the bottle of his memory. He grins darkly. No, not that way. It'll come to him eventually, he's sure of that. His memory is like a Chinese puzzle, with blanks and blind alleys and false walls, but nothing ever escapes from it. But, damn, there's more to it than just that—there was something funny going on about the death, something funny about the way it happened and the way people were reacting to it, people like cops and coroners and Crown prosecutors. Sweeny had been a reporter long enough to smell a story when his nose was shoved into it. If he came up with a good one, it just might impress his new bosses, get him in a bit more securely at the *Chronicle*, where he knew they were keeping an eye on him. He was doing okay, he knew that, but was *okay* enough when you're sixty-two goddamn years old and you're getting what's probably your last chance?

Sweeny gets up to change the channel and raise the volume. The new picture is of a girl in a low-cut long dress singing, but he returns to the chesterfield. The sound is still so low he can barely make out the words the girl is singing but he can see her mouth clearly, opening and closing like a black-and-white fish at feed. Yeah, there's something funny going on there, a story of some sort, but is it gettable, that's the question. And, once got, will it be worth anything? Strangers die all the time. What's so special about this one? Who cares, Sweeny? On the screen, the girl is bowing, the weight of her breasts seemingly threatening to knock her over. Sweeny's eyes open wider. *God, he needs a drink.*

❖

"Boo!"

"Jesus Christ, Sweeny, you scared the shit out of me."

He had walked past the Queen's on his way home that afternoon and poked his head in the lobby to see Charlie Cook's spindly back draped over the front desk, resplendent in the same red-and-green plaid jacket as the day before. Sweeny didn't creep up on him, exactly, but Cook was engrossed in the girl with the blonde hurricane, who was sitting behind the desk. Beneath the chaotic hair were startling green eyes gazing past Cook's shoulder at Sweeny, who held up a finger beside his nose and leaned forward quietly.

"Any more ghosts?" he asked as Cook wiped his face.

"Ghosts, hell. If you're referring to Nicolas Limousine or whatever the hell his name is supposed to be, or *was* supposed to be, I'm chalking that one up to just another bad debt. Just a cheap grifter is all he was. Maybe he ain't even dead—I should check with Benno's and see if he ain't up and walked away yet, leaving them with a bad bill, too."

"Wait a minute, didn't you charge his account to a credit card, like I said?" Sweeny was laughing at Cook's red face.

"Yeah, sure, just like you said, charge it to his credit card. Sounds like a good idea. Think I'll do that, I say to myself. Not so easy, but if there's a way, Charlie Cook will find it. The police have his wallet, so I couldn't actually put my hands on one of those credit cards, but there is a spot on our check-in forms where you're supposed to write the number of the card you're going to be using, if you're planning on using one. We don't insist that people fill that out, since most people pay in advance anyway, but I remembered this fella had, because he asked if he could use American Express, I think I mentioned that to you. We accept American Express but you don't see it too often around here, so it made an impression on me, even then, before I'd seen the stack of other cards he was carrying. I thought to myself, this is a swell customer, Charlie, be sure and treat him right. Ha. He treated us right, all right."

"You're talking in circles, Charlie. What happened?" They were standing side by side with their elbows propped on the counter. Sweeny smiled at the blonde, who smiled back.

"Well, after I talked to you yesterday, I checked and sure enough, just like I remembered, he *had* filled the number in, and there it was, big as life, an American Express number, something I could hang his bill on, including ninety-seven dollars and forty-five cents in long distance calls. But, of course, I didn't actually have the card, just the number, and a credit form hadn't been stamped, so I figured I'd better call American Express and verify the account, we'd do that as a matter of course with a bill that large anyway, and see what they advised doing in a situation like this."

"You mean a situation in which the customer is deader than an IBM card?"

"That's it. Does the estate take care of the bills or does the credit card company take the loss, that sort of thing. *I* don't know."

"So?"

"So I called." Cook set his mouth and folded his arms.

"Yeah?" The girl, who was standing just behind Cook's left shoulder, out of his line of sight, was rolling her eyes, and Sweeny had to concentrate hard on what Cook was saying. She was about half Sweeny's size and weight, maybe one third his age. She was wearing a short black skirt and wine-coloured sweater. There was a black plastic square pinned just above the tip of her left breast with her name on it: *July*.

"Well, they never heard of our friend Nicolas P. Limousine, have no record of him, never have."

"*P*? Nicolas *P*?"

Cook waved his hand in an impatient gesture. "That's just an expression."

"Well, what about the number?"

"Oh, yeah, they had a number like that, but it was an old one, discontinued. And it hadn't belonged to Nicolas P. Limousine. Not ever."

Sweeny shrugged, taking his eyes off the girl, who was reaching for a ringing phone. "So he was a credit card forger among his many other accomplishments, not that we know too much about the others. At least now we know something. What about the other cards?"

"Don't know about them, but you can bet your life I let the police know what I'd found out from American Express, and they said they'd check out the other cards. Don Stanfield is handling the case, one of the detectives. Know him?"

Sweeny shook his head.

"But I'll bet anything those other cards come up just as phony. That grifter even had a Carte Blanche card. That's a *good* card."

"What about the suitcase, Charlie? You said you had Limousine's suitcase in your office. I'd like to take a look at it."

"Oh, Stanfield took it. Sorry, you shoulda asked me yesterday."

"Yeah, wasn't thinking fast enough. What kind was it, what'd it look like?" He frowned, shaking his head. *Stupid, Sweeny. You're getting slow.*

"Nothing special. Leather, expensive, but not out of the ordinary. Sort of reddish brown, with a strap. Had a lot of stickers on it, though. It had done a bit of travelling—London, Paris, one from Madrid I noticed, a bullfighter with a red cape."

"I don't suppose you went through it."

"The suitcase? Go through a suitcase? *Sweeny.*"

"Okay, okay. Just wondering. It was sitting in your office, and I thought maybe you'd gotten curious, especially since its former owner owed you some dough." The girl was sitting at a desk now, talking on the phone and writing on a pad with a ballpoint pen. Her legs were crossed and plenty of them was showing. Her blonde head was tilted to one side, revealing the smooth whiteness of her neck. When she talked, Sweeny could see her small, even teeth in a blur of whiteness. He could hear the dry, flat tone of her voice without making out any words.

"Well, sure, I was curious. But no, I wasn't about to open a guest's suitcase."

"Even a dead one? Charlie, you've come a long way."

Cook grinned. His nose, the only portion of his face with any excess flesh on it, reddened slightly, whether in embarrassment or pride Sweeny couldn't tell.

Sweeny slapped him on a red-and-green-checked arm and turned to go, stopping himself with a snap of his fingers. "One more thing, though. Can I take a look at that check-in form. I never did hear what he used as an address."

"*That* I can provide you with. The police took the original, but we kept the carbon copy. I don't know if the address will be too helpful, though. It's a Washington address. I mean Washington, DC."

Sweeny raised his eyebrows. "I happen to know Washington pretty well, lived there for a bunch of years. Let's see."

"Sure. Hold on." Cook opened the swing door and went behind the counter. He brushed past the girl, who was just hanging up the phone and getting to her feet, and disappeared behind a partition into a back room.

"You're Mr. Sweeny," the girl said. It wasn't a question, but it wasn't an accusation either.

Just the same, Sweeny looked around him, as if unsure who she was speaking to. "Guilty as charged."

Her smile was radiant, sending off heat. "I read your story about the daffodils. It was sweet."

"Oh, thanks." He had done a story earlier that week on a woman who had a yard full of daffodils in front of her house, more of them, and more different kinds, than anyone in town, and, this year, earlier than ever before in memory, long before flowers should be up, even daffodils, with patches of snow still on shaded sidewalks. Every April, her front yard became a town showplace, and every year, his check of the files showed, the *Chronicle* did something on her, a story or a picture at least, frequently both. This year, Sweeny had done what he thought was a slightly different approach, focussing more on the woman than on the flowers. "You like daffodils or stories about crazy ladies?"

She laughed. "Crazy ladies. I'm one myself."

"You, July, are a *young* crazy lady," he said, letting his eyes stray down to the nametag. "And a very pretty one, if I might say."

The girl rolled her eyes and made a groaning sound.

"Hey," Sweeny said quickly, "that was a dumb thing to say." But then he was caught in the apology, unsure of which direction to go. The girl neither smiled nor frowned, looking at him levelly with her cool green eyes. He was relieved to see Cook's bulging nose come around the partition.

"Here 'tis. Whatcha up to?"

Sweeny took out his glasses and put them on to examine the small sheet of paper. He was oddly pleased that the girl, after breaking into a final smile, had slipped into the back room and didn't see the way he looked with the lopsided wire frames sliding down his nose. "Nothing special. You know me, just a snoop. Reporter's instincts and all that."

It was a standard hotel check-in form, with a line for name, address, number of people, car make and licence number, company represented, number of days, rate, credit card and number. And a final line for signature.

Limousine's printing hand was neat, meticulous, but his signature was almost illegible. Sweeny pursed his lips. There was something familiar about the signature that sent goose-bumps skittering to the surface of his skin. He forced his eyes to move up and take in the address. It was a post office box.

"That's kind of a funny address to give a hotel, isn't it? I mean, that's obviously not a living address, just mailing."

"Kind of, yes. It makes sense now. He sure didn't strike me as a grifter or I wouldn't have let him get away with that. It's not all that unusual, though, with travelling men, and that's what he looked like, a travelling man, prosperous, though, not a grifter. But I guess that's what makes a good conman, he *don't* look like one."

Sweeny took another look at the signature. "Hmmm. Mind if I borrow this thing for a few days?"

"Nope, go ahead, keep it. Fat lot of good it's doing me now. I need a copy for our files but the police should be giving me back the original."

"Thanks." Sweeny turned to go again. "Hey, that little girl, July." He gestured toward the back room with his thumb. "She for real?"

Charlie Cook grinned, the nose reddening again. Over thirty-five years before, the skinny little bellhop had walked right into the fist of a man whose drunken wife had called for room service and gotten carried away. The nose had been a lopsided bookmark ever since, keeping Cook's place in the daily pages. "Is she ever."

❖

A grey, fuzzy static is coming from the television screen, and Sweeny swings to his feet, shaking his head, coughing. His mouth is a desert floor swept by wind. He remembers what he wanted before and stumbles to the bookcase, rubbing the pins and needles out of his leg. His wallet, keys, and change are in a pile on one shelf, next to the screwdriver and hammer he borrowed from the caretaker. He wants to fix the leak in the toilet, maybe hang a few pictures on the drab walls. Maybe this weekend, after the funeral. *The funeral.* The hotel form Cook gave him is in his wallet and his thumbs get in the way as he fishes it out. He makes sucking movements with his mouth, flushing saliva over his tongue, as he unfolds the form and stares at it. *Limousine. Nicolas Limousine.* The scrawled signature floats before him like a caterpillar rolling in the wind. *Thank God there's no bottle in the house or it would be all over now. Thank God for that.* The only other living thing in the room is the television screen and it is blind, so there's no one to see Sweeny fall to his knees.

❖

In his dream, Sweeny is the boy again, standing in the doorway of the office above the print shop, hands sweaty around the newspaper, staring at ominous shoulder blades hunched over a battered desk, the arm barely moving as the pencil in the gnarled hand races back and forth down a narrow column of type. The snowy head between the shoulder blades rises and a craggy face with sunburned cheeks turns toward him, and intense blue eyes, eyes like holes ripped out of the face so you can see straight through to heaven, are looking at him. There are deep cracks in the leathery cheeks, the face and turkey-drumstick neck beneath it burned red, as if they belonged to a man who carries his head closer to the sky than most people. The mouth opens and releases a voice like ice cracking on the river in spring. Words buzz around the boy's head like gnats, too many to count or deal with, and an arrow of pure delight pierces him. His hands are on typewriter keys, his fingertips cold on the smooth pebbles, sparks flashing into darkness, stars like sparks above him. He is cold, shoulders arched, the floor hard beneath them, the sooty window above and beyond it empty with the darkest night. He is alive, alive. There is a hand on his arm—*Oh, God*—and the old man's face is beside his, the granite cheekbones, white hairs in the fierce nostrils bristling, corncob pipe clenched in his teeth like the stoic victim of some extinct bird of prey. The boy's eyes close, open, close again, but the darkness remains, swimming above him, darkness studded with stars, cold pinpricks in the darkness that covers the earth and air like a frown from the sun. But the floor is there beneath him and his head is exploding with pain. He is alive.

IV

Friday

"WORKING ON SOMETHING?"

Sweeny had been head-bent over a note pad, running red lines under a list of words, and hadn't heard Callan approach. The jacket of his new grey suit was draped over the back of his chair, and he'd loosened his necktie.

"Sort of." Shit, that was the wrong thing to say. Callan had a fistful of papers in his hand and was making the assignment rounds. His title was ME, but at the small *Chronicle* that job, the news editor's, and city editor's were all rolled into one. Sweeny frowned and glanced at his typewriter. There was a sheet of paper rolled in, blank, just out of habit, but that trick didn't work anymore.

"Whatcha got?" Callan tilted his hip and allowed his body to fold down onto Sweeny's desktop in a smooth, easy motion, depositing the seat of his no-iron slacks between the typewriter and the phone without disturbing a pencil or a piece of paper. He was a thin, anemic-looking man with a pinched face and a grey-brown moustache that belonged to someone rounder. He was a closed-in man, filled with partitions, and Sweeny hadn't figured him out yet.

"Probably nothin'. Probably just wasting my time. Got somethin' for me?" Sweeny swivelled around, his hand on the notepad, and pushed his chair back, easing the angle between them. He'd been playing this game with editors for a long time.

"Nothing that can't wait. A couple of features I think you can do a good number on, but nothing special. You look like you got something by the tail."

Sweeny smiled slowly. "Maybe. Maybe it's got me. Don't know." The important thing was not to appear too eager.

"Shoot."

"Well," Sweeny shrugged. "Remember the guy who blew out in the Queen's Hotel the other night?"

"Yeah, had some kind of funny name."

"Limousine."

"Right. What'd he die of, after all?"

"Well, that's it, I don't know. They did an autopsy yesterday but they haven't said. And there's a bunch of other funny things swimming around."

"Like what?"

Sweeny shook a Player's out of the pack on his desk and offered one to Callan, who shook his head.

"Like first they weren't going to do an autopsy, then they did. Like the cops are being quiet on it, they don't offer anything to De Lisso on it at all, I have to call and ask specifically."

"Well?" Callan made an impatient gesture with his right hand.

"That's just part of the smell. The guy had no identification on him, I mean none, zilch, not a driver's licence, not a library card, not a laundry ticket, just credit cards, enough to take you around the world."

"That's identification."

"Yeah, but they were phony. At least one was. The cops took his wallet, but he'd used one of the cards at the hotel, and they checked it with the company, American Express. No such number, no such name."

"A forger," Callan said. "Comes into town to do a bit of credit card shopping, pass a few bum cheques."

"That's what I was thinking, too. But no chequebook. And a conman would have all sorts of phony ID, not none at all. They don't even know for sure Limousine's his name. I didn't see these credit cards, but someone at the hotel did so I presume they all had the same name on them. Maybe that proves the guy's name really was Nicolas Limousine, but conmen working credit card scams don't have the same name on all their cards, and never their own names. No, it don't wash that way."

"So what else?" Callan looked more interested.

"Gives a post office box as his address. A post office box in Washington. Washington DC."

Callan arched his eyebrows, sucked at his cheek.

"Had travel stickers from all over the world on his suitcase. Bunch of other stuff I haven't put together yet, too."

"Okay, sounds interesting. Where's it going, though? So far what you've got, maybe, is an eccentric man who dies away from home. Not much of a story."

Sweeny shrugged. He had Callan's mouth around the hook, now all he had to do was jerk the line so the hook caught. He cocked his head. "Well, maybe it'll turn out to be nothing. Even then, maybe I can spin it into a feature . . . the lonely death of a travelling man, that sort of thing. But . . ." he hesitated for effect, ". . . it smells like maybe a little Mafia to me."

Callan unfolded his limbs, stretching his legs out straight in front of him, his hands clasped in front of his belt buckle. "Hitman? That sort or thing?"

"Maybe, maybe an enforcer of some kind. Maybe an advance man for somebody big coming to town, maybe a messenger of some type, maybe somebody big travelling on the sly for some reason. Drugs, maybe. It's getting big on the coast. I gather, and we're on the route. And we're getting to be a pretty big town, too." He shook his head. "I'm just guessing now, but it has a little of that smell, though, complete with the cops forgetting to tell things, like maybe they're sitting on something big they don't want to get out."

Callan got up. "I like that, Sweeny."

He smiled. "Maybe it's just a wild goose chase."

"Maybe, but chase it for a while, see what you can do with it. Like you say, it might be a good feature."

"I'll need a bit of time, have to make a few long distance calls."

"Lemme know how you're doing."

Callan moved away, the shoulder-blades looking lethal beneath his striped shirt, making Sweeny think, not for the first time, of Highmountain. He stopped at another desk, bending his balding head over his handful of papers.

Across the newsroom, Gene the copy boy had just emerged from the wire room with a startled look on his face. "I can't believe it," he announced to no one in particular. "The Beatles are breaking up. Paul quit." Callan straightened up, turned around.

Sweeny reached for the phone, blowing softly against his lips. If there was going to be a reaction story on that, he didn't want to be the sucker doing it. Kramer wasn't in his office but was expected back shortly. "May I have him return your call?" the receptionist's voice asked. He looked at the clock, calculating. It was almost ten. "Yeah, sure, I'll be here all morning. It's Sweeny, S-W-E-E-N-Y, at the *Chronicle*." He gave her the number. Then he dialled long distance information for Washington.

❖

"Police department."

"Detectives, please. Don Stanfield."

"Just a second, I'll connect you."

"Detectives."

"Hi, this is Wilf Sweeny, at the *Chronicle*. Stanfield there?"

"Yeah, hold on. Stan, phone."

"Stanfield."

"Hi, Wilf Sweeny, at the *Chronicle*. I'm the new guy—we haven't met. Stan, is it? I thought it was Don."

"Yeah, Don's my name, but people call me Stan."

"Okay, I'll try to remember that. I understand you're handling the Limousine investigation."

"I wouldn't exactly call it an investigation. Just a routine look-see."

"Uh huh, I see. There seem to be a couple of funny things, though."

"What's that?"

"Well, I understand an autopsy was performed. Can you tell me the results?"

"Not the cause of death, you'd have to get that from the coroner's office, but I can tell you that no foul play is suspected at this time."

"Okay, no foul play. Good. At this time . . . does that mean it was before?"

"I didn't say that."

"I know you didn't, Stan. I'm asking."

"I'll pass on that one. Whenever there's a death that isn't immediately explainable, there's a possibility of foul play, you know that."

"Sure, but it isn't always suspected."

"Whatever you say."

"Okay, fair enough. Couple of other things. I understand that this Limousine guy had a wallet stuffed with credit cards on him, but no other identification. Have you been able to confirm his identity?"

"What exactly do you mean?"

"Well, I gather that the name on the credit cards is Nicolas Limousine. Is that really who this guy is?"

"We don't have any reason to think not."

"Does that mean you were able to contact his next of kin?"

"They've been in contact with us."

"*They* called *you*? That's interesting. How did they know he was dead?"

"That I couldn't tell you."

"And it was his family?"

"Not family, exactly. Business associates, I believe."

"Uh huh. A Mr. Harriman, was it?"

"I don't recall the name right off."

"But you were able to get a positive ident, eh?"

"We're satisfied."

"Okay. Good. Now, Mr. Cook, the assistant manager of the Queen's Hotel, tells me that the credit card that this Limousine used when he checked in turned out to be a phony, that he contacted the credit card company and there was no Limousine listed on their records and the number was an old one or there was no such number, something like that. And Mr. Cook tells me he passed this info on to you. That right?"

"Charlie Cook seems to keep you pretty well informed."

"No law against that, is there?"

"Nope."

"So, have you checked out the other cards, to see if they're legit?"

"I can't comment on that."

"Why not?"

"That's part of an on-going investigation. I can't talk about it, simple as that."

"Okay, fair enough. On-going . . . couple of minutes ago, you said you wouldn't call this an investigation. But you just did."

"That's an expression. Figure of speech."

"Okay, I know a little something about figures of speech, Stan. How about the suitcase?"

"How's that?"

"Limousine's suitcase. I understand you have it."

"Uh, yep, we do."

"Anything unusual in it?"

"How do you mean?"

"I mean, anything out of the ordinary, anything, well, illegal, or suspicious?"

"I can't comment on that, either."

"Okay, of course not. Now, let me get this straight. Just a sec, hard to read my own handwriting sometimes. Lemme just go over this one time. It's not an investigation, just routine. Foul play not suspected at this time but you don't know, excuse me, you don't have the cause of death. You didn't contact the family but friends contacted you. You didn't get a positive ID, but you're satisfied the stiff is who he's supposed to be. You can't comment on the credit cards or the suitcase because they're part of an ongoing investigation. Is that about right?"

"That's what you said."

"Well, Jesus, Stan, what the hell's the big mystery here?"

"I can't comment on that."

"Well, Jesus . . ."

"Well, Jesus yourself. Lemme ask you something. Sweeny, is it? What's the big interest in this, Sweeny? It's just a natural death, a dime-a-dozen kind of thing. It's just routine. We don't mind co-operating with you newspaper boys on something real, just ask Jim De Lisso, but this is nothin'. You're just blowin' in my ear. What you getting your nose all out of joint over it for?"

"That's a good question," Sweeny said. "But it ain't me whose nose is out of joint, Stan. And as to why, I guess I'm just fascinated by routine."

After he hung up, he sat staring at the keys of his typewriter, smoking, his index finger rubbing the ridge of his jaw. It was hot in the newsroom. There were no windows in the big room so he couldn't see for himself, but the last few people to come through had their coats open so he guessed it was warming up outside. He made a note on his pad, then picked up the phone again.

"Good afternoon, American Express."

"Making a credit check."

"One moment."

"Credit, Mrs. Sears." A crisp woman's voice.

"Hi, got a little problem here, maybe you can help me out. Wilf Sweeny at the Georgia Hotel in Vancouver. One of our maids found one of your cards in the back of a dresser. Looks like it might have been there for a while. The name is obscured, but I can just make out the number. Think you could track it down for me? We'd like to be able to return the card to our guest, whoever he was. Little service of the hotel."

"I'll check it, sir. Let me have the number."

Sweeny read it out slowly, holding the crumpled check-in form close to his nose. "Like I say, it might be an old card, might not be active."

"Would you like me to call you back, sir?"

"No, that's okay, I'll hold."

Sweeny kept his eyes on the second hand of the clock above the copy desk as he listened to the phone's silence, the receiver pressed loosely against his ear. The sweeping hand went almost three times around the face of the clock before the voice came back.

"That card is inactive, sir. Is there any credit involved?"

"No, no, nothing like that. We'd just like to know who it belonged to. Even if he doesn't use it anymore, getting a word from us that it's been found would be a good plug for us. A little public relations, you know?"

"The account was in the name of Ormand Harriman."

Sweeny sniffed. "Uh huh. Is that with two Rs?"

"Yes."

"Uh huh. Got an address? Like to be able to write to him."

"It's a post office box, in Washington."

"Post office box?" Sweeny sucked in his breath, looking down at the check-in form on the desk. The address Limousine had given was P.O. Box 3011, Station D.

"Box 4367," the crisp voice said. "Station D. The postal code is 20090. You might want to check with the post office before writing to him, though, sir. This account has been inactive for several years. This is interesting, though. You say the card was just found?"

"Yes, by a maid. Why?"

"There's a new note in this file, just from yesterday. Another British Columbia hotel was inquiring about that number."

"Is that right? Must be something in the air. Box 4367, you said? Okay, I got that. Hey, thanks very much, Miss, you've been a real help."

He put the phone down gingerly and stared at it, as if it had spoken to him in a foreign language, or said something obscene. It rang almost immediately.

"*Chronicle* newsroom, Sweeny."

"Mr. Sweeny? This is Dr. Kramer's office. Hold for Dr. Kramer, please."

"Sure." He picked up his pencil and flipped the page on his notepad.

"Mr. Sweeny? Lloyd Kramer here. You've been trying to reach me?"

"Yeah, thanks for returning my call, Doctor. It's about the autopsy you performed on Nicolas Limousine yesterday."

"Yes, Mr. Limousine. A very interesting autopsy."

Sweeny leaned forward. "How so, Doctor?"

The coroner laughed. "Oh, nothing like what your voice sounds like you think. I didn't find any daggers sticking out of his heart, if that's what you mean."

Sweeny chuckled politely.

"But the man was in remarkably good health. For his age, I mean. Of course, he wasn't really in good health. He was dead. But he had been."

Sweeny made a face. A comedian. "For his age, you say. How old was he?"

"Couldn't say for sure. Fifties, possibly late fifties, early sixties, but in many ways he had the physique of a man in his forties. You could get the exact age from his family."

"Family?"

"I understood the family had been in contact with the police and arrangements have been made for a funeral."

"Oh, yeah. Not the family, but I know about that. Tell me, Doctor, if it wasn't a dagger, what did kill Mr. Limousine?"

"Can't tell you exactly, but death was from natural causes. There's no reason to suspect foul play of any kind. I don't know exactly what caused it since the muscle tissues of the heart exhibited no evidence of prior weakness or disease, but there was heart failure."

"That's pretty much what you had thought prior to doing the autopsy, wasn't it? I happened to be discussing the case with Hal Benno the other day, and he said something to that effect."

"Well, yes, frequently an autopsy confirms what the pathologist surmised."

"Then why do one?"

"The law requires that an autopsy be performed whenever there is a case of death in any sort of unusual circumstances, where there might be some question, no matter how slim that question might be."

"And dying in the middle of the night in a hotel room in a strange town is considered unusual enough?"

"I'd say so. Wouldn't you?"

"Yes. I would. That's why I wondered why there wasn't an autopsy ordered immediately. I understand you hadn't intended to, then changed your mind after talking with Frank Farr, the Crown prosecutor."

There was a pause on the other end of the line. "That's not exactly right. This is a good example of how you fellows in the media get things twisted around. Don't get me wrong, I'm not chastizing you, just making an observation."

"No offence."

"Good. I confer frequently with Mr. Farr. In my capacity as coroner, I'm an arm of the court, just as he is. So discussing this particular case is not unusual. In fact, if I had to characterize it, I'd say it was very *usual*. You probably know, in British Columbia you don't have to be a pathologist to be a coroner, or even a physician, for that matter, but I happen to be one, so I'm my own pathologist. Sometimes, wearing two hats, the coroner's and the pathologist's, it gets a little confusing."

"I can see how that could be," Sweeny said.

"I may have mentioned to Mr. Benno that I thought an autopsy would be a waste of time in this particular case. But that didn't mean that I didn't intend to perform one. As it turned out, I was right. It *was* a waste of time, although, as I said, it was an interesting cadaver, and there's always something to learn."

Sweeny held the phone a little away from his ear and shook his head, smiling. "Thanks for the lesson, Doctor, I'll remember that. You think, then, that I'm off base in thinking there's anything worth smelling here, is that right?"

"The only smell surrounding the death of Mr. Limousine, from a medical point of view, is that of embalming fluid, Mr. Sweeny."

Sweeny groaned to himself, chuckled audibly.

"Okay, I'll buy that. Just for my own information, though, to satisfy my undying curiosity, what did you list as the cause of death?"

There was another pause, during which Sweeny thought he'd have to go over and meet Kramer one of these days, maybe pull a feature story out of him. Seemed like a fairly decent sort.

"Well, I'm a little, ha ha, embarrassed to say. It sounds kind of funny when you say it out loud, to the layman, but we do this every once in a while when we don't really know what, but we do know it was natural."

"What's that?"

"Well, it's sort of a bookkeeping shorthand."

"What's that?"

"Well, we write GOK. That's what I put on Mr. Limousine's death certificate as cause of death."

Sweeny scribbled on his notepad. "GOK. Don't think I ever saw that before. What's it mean?"

Kramer tittered. "God only knows."

"Eh?"

"God only knows. GOK. That's what it means."

❧

"Ever hear of a cat named Harriman?"

Sweeny was draped over a cup of coffee, blowing smoke clouds into the liquid to cool it. On the other side of the counter, Delancy had his foot up, a damp towel in his hands as always. His bald head glistened under the fluorescent lights and his onion eyes swam in a clear, salty broth.

"Sure, he was governor of New York a few years back, right? A very well-upholstered fellow."

"That's not the one I had in mind. Ormand Harriman. Any bells?"

"From around these parts?"

"Don't know. Might be. Maybe once, long time back."

Delancy squinted, indicating that he was thinking hard. "I keep thinking of Harry Mann, remember him?"

"Harry Mann?" Sweeny made a sour face. "You're kidding."

"No, you don't remember him? He was in our class at school, except I think he flunked once or twice and fell behind. We used to call him Wo Mann, remember?"

"Oh, yeah. Wo Mann. A little guy. Jesus, when was that, anyway? About five hundred years ago?"

"Oh, easy. Maybe six."

Sweeny sipped the sour coffee. He took his notepad out and put it on the counter, rubbing his ear as he leafed through the pages.

"Yesterday it was Limousine, today Harriman," Delancy said. "You getting set for a quiz show?"

"Yeah, *Twenty Questions*."

"I don't think that one's on anymore."

Sweeny looked at him.

"Matter of fact," Delancy said, "that one was never on TV."

Sweeny shook his head.

"And I don't think it's on anymore, on radio."

"Okay, I get the picture."

"Don't get sore. I'm just trying to be helpful. What's the problem, Sherlock?"

Sweeny shrugged. "I don't even know if there's a problem. Maybe I'm chasing smoke clouds. I told you about the stiff in the hotel."

"Mr. Limousine."

"That's the vehicle. Limousine. Very swanky. Something about him bothers me. Something about him and the way he died and about what he was doing here, something about the way the cops are handling it, something about the way the funeral's been arranged, something about the whole fucking thing bothers me. *Damn it.*" He banged his hand on the counter, making his coffee cup clatter in its saucer. "I know I know that son of a bitch."

"So look through your address book. And would you mind keeping it down to a gentle roar?" Delancy looked down the row of customers lining the counter and smiled reassuringly.

"Jesus, Delancy. My address book. You should be in New York, you know? You should be Jewish and this should be a delicatessen on East Broadway."

"Not on Delancy Street?"

"Address book. I wish I had one." He stared at his coffee cup, tapping the rim with a finger. Those fucking telephone calls Limousine made—now where the hell were they to? Maybe he should check them out.

"Delancy's Deli. I like the way that sounds, but it don't sound Jewish."

"Huh? Oh, you don't have to be Jewish." Sweeny laughed. "You know, I took a long reach and told my boss this morning maybe Limousine was in with the Mafia, now I'm beginning to think that may just be right."

"Mafia? A whatchamacallit, a Mafioso here?"

"I don't know. I wanted some time to try to track this down so that's what I told Callan. There isn't an editor alive can resist that word, Mafia, when you whisper it in his ear and tell him it can be on the front page. But maybe I had it right. There sure as fuck is something shady going on."

"Foreign intrigue, eh?" Delancy said. "Sure, a spy, like Walter Slezak in that movie I was telling you about. Cloak and dagger stuff."

"Huh," Sweeny said. He looked at the notepad again. On two different pages there was a post office box in Washington, underlined. "You know, you might not be as dumb as this coffee tastes."

"More dumb coffee?"

"Sure."

He headed for the Queen's when he left the Coffee Pot, letting spring seep into him. The air here was uncannily clear and sweet after New York, the sounds muffled. People smiled at him on the street, walking slowly, their arms dangling at their sides rather than in the distinctive huddled style of the cities. Sweeny was just beginning now, after two months, to get used to the slower pace. He enjoyed the courtesy, the patience, people waiting at corners until the green walk sign flashed, people standing idly in line at bus stops, even in bad weather, without jostling for position. There was a girl standing on the corner he now approached, beside a bus stop sign, her eyes on the street. She wore a blue polka dot dress under her open blue cotton coat, and carried a rolled up copy of the *Chronicle* under her arm, making Sweeny think lewdly that words he had written were nestled snugly against her breasts. He shook his head to dispel the idea. That was New York thinking, big city thoughts. He wanted to go up to the girl and kiss her, gently and purely, like the telegraph company manager did in the Saroyan novel—what was it? *The Time of Your Life?* No, *The Human Comedy*, that was it—then thank her for being young and pretty and go on his way.

He wanted to get a copy of the numbers Limousine had called, but Charlie Cook wasn't in and the dumpling woman sorting mail behind the counter said he'd be gone all afternoon. Sweeny made a clucking sound and turned to go, but the girl on the street had made him think of the funny blonde who worked here. He went outside and, on an impulse, around the corner to the coffee shop entrance and put his nose against the glass. Sure enough, July was at the counter, alone, busy with a sandwich. Sweeny straightened his tie, glancing both ways along the street like a boy about to enter a dirty movie, then barged in.

"Hey, how ya doin'?" He sat down beside her, reaching for a menu.

"Mr. Sweeny, hi." She was wearing the same black skirt as the day before. The hem rode high up on her thighs and her knees were pressed close together. Sweeny had to struggle to keep his eyes high.

"Please. *Mr.* Sweeny was my uncle. Just Sweeny is fine."

"Sweeny. What is that, anyway? Irish?"

"Irish as all get out, Black Irish if you know what that is. Except I'm Swedish on my mother's side. When I was little I used to get it confused, thought our name was Sweedy."

The girl laughed. "You don't have a first name, I suppose."

"I do, but I forgot it. And you, is your name really July, or did you start out as April or May and graduate? Or were you a Julie or Julia?"

"It's really July. Now, anyway." She shrugged. She was wearing a baggy white fisherman's sweater that obscured the shape of her breasts. Her teeth were tiny and white on the soft brown bread of her tuna salad sandwich.

"How is that?" Sweeny asked, pointing his chin at her plate.

"This fish's mother would never recognize him, but it's edible."

Sweeny took a deep breath. "Hey, I'm gonna like you. Your jokes are as feeble as mine, but they're just as steady."

July gave him a mayonnaisey smile. There was a whitish smear thin as dew along her lower lip.

He waved to the waitress, bringing his hand down to point at the plate beside him. "She's still kicking, so I'll try it too."

"Very funny." The waitress had a sandpaper voice. "Coffee?"

"Sure. And lots of lettuce. On the sandwich, not in the coffee."

The waitress was no older than the girl he was sitting next to—they were both no more than twenty, he supposed—but she seemed coarse and clumsy as she brought a mug from under the counter and banged it in front of him. Her fingers, he noticed, were thick and graceless, and she spilled a bit of coffee as she filled his cup from a stained glass pot. She made a face at him.

"Neat," Sweeny said, grinning. He didn't really want more coffee, or the sandwich either. He'd just had one at Delancy's. But now what was he supposed to do? He was sitting next to this girl who was one third his fucking age and half his fucking weight and he could barely keep his hands off.

"This is your second time around, I hear," July said.

"Huh?" The sound of her voice, more than what she said, startled him.

"You've been in the States, I guess. For a long time?"

"How do you know that?"

"Oh," she waved her sandwich at him and Sweeny stared first at the delicate pattern of teethmarks on the bread, then to her mouth. "I'm a big detective." She shrugged. "You said *huh*."

"Oh, yeah," Sweeny smiled. "I should be saying *eh*, eh?"

"Yeah." She grinned, a light coming on behind the green lustre of her eyes. Her blonde hair wasn't blonde at all, he noticed. Along the part down the middle of her head the hair was dark brown and straight. Along the side of her narrow head, though, it took off into a round swirl of canary curls.

"Well, yeah, I've been in the States for a while."

"But Mr. Cook says you come from here originally. That's why I said 'second time around.'"

"Yeah, I heard you. It just didn't register. Yeah, this is my hometown. It was a while ago, though."

"Before my time, eh?"

"Yeah, before your time. Most things were, weren't they?"

She made a face and sipped at her coke. The waitress brought Sweeny's sandwich and placed it in front of him with a shrug. "Lots of luck."

He nodded ruefully and picked up half of the sandwich, taking a small bite. Okay, this was giving him something to do—now what?

"So?"

"Huh? I mean eh?"

"So aren't you going to tell me all about it? I mean, I like ancient history."

Sweeny swung around on his stool and looked at the girl. She was patting her mouth with a napkin and beaming at him. He felt like he was about to make a fool of himself but he couldn't stop.

"Are you putting me on?"

"I'm trying to make it easy for you," she said quietly. Her voice dipped so low he could barely hear her, but the words cut through the dense air between them like an electric spark. For a moment, the smile was gone and she looked at him the way a lover might, a look that Sweeny could only faintly remember. Then, just as quickly, it vanished. "No, really. I'd like to hear about your adventures. I'm interested in writing, and I guess you've been all over, seen everything, know everything there is to know." The smile sprung back suddenly, a light bulb being turned on. "Besides," she put her hand on his sleeve, "I like older men."

Sweeny laughed and swallowed a mouthful of tuna salad. "You come to the right place, baby. I'm the original older man."

"And I'm a little horny, too."

This time, Sweeny almost choked. He coughed, took a swallow of coffee.

"Hey, I was right, I *do* like you."

"Well, don't get your hopes up yet. I haven't decided if *I* like *you*." She took a du Maurier from her purse and lit it with a tiny gold lighter. She swiveled and pressed her bare knees against his leg. "Have you noticed,

Mr. Sweeny, how life is like a mirror image sometimes?"

Sweeny chewed thoughtfully. "Yeah, it stares back at you."

"That isn't what I meant. I mean, you know how certain things are supposed to happen? Life is laid out in an even, orderly way, like the script for a soap opera."

"I don't watch them."

"Okay, like a movie with . . ." She narrowed her eyes as if measuring him for a coat. "Lana Turner. Certain things happen, in a certain order. You can expect them, one right after another. But sometimes"—she took a drag on her cigarette and tilted her chin to exhale—"things get twisted around and work just the opposite way of the way they're *supposed* to."

Sweeny sipped coffee and stroked the rim of his jaw with a finger. "Okay, I follow that. What're you leading to?"

"Well, I'm the pretty little innocent girl with the nice body and you're the dirty old man, right?"

Sweeny rubbed his eyes and put his chin in his hands. "Say, do you know Delancy?"

"Beg pardon?"

"Never mind. Yeah, yeah, I'm the dirty old man."

"And if this were a movie, you'd be a private eye or a secret agent or a soldier of fortune or something like that, and you'd have something I want, a document or something, a stolen gem, a little black book. Something, maybe just help."

Sweeny pushed his plate away and lit a Player's. "Yeah, I think I've seen this movie. I've got the Bogie part."

"Now you're talking. And *I*," July said demurely, putting her fingertips to a point just below her throat, "would have something *you* want."

"What's that?"

She didn't say anything but her smile widened and she spread her hands apart, forming a frame.

"Okay," Sweeny said. "I get it."

"But life doesn't really work that way at all. Sometimes, lots of times, it's just like a mirror. Everything is there, in order, but it's all bass-ackwards."

Sweeny blew smoke to the side. "Okay, thanks for the philosophy lesson. What's the kicker?"

"Well, simply that, in this case, *I've* got something *you* want, and, um, I like older men."

"One of which I happen to be."

"You're the original."

"Yup."

"And I'm a little horny."

"Well, so am I, but . . ."

"That's beside the point. In that movie, when Lana gives up her body, maybe she likes the fuck she gets out of the deal . . ."

The word went down Sweeny's gullet like an ice cube slipping out of a drink with a splash and startled swallow.

"What's the matter, you never hear a pretty girl say 'fuck' before?" She was grinning, enjoying his discomfort.

"Not quite the way you say it."

July laughed. "Yeah, it's my Canadian accent, eh? Anyway, as I was saying, *maybe* she likes the fuck . . . but that's only incidental. She does it to get back the little black book so she can protect her father's good name. After all, it wasn't *his* fault he sold those secrets to the Russians. He was being blackmailed by the janitor, who happened to barge into the lab and catch Poppa with that cute blonde supplier of white mice. But, mercy, that was *years* after Mum's death, and a man does have needs, and besides. . . ."

"Yeah, I *saw* the movie, July."

"So the point is, it doesn't matter if you're horny. That's beside the point. That wouldn't be why you're doing it. If you liked me, if you wound up liking *it*, that would only be a fringe benefit."

"Some fringe."

"You only say that because you're playing the part of the dirty old man."

"It's a habit that dies hard."

"Well, forget it." She leaned forward to put her hand on Sweeny's knee, a touch he could feel all the way up his leg. "From now on, as far as *this* relationship goes, I'm the dirty young girl and you're the sweet, innocent old-timer."

"A virgin, no doubt."

July rolled her eyes upward. "That would be nice, but unrealistic, I guess."

"I guess."

"But sweet."

"And innocent."

"Definitely innocent."

"As innocent as can be, under the circumstances."

"The circumstances that innocence is somewhat a reverse function of age."

"And I've got enough age to reverse a bunch of functions."

"Something like that."

"Okay. Just one thing, though. What's this thing you've got that I want so much that I'm willing to sacrifice my honour for it?"

"Oh, that." July swiveled her stool so she was facing ahead, gazing at the mirror above the counter, a real one, not a metaphor. Sweeny looked at the sweep of her profile, admiring her nose. It was the kind that didn't make a big fuss about the nostrils, small, neat black openings barely noticeable. Sweeny liked that.

"Yeah, that."

"Oh, that's just a map," she said lightly.

"A map. Okay, I can see giving up your honour for that. A treasure map, eh?"

"Maybe."

"Let's see it."

She turned her face to him, causing his heart to thump against his chest.

"Oh, no. Not yet."

"How do I know it's worth the sacrifice, then?"

"Oh, you'll think so."

"I will, eh? Where did you get this map?"

"From his room."

"Room?"

"At the hotel. Upstairs. *His* room."

"I'm not following you, July."

"I can see that."

"Well, good for you."

"You should be, though."

Sweeny narrowed his eyes at her. "You mean your hotel? The Queen's?"

"Sure, the Queen's, silly." She put her hand lightly on his knee again. "The maid found it. In his room."

"Whose room?" Sweeny asked, but even as he pronounced the words he knew the answer, the skin tightening along his spine.

"Limousine's," July said. Her eyes were wide, the irises green as a field of corn in late spring.

❖

Walking back to the office, Sweeny felt like he'd been to a steam bath, had lost pounds, was floating on air. He couldn't remember the last time he'd felt that way. He'd known all kinds of women—school girls, office girls, women reporters, friends' wives, sisters, mothers, waitresses and actresses and models, whores, tramps, lushes, nymphos, ambitious girls, girls on the way up and girls on the way down, winners and losers, beats and hippies, artists, writers, dancers, singers, dopers, free-lovers and no-lovers. But July wasn't like any of those, and she sure as hell wasn't anything like the garment district models he'd been consorting with just a few months ago. It wasn't just that she was such a nut that had his heart galumping against his ribs, that or the faint aura of danger radiating from her like a back light. No, it was the youngness of her, the freshness evoking a life that seemed so distant from Sweeny's own.

And the map—that was something else again, too. She didn't have it with her, of course, couldn't describe it, didn't know what it meant, but they'd made a date to meet that evening to look at it. *Jesus.* Sweeny slapped the palm of his hand against a streetlight pole and swung himself around it. "Hey," he said out loud, his cheeks reddening. "Eh?" A woman in a suede coat and fur hat gave him a sharp look as she walked past. "Hey, I'm not drunk," he called after her. She didn't turn and he wanted to shout it again, louder, "Hey, I'm not drunk, I'm not," but he thought better of it.

There was a phone message on his typewriter to call operator 39 in Washington, DC. He did and she put him through to *The Star*.

"Hey, Pat."

"Sween, you weren't around."

"Man gotta eat."

"Eat, sure."

"Hey, I told you this morning, Pat, I'm dry as a sponge."

"Sponge, maybe. But dry?"

"Dry. I'm dry. And maybe I'm in love, too, but that's another story. What'd you find out for me?"

"Something. I checked out those post office boxes. Had a bit of trouble, they're blind boxes, not supposed to be such numbers, ya know? But I got a friend. You were right. They go back to this fellow called Harriman, Ormand Harriman."

"I knew it," Sweeny said.

"So whadya take up my afternoon for?"

"That's an expression, Pat."

"Yeah, yeah. Anyway, this Harriman is a very slender fellow, no shadow."

"Nothing at all?"

"Practically nothing. He's not in the phone book for the district or any of the suburbs. Not in any of the directories. He's not on the roster of any of the government agencies that I took a quick look through, and he's not in our files or the *Post*'s, I called someone there and checked. And no one around this place ever heard of him."

"But he's got a couple of post office boxes," Sweeny said. He was chewing on the eraser end of his pencil, gazing across the newsroom at the young girl from Women's, Karen, who was leaning over the water cooler, her orange hair cascading down like fire. She was nice, but not *as* nice.

"Several."

"What's that?"

"He's got several post office boxes, different numbers, no special sequence. All blind boxes, they're not supposed to exist."

Sweeny blew against the mouthpiece. "What does that all add up to, Pat? I've been thinking Mafia, maybe, based on some stuff I got here since I talked to you."

There was a laugh on the other end of the line. "Mafia, yeah, well, maybe. But, Sweeny, baby, you are a little behind the times."

"Okay, so whatever they call it these days. Casa, whatever."

"That's not what I mean."

"So?"

"So don't be a klutz. You ever hear of spies?"

"Someone else suggested that, but I haven't given it much thought yet. CIA?"

"CIA maybe. FBI maybe. Or army intelligence, navy intelligence, air force intelligence. Take your pick. Or half a dozen others I don't know the initials for. Or your own boys, the ones with the funny hats?"

"Mounties, Pat."

"Yeah, those jokers. Or some other country, maybe. The KGB, the Ruskies call theirs. Point is, it's the MO."

"You think?"

"Think? I don't think about stuff like that. I'm just a broke-down deskman who spent a lot of sweat on the cop beat, buddy, and I know who to ask, just like you. You call up and ask me, I turn around and ask someone else. They tell me, I don't know, but they tell me, it's the MO. When a guy appears not to exist, when he leaves no shadow, then he's probably standing behind a pillar."

Sweeny spit out a piece of eraser. "Okay, I get it. Sounds nice. How about Limousine, anything on that name?"

"Ha. That one's even tougher, ya know? It don't exist either, and it don't even have a sling of post office boxes. There's one thing, though, maybe that's MO too."

"How's that?"

"Well, this guy was tellin' me, the name *sounds* right."

"It sounds right," Sweeny said.

"They like puns, these no-shadow boys, that's what this guy says. They like names with double meanings, play-on-words stuff. So, Limousine, that could be the kind of name they'd make up."

"Play on words. Why?"

"It's a game, I guess. Puns don't translate well, maybe not at all. So they like to tease the other guys."

"So you think I've stumbled into a covey of spies, eh, Pat?"

"Like I said, Sween, I don't think. I'm just passing along the dope. But, Sween, a word of advice. You're too old to be bucking for a Pulitzer, so be careful what you do and say."

Sweeny laughed. "This is Canada, Pat. They don't give Pulitzers up here."

"Why, wasn't he the guy who said 'Go west, young schmuck?'"

"No, and anyway, this is north and west."

"Same difference."

"Yeah, well, I'll be careful anyway."

"Not if you say you're in love, you ain't being."

"Yeah, well," Sweeny repeated. "Hey, listen, Pat, you remember that time they found that real estate cat all tied up and a rose sticking out of his ass?"

The voice on the other end of the line laughed so loudly Sweeny had to move the receiver away from his ear. "*You're* the asshole, Sween. The rose was in his *mouth*, you schmuck, the asshole was just a story we told around the office."

"Oh, yeah, I forgot that. Sometimes the story you tell is a hell of a lot better than the one you write, right? But, anyway, wasn't that a hell of a case? And, Jesus, that was before they even started coming into fashion, that sort of thing."

"Yeah, that was something," Pat said. The last time Sweeny had seen him, he was a skinny man with a protruding Adam's apple and a perpetual sheen to his upper lip. He was a hell of a police reporter, not like this bloodless bastard De Lisso. Now, his voice sounded heavier, as if his vocal cords, at least, had put on weight. "What's that got to do with this?"

"Eh?" Sweeny said. "Oh, nothing. I was just thinking about it before, when I was talking to some dumb dick. Remember that cop who gave us the hard time on that one, Pat? They didn't want to talk about it 'cause of the fag thing, and there was this one guy, a real piece of beef . . ."

"Hallernan," Pat said. "He was okay, just quiet."

"Quiet, hell. I always thought he protesteth too much, know what I mean?"

"That was a good case, all right," Pat said. The long-distance line crackled sharply, as if someone listening in had snapped gum into the receiver. "But you know what else it was, Sween?"

"What's that?"

"A long time ago, man, a long time ago."

"Well, yeah," Sweeny said.

"Hey, Sween, you really dry?"

"Sure, that's what I said, didn't I?"

"Yeah, you did that. And good luck to you, man."

"Yeah, thanks. Hey, just for fun," Sweeny said, picking up his pencil, "before I let you go, why don't you let me have all those numbers."

"Which numbers is that?"

"Those post office boxes of Harriman's. Lemme have the numbers."

"Sure, got 'em right here. Just for fun, right?"

"Right. What else? Just for fun."

He began to write.

V

AT A QUARTER PAST SIX, FIFTEEN MINUTES EARLY AND feeling a bit like a high school boy on his first date, Sweeny finds himself standing outside the beer room of the Heights Hotel, a gloomy but amiable landmark in the older section of town. It was the kind of place where the beds would be sharp with springs, roaches would roam the floor, the chambermaid would rattle in the hallway in the morning, and pipes would gurgle all night. He'd stayed at too many places like it.

Sweeny inspects his reflection in the window. A few minutes before, he'd been on the corner, watching the sun sink into the clutches of the mountains in an almost cloudless sky, and already the temperature has dropped a few degrees. His trenchcoat is buttoned up tight, cancelling out the effect of his best sports jacket, still crisp from the dry cleaner's plastic wrap.

He frowns at the image he sees—a tall man with sloping shoulders, the illusion of strength obscured by the shapeless coat, a lopsided snowman beginning to turn to slush, its life trickling away. He peers closer, unhappy about the battered face, too frayed, too *old*, with black hollows for eyes—nothing there for a young girl. The word "Tavern" cuts his body in two, and behind the reflection he can see cars moving slowly past on a windy street.

He walks back to the corner and gazes down the hill, southeast toward the city centre. Clouds are starting to congregate around the pair of peaks behind which the sun disappeared, the last rays bathing them in streaks of vermilion. Behind him, the neighbourhood seems to sigh, its bones creaking with age and regret. A few blocks away, further up the plateau, is the spot where his uncle's feed-and-grain had stood, buttressing itself with whitewash and advertising calendars for as long as it could, until it made way for a little shopping mall: a convenience store and a sandwich shop and a dry cleaner. Sweeny kicks at a page of the *Chronicle* fluttering up the street as it tangles itself around his foot. Two Indians in scruffy jeans and cowboy boots walk past, their heads lowered, then a boy with a beard and a girl, both with the same sort of birdsnest hair. A college has sprung up here in the years since he left, the campus not far from where he stands.

Sweeny glances at his watch, then back up the street toward the hotel. The Indians are pushing through the door of the tavern, the boy and girl walking on, and there is no sign of July. He shoves his hands into his coat pockets and crosses the street, turning north. He doesn't want to go all the way to where the feed-and-grain had been, that would make him late, but he'll go a block or two, then swing back to the hotel from the other direction. Maybe he'll come upon her in the street.

Where he walks, on a plateau above the first loop of the river in whose valley the city nestles, there was, even as late as Sweeny's childhood, a forest of hundred-year-old pine and birch. Then the growing town reached out and up, sucking the closest ones down. Where Uncle Tomas built the feed-and-grain there was nothing else at first, just a clearing, the wooden buildings and a rutted, muddy road leading to them. Then, in a rapid expansion, the town puffed up the hill to clear its lungs, take in the view and gather around him. In front of the store was a street with children playing, in Sweeny's earliest memory of the place, but Uncle Tomas could look up from his ledger in the rear office and gaze out the window at green, loping hills fringed by pine, dotted with cattle and yellow wildflowers in the spring, the icy-blue tips of mountains not far away. By the time Sweeny came to live with him and Aunt Alice, at sixteen, the store was locked into the town on all sides, a piece in a jigsaw puzzle. The houses had been new then, the neighbourhood hopeful; now they are worn, in need of repair.

Sweeny pauses to inspect a rambling house with half a dozen or more gables. It appears to be a rooming house, its once spacious, airy rooms partitioned into cramped suites for college students. He walks on, past one ramshackle house after another, his hands deep in his pockets. A sense of familiarity envelops him, like the warm smell of milk in Aunt Alice's kitchen. He'd been a pilgrim then, and everything had been strange, just a stop, not a place to stay. All the staying he had ever wanted then was behind him, on the porch of his grandfather's house, beside the creaking rocker.

He had been on the Heights once before that, during the weeks of dull blur that came after his mother's death, when he was eleven, and all the hurt in the world was raining down on him, but all that remained with him of that sad, brief time was the fluttering of the blue curtains in his cousins' bedroom, where he would spend whole mornings in bed, buried under the covers like a mole in Aunt Alice's garden. And why shouldn't he have hidden? He'd been deserted not once but twice, first by a father he could barely remember, then by the mother who had become the centre of his existence. And then it was as if he had gone directly from that warm sanctuary behind the curtains to the beaten-down grass in front of the old man's porch where he was getting out of Uncle Tomas's car, clutching a cardboard suitcase in one hand, a paper sack in the other, and Greta was coming toward him down the steps, going down on her knees and enfolding him in her massive arms, engulfing him in the smell of warm milk. "Poor baby, poor baby," she kept saying, alternating the expression in Swedish and English. Finally, she rose, giving him air, taking the suitcase from him in one big, callused hand, his small, soft one in the other, directing him toward the porch steps. Uncle Tomas and the car were gone from the memory, and Greta was whispering: "Come, Grampa is waiting."

He had climbed the steps to the porch, pausing on the next-to-the-top step, his eyes level with those of the old man in the rocker, his body cramped into a comma. "He has the bad rheumy pain in the neck," Greta's voice whispered in his ear, her accent thick as cream. "He cain't turn his head so good. You be careful not to hurt him."

Sweeny remembers now how he had to edge slightly to the left so he could look directly into his grandfather's immobile eyes. "I've come to live with you, Grampa, is that okay?" he said after a moment, when Greta's sharp finger prodded his ribs, his voice so soft he wasn't sure the old man had heard.

There was no immediate response, the old man's eyes blinking slowly, as if repelling the smoke drifting up from the corncob pipe clamped in his toothless mouth. The boy's mouth was opening to speak again when the old man lifted his arms with visible pain, his head rocking on his thin shoulders, and the pipe sagged. "Ya, boy, ya, come, come here." Then he had been engulfed by the old man's thick smells, raw wood and smoke and sweat and some mysterious something else, smells so unlike the starch and strong soap of his mother, the old man's daughter, so unlike those vaguely remembered antiseptic smells of his own father, and his chin was in the brown hollow of his grandfather's collarbone and he could feel the thick, twisted old hands gripping his shoulder blades like they were dear life itself. Beneath them, the rocker swayed and creaked. "It be okay now, boy," the old man said, "it be okay now."

The boy believed him, and for the next five years they were his family, the old man whose life had spun down to a bed, a chair, and a place at the kitchen table, and the old dumpling-shaped woman who took care of him. His wife was dead, two of his three sons dead, killed in the war, and now even his daughter dead. He was an old man too stiff and bent to even walk across his land, let alone work it, who spent most or his time, even in winter when he bundled up in a grey wool greatcoat and a Hudson's Bay blanket, rocking on the porch, staring with vacant eyes at the road leading away from the house, as if expecting someone. And if that first moment in the old man's arms was the clearest memory Sweeny had of his childhood, another was almost as strong, though there was no specific time attached to it. It could have been later on that first day or any day after that over the next few years, the time it took for the old man to finally be squeezed so tight by the hand around his middle that he died, any day at all that the weather was tolerable: sitting on the porch, the two of them, the grandfather in the rocker, the boy on the steps, his shoulder just an inch from the old man's foot, his head right where the old man could see its crown, just below the line of vision. Sitting in silence, smoke from the old man's pipe blowing blue and fragrant across the porch, the creak of the rockers in the boy's ears like some vague, foreign music, a melody from far-off Sweden, the two of them together and alone, hushed and still, hanging in space, as if waiting for someone, some thing. Far in the distance, there was a hill with a towering blue spruce reaching for the sky like the hand of a drowning man. The boy would stare at the tree, imagining stories about it, but it wasn't until after the old man died that he realized his grandfather had been watching it too. They buried him there, right below the tree's curling roots, beside the woman who'd been his wife, the grandmother Sweeny had never known. "Now they can both be happy," Greta said.

It was funny, Sweeny thinks now, that he could remember the woman saying that, but he had no idea what had become of her. The farm had been sold, the boy bundled off to his aunt and uncle's again, the old woman who had been so dominated by the man she worked for dissipated almost entirely in memory. The Heights was in front of him then, at his uncle's house for the next two years, till he finished school and was old enough to be out on his own, in a small set of rooms over a hardware store not far from his uncle's. Then, after Highmountain, that other old man in his life, died, he all but moved into the office above the print shop—had, in fact, taken a room in a boarding house two blocks from the newspaper so he'd have some place to go when the paper became too much for him, but spent hardly any time there—and that had been that. He'd continued to come up here to visit his aunt and uncle, of course, and occasionally on stories, but it was different. It wasn't home anymore, not that it ever really had been. Just a stop. Now, his aunt and uncle long dead, his cousins scattered, the house they'd lived in torn down, it was barely even that, just a neighbourhood, a section of town that was a little out of the way. Up to now, Sweeny hasn't even bothered, since his return to town, to visit it.

He turns back toward the hotel, his steps quick on the almost-empty street. Now *he's* the one who's late. As he walks down the hill, he can feel the neighbourhood sigh again, this time over his passing, the buildings hovering in space and time like animals gathering strength to lunge or slink away and die.

❖

It was twenty minutes to seven and almost dark when he got back to the tavern, and there was still no sign of July. He glanced around anxiously, but there was no one in sight. Then suddenly she was there, stepping out of the shadows of the doorway and right up beside him, setting his heart pounding.

"Hey, good-looking." Her swirl of hair was neatly patted down, and she'd changed the skirt and sweater for brown corduroy jeans, a wine-coloured T-shirt, and a fringed suede jacket. She looked even younger, even prettier than he remembered. "Buy a girl a beer?"

"I thought maybe you'd forgotten," Sweeny said.

"You did, eh?" When she smiled, her face was bright as a theatre marquee. He took her hand and led her through the "Ladies and Escorts" entrance into the tavern, through the semi-darkness and noise, to a table halfway to the bandstand, where a five-piece band was demolishing "Purple Haze." Sweeny was far from being a connoisseur of popular music, but even he knew the guitarist was no Jimi Hendrix.

July grabbed a waiter's arm and shouted at him: "Four draught."

Sweeny held up his hand. "Make it two, and a Coke."

"Hey!" July said quickly.

"Take it easy, the Coke's for me." He had to shout to be heard over the band.

"I thought you were going to play poppa on me."

"Hardly." Sweeny grinned. "I wouldn't know where to begin. Anyway, if you're old enough to talk dirty, you're old enough to drink."

July grinned back, arching her shoulders against the chair. "And you're not old enough, I guess."

"Oh, I'm old enough, all right. I'm just trying to get into my role. Sweet and innocent, remember?"

The waiter sloshed three glasses down between them. July took a swallow from one of her beers and mouthed a silent, satisfied "ah" as she surveyed the people sitting at tables near them, but Sweeny let the Coke sit where it was. The band stopped playing with a sudden lurch and a rush of voices poured into the vacuum. Sweeny took off his coat and laid it carefully on a chair. "You know, I used to drink in this place when I was even younger than you. The dust has gotten a little thicker, but the place hasn't changed much."

"Younger than me," July mimicked. "That must have been centuries ago, eh?"

"I'm still alive and kicking, so it couldn't have been more than two or three centuries." The band took up again, a roaring "Hang on, Sloopy," and he brought his hands to his ears. July laughed.

"Well, I don't know." She sipped at her beer, studying him solemnly over the rim of the glass. "Charlie Cook says you're preserved in alcohol, so maybe you're old as the hills, for all I know."

Sweeny winced. "That hurt. I've been known to take a drink or two, sure, but it's none of Charlie Cook's business. He was just a shitty-assed bellhop selling booze and condoms on Sunday when I was a newspaper publisher in this town. I don't remember us doing too much drinking together, though he probably got a few for me. And he hasn't seen or heard word one from me since then until a few weeks ago, so I don't think Charlie Fucking Cook qualifies as any kind of an expert on me, on my drinking or anything else about me."

He was glad the band was drowning out the anger that had slipped into his voice. He looked away, but when he looked back she was smiling at him, her small, even teeth bared.

"I exaggerated a *bit*, perhaps," July said sweetly, running a finger lightly along the rim of her glass. "He said, if I remember his words right, that you had the *look* of a drinker."

Sweeny gave her a fierce grin, his anger hissing away. "The look, eh? You *are* a delicious little liar, you know? I've got to learn to control myself around you."

"Not completely, I hope." She finished her beer in two big swallows, put down the empty glass and reached for the second one. Sweeny beat her to it.

"Think I'll show you what a drinker really looks like." He gulped the beer down and banged the glass on the table. He raised his hand, signalling the waiter with four fingers.

"Hey, you're supposed to be sweet and innocent, remember? I'm the dirty young girl. But you're starting to talk like you're about to start talking dirty, lapsing back into character. You've got to do better, Sweeny. We've rejected that character, please keep that in mind."

"It ain't easy, baby. It's a skin now. Hard to shed."

"Bang it against a tree."

"Huh?"

"You know, like bucks do in the spring so new antlers can grow."

Sweeny laughed, just as the round of beers arrived. "You've really got a one-track mind, baby. You're onto horns again."

July grinned, letting the pun pass. The smile faded suddenly and she looked at him solemnly. "Don't call me baby. Not yet, anyway."

They clicked their glasses and Sweeny let the beer rush into him like seawater into the lungs of a drowning man who's given up and welcomes what now must come. He had started and was as helpless as that drowning man, being swept along by a tide. Might as well enjoy it.

"How about that map?" The band had chugged to the end of "Smoke on the Water."

"Patience," July said.

They finished off the beers, Sweeny and July matching each other swallow for swallow. Sweeny looked up for the waiter, but July touched his arm. "Let's blow. I'm hungry." They went up the street to a health food restaurant, where ferns hung beside lamps with stained-glass shades. As they waited for one of the few tiny tables, July went off, leaving Sweeny to admire an old-fashioned spring scale, the kind that told your weight for a penny. It had been rigged to work for free, he saw, and, looking around, he stepped on gingerly. The needle spun crazily, shooting up past 300, swinging down to 100, then up again, gradually diminishing its arc. It took a long time to finally settle at 235. Sweeny sighed as he watched the needle quiver, as if it were still undecided. He stared balefully at his face in the mirror centred in the scale and recognized it from the one he had been examining not long before in the tavern window. The eyes were clearer now, dark but clear.

"A big man," July said softly.

She was standing beside him, looking solemnly at the scale. Except for the shape of her breasts in the T-shirt, she looked like a child, and Sweeny had an impulse to hug her, right there, the hell with everyone else. "Too big," he said.

"Afraid you'll crush me?"

"I wouldn't have said that, but yeah, I suppose so." He stepped down.

"I can be on top, you know," she said, winking. Sweeny felt an ache about the size of a quarter slip between his ribs and begin to grow.

A young woman almost as tall as Sweeny wearing a jade-green dress that went from her throat to the floor in one sweep of shimmering cloth took them to a corner table where a candle flickered in a dish. July ordered for them both—vegetable curry and rice, cucumber and yogurt salad, a pot of jasmine tea. Sweeny watched her face as she scrutinized the menu and talked to the waitress—it was amazing how much light her face seemed to reflect.

"You know, you must be crazy," he said when the waitress left.

"Because I like beer and health food?"

"No, not that. I mean you must be crazy to be sitting here wasting your time with me, an old, overweight used-up hack, old enough to be your grandfather."

"But sweet and innocent."

"Yeah, I keep forgetting about that game we're playing."

"It's no game." July looked hurt. She stuck out her lower lip and pouted. Sweeny wanted to reach over and touch that lip with his fingertips. "This is serious."

"Yeah," he said, without much conviction. "Okay, you want to get serious. *Seriously*, most girls your age look at an old fart like me and all they see is a pile of rubble. What's the attraction?"

"Maybe I like rubble." July grinned. "Like some of this art you see in galleries these days, sculpture made from scrap iron? I like the possibilities. Anyway, it's grist for my mill."

"How's that?"

"That's something my dad says. 'It's all grist for your mill, sand to chew on.'"

"Sounds like a great philosopher." Sweeny lit a cigarette and tasted the smoke mingling with the fading flavour of beer still in his mouth.

"Oh, he is." She paused. "You know how hacks are."

Sweeny cocked his head, blowing smoke. "Ah ha, the plot thickens. Your dad's a newspaperman?"

"Was."

"So I'm just a father figure, eh? Here, I thought I still had some sex appeal, turns out I'm just a surrogate father."

"That's not exactly right." She sounded angry. "You do remind me of my dad a little, *just a little,* and maybe that's what made me first pay attention, but after that, that's all there is. I don't have a goddamn Oedipus complex. . . ."

"Electra."

"Whatever. I don't have a secret yen to fuck my father. I do have a secret yen to fuck you, though."

"Some secret." Sweeny shook his head.

"Not at all." She lowered her voice, looking around. "I guess the whole restaurant doesn't have to know about it, though."

"No, you don't want to put ideas into people's heads. They'd be lining up outside my bedroom door, and I don't think I'd have the strength to last for long."

July's grin returned. "You look strong enough."

"Yeah, well . . . let's get back to your father. So he's a hack like me."

"Not like you."

He looked at her hard. "Who is he? What's his name?"

"I'm not going to tell you."

"Ah ha, more mystery. Do I know him?"

"Maybe."

"Well, that narrows the field down to twenty thousand. And, lessee, he'd have to be, well, at least forty I guess, so that narrows the field down to fifteen thousand or so. Okay, I'll start reeling off the names as they come into my mind and when your eyebrows jump, I'll know I hit it. Just like a lie detector, eyebrows. You know that?"

"I don't have eyebrows."

"Yeah, those are caterpillars crawling over your eyes. Everybody has eyebrows. Except a woman I did a story on once, in New York, Newark, New Jersey, actually. She was in a fire and her eyebrows were burned clean off." He rubbed his own eyebrows. "And the hair off her head, too, but that grew back. The eyebrows never did. Made her look like a doll, you know, one of those Barbie doll things."

"You did a story on the fire?" July was leaning forward.

"Hell, no. The fire had been a couple of years before. She was burned when she went back into the house to save one of her kids. There were three of them, if I remember right, and one was already out, she saved one and the third one died."

"So what . . . ?"

"This was when she killed the other two kids. Because they'd been burned and had pain and cried at night. Put a pillow to their faces and that was that."

In the silence between them, they could hear the murmur of talk from the next table, where two women and a child were attacking a massive salad. "I don't have eyebrows either," July said quietly.

"Sure, just those caterpillars. But stop changing the subject. It's your dad I'm interested in. Let's narrow it down more, geographically. Do I know him from here?"

"I didn't *say* you knew him. I said *maybe*."

"Okay. *If* I know him, where would it be from? Here?"

July shook her head.

"Toronto?"

She shrugged, raising her hands. When her shoulders went up, her breasts moved like water under thin ice beneath her T-shirt.

"New York? Washington? Miami? London? Paris? Madrid?"

"Nope, nope, nope. Hey, were you really in all those places?"

"Sure." Sweeny grinned and sipped at his tea. "I got on a train here, right here in this little burg, one day, and one thing sort of led to another. Paper in Toronto sent me down to Washington to cover that nonsense and I never bothered to come back. Then there was a war over in Europe, maybe you've heard of it, and I forgot to go back for a while after that shooting match was over. And then . . ." He raised his hands in an imitation of her gesture. "So where do I know your old man from?"

"Oh, I'm not telling."

"C'mon."

"No, we'll see how smart you are. I bet you'll guess."

"How much time do I have?"

"I don't know. That's a good question." She laughed. "It depends on how much grist my mill can take."

"How much grist you in the market for?"

"I don't know if there's any special ration. You're a good character. I'm going to pull as much out of you as I can and use you somewhere."

"Character, okay, I get called that a lot. But use me?"

"In my novel. Didn't I tell you?"

"Oh, I see." He laughed. "I should have guessed. I wrote one once too."

He stopped suddenly, blinking, and tugged at his ear.

She gave him a quizzical look.

"Something flipped through my head so fast I couldn't see what it was." He grinned. "I haven't thought about that thing in years. I'd forgotten I wrote it. Actually, I was just thinking about it last night, but without *really* thinking about it. Know what I mean?"

"Sure. What happened to it? Did you publish it?"

"Naw. I never even . . ."

The tall waitress interrupted him with their salads and the thought vanished. Sweeny examined the yogurt mixture with suspicion. His mouth was parched, the roof tight as a boil, but the cool, soupy stuff he spooned in brought no relief. He'd made a mistake having those beers, showing off, he knew that. He'd come dangerously close the other day at the Queen's, but he'd stopped just short of too many, and it was the middle of the day, with plenty of hours left to work the stuff out of his system before it did any harm. This time, he knew, it was too late in the day. It didn't make sense. He was a grown man, sitting up at a table like the big people, eating with knife and fork, carrying on an intelligent conversation—he didn't *look* like he was hell bent on being drunk, losing all control of himself, giving up any claim to manhood or humanity or whatever you wanted to call that thing that belongs only to *us*, that the other animals don't have. He didn't *look* that way, but he was, Sweeny knew that, just as sure as night follows day—or was it the other way around?

He was smiling at July, eating, making conversation, feeling the ache that had begun as a tiny spore between his ribs spread through him like a buttered cancer, but he was kicking himself at the same time. Falling off the fucking wagon was as easy as falling off a log, as they say. But still, after two dry months of hell and murder, he should have been stronger. Now that he had started—and with this Limousine thing to propel him along, tugging at his sleeve till he bent over and fell—there was no telling when he'd be through. And where was there to go lower than here?

An image slipped into Sweeny's head like a penny into a slot: a sooty window, staring down at him like the vacant eyes of a lunatic, and behind it, clear, black winter night, frosted with stars, matches crackling into distant fire in the cold. He could feel the floor hard beneath him, the cold nostril breath of the night snorting in through the cracks in the window. He could feel his blood, his skin, his bones. He closed his eyes but when he opened them, a moment later, it was all still there: the window above him, filthy grey and yet, somehow, clear as a pencil stroke on white paper, and the night beyond. He was alive and, somehow, miraculously, he was sober.

He was in his own apartment, in New York's lower east side, the dust around him thick as the taste in his mouth, on the tail of a beast he'd been riding for almost two weeks. He had climbed on when his job—the latest in a spinning series of dismal failures—as a press agent for a garment district factory had evaporated, leaving him blind with tears and anger. Sweeny's job had been to get his boss's name into the gossip columns and the label's name into the fashion pages—an all-but-impossible task he had claimed he could accomplish by virtue of all the old friends he had in the business. At the very least, he'd get his boss into the models. He'd been at it for three months, maybe a little more, and was doing best in the last department—with the models—having already cashed in most of his old friends' debts on previous jobs. It was an easy trade-off he had with the girls—if they'd make the boss happy, Sweeny would try to get *their* names into the gossip columns, a job that was easier to do because the gossip columnists were more interested in hearing about models who fucked than about clothing manufacturers who fucked, though not *much* more. Just enough to keep Sweeny going. His wants were few: a bed to sleep in, something solid in his belly to sop up the other stuff, and, yeah, the other stuff, a certain amount each day, just enough to keep doubt from the door.

It could, he knew, have gone on forever—sliding along the bottom rail, greased by his own excretions—except that nothing goes on forever, certainly not this kind of scam. The boss would get wise, or he'd get tired of redheads—they were the ones the gossip columnists and their runners seemed to like best that season—or his wife would find out, or he'd have a heart attack in some redhead's bed. Something would happen to jinx the deal, it would have to. What *did* happen was simpler. The dress factory moved south, where labour was cheaper—moved lock, stock, and barrel, taking sewing machines, patterns, dresses, needles, and thread, even one of the models. But not Sweeny.

The unemployed pimp climbed on the beast.

Not just a drunk, not the usual nine-to-five swim, but a meatgrinder— he took two weeks of what was left of his life, crumpled them into the metal jaws, added booze to taste. There had just been, for the past few years, too much *down* for him to resist. And it had been a long time since he had resisted at all.

The two weeks were a blank, but now, almost four months later, sitting in the light, the memory of the darkness of his wakening was as sharp as the taste of the hot spiced potato on his tongue. He had come to, some-how, still alive, aware that he was an out-of-work pimp but with little rec-ollection of his last days. He was in his own apartment, remarkably, with all his limbs intact, remarkably, even his cock still screwed into his lower belly where it ought to be, and his head as big as the Ritz but still, remark-ably, clear. He could think, *he was thinking*. He was alive. It was night, he was lying on the floor in the kitchen, on his back, a spider exhausted from railing at the glass walls of a jar. The window shade was up and the kitchen window stared down at him like the loose smile of an idiot. He could feel the rough texture of the buckled linoleum beneath him and some little thing skittering across one bare foot. One pane of the window was cracked, a jagged black line like a lightning bolt in a cartoon. On the other side of the sooty window was clear, black winter night, frosted with stars. Sweeny lay on the floor, his head huge and throbbing but clear as the cold night, his eyes open, staring at the sooty, hoary stars until his vision blurred from tears. His life hung just beyond the cracked glass, barely out of his own reach, each moment shimmering and clear, distinct as a star, like a map spread before a lost sailor in the moment before the mast falls and all is lost, as the wind pounds down without heart.

The night—the moment—went on and on, wheels spinning silently in deep snow, but morning eventually came, the points of light the stars depicted drowning in grey sky. When Sweeny got to his feet and went to the window, all he could see in the alleys below was laundry hanging like listing flags from webs of clotheslines. He made coffee, took a long bath, shaved, drank the coffee, and made another pot, and finally sat down and typed the letter to the *Chronicle* he'd been composing for hours. It was an idea he'd had in his head for some time, but never had the courage to act on. And he promised himself, as he wrote, that if he got the job—this last chance—he would give up the booze forever. But, of course, he hadn't really expected to get it.

"Something wrong?" July asked softly.

Sweeny shook his head, blinking. "This curry's *hot*."

"A cold beer sure would go good with this stuff," she said, smiling ruefully.

"Yes, it would." He finished what was on his plate and pushed his chair back. "Wow. Hot. How about that map, by the way?"

"Patience, patience. I don't have it with me, anyway."

"What? I thought the whole . . ."

July cocked her head. "Here I thought you wanted to be with me."

He bit his lip. "Sure, I do. I really do. But I am kind of anxious to see this map, too."

"Okay, I don't want to disappoint you. We can have tea at my place. It's not far. That's where it is."

Sweeny smiled. "Ah ha, the plot thickens again."

"Well, there is the little matter of the, ah, *payment,* if you recall."

"That's right. I forgot I was with a dirty young girl."

The waitress gave him the bill at the register. "Enjoy your dinner?"

"Not bad, but I could eat for a week on what this cost."

The woman smiled. Glistening earrings the shape of half moons framed her narrow head. Her eyes, Sweeny noticed, had the same silvery sheen.

"But it's peanuts compared to what the astronauts get for chow, so forget it."

July took his arm as they went through the door. Sweeny hunched his shoulders against the cold and felt a glow emanating from his side.

"What're you laughing at?" she asked.

"Eh? Oh, nothing. Just myself."

She looked at him hard, squeezing his arm. She had to tilt her head up to look him in the face. "It's not to laugh," she said softly.

They walked one block up the hill, then took a turn to the right. They passed a vacant lot and the city suddenly hung below them, its lights shining coldly through the darkness. Timber had changed so much in the years since Sweeny left, yet it still took his breath away when he caught glimpses of it like this, not because it was so large or so grand, but because it was *his* and yet so foreign. They were a mile away, at least, but the yellow neon sign hanging from the Queen's was as clear as the full moon above them.

"That moon," Sweeny said. "What a target it'll be for those guys tomorrow. But . . ."

"What?"

"They don't usually have these moon shots when the moon is full, do they?"

"I dunno, why not?"

"Something about the angle, I don't know. Something I read."

They walked on in silence. Above them, clouds darted across the sky like racehorses.

"It's funny, those places you said you worked in?" July said suddenly.

"Huh?"

"All those places you worked in—Washington, Paris, London?"

"Yeah, what about them? They're just places where it gets dark at night, just like this one."

"Yes, I know that, Mr. Sweeny, sir. I mean, they're the same places that Mr. Limousine had stickers from on his suitcase."

Sweeny stopped walking. "Wait a minute. You saw Limousine's suitcase?"

"Sure. It was leather, real leather, I mean. It had lots of stickers on it, that's why I noticed it. I'm trying to visualize it right now, sitting on the floor by the post in the lobby. I was admiring it because it was very colourful, like something you might see in a travel agency window. There were lots of stickers, and I think there was one from every one of those cities: Paris, London, Madrid—that one for sure because there was a matador or something, and a red cape—and New York, Washington . . ."

"Toronto?"

"Could have been. I'm not sure. And what was the other one? Miami. Yes, except the sticker might have been from Miami Beach."

Sweeny was lighting a cigarette, cupping his hands around the match to protect it from the wind. "Any place else? From East Europe, maybe?"

"Well . . . yes, Berlin. But I don't think it said East or West."

"Berlin, huh." He had a vision of his hotel room in the American sector, of the neatly painted furniture and the crisp white curtains fluttering in the breeze from the open window, and of the view through the window, the crater across the street, the barbed wire, the smoke hanging heavily across the horizon, the constant feeling that the war was still on, even though the fighting had stopped. The curtains, he remembered, had been starched. They moved stiffly against his face as he stood by the window his first night there, watching a woman with a small child in tow come slowly down the empty street and pause in front of the crater, peer in, the fidgeting child suddenly still. Their heads were bowed as if they were in prayer. The next morning, he stopped at the crater as he left the hotel and let his eyes wander over the rubble, looking for some sign of what the woman had been seeking. An old man came tottering down the street toward him, his eyes suspicious and bleary under an alpine hat with a feather. He stopped beside Sweeny and the two men gazed into the crater in silence.

"Many people die here," the old man said finally, in rough English, the feather in his hat bobbing comically.

"Bombs?" Sweeny asked, feeling foolish for asking such an obvious question.

"Ya," the old man said, looking at Sweeny with eyes suddenly clear and filled with pity. They merely lost their lives, he seemed to be saying; you have them on your conscience.

Sweeny stayed away from the crater after that, though he often looked at it from the window, gazing out at the broken grave without bodies that most people walked past briskly, without pausing. The woman and child didn't return, though he watched for them every evening of the two weeks he was in Berlin, writing stories about a city rebuilding. Rebuilding was something Sweeny knew a bit about.

He shook his head. "Any place else?"

"Not that I remember. No, I don't think so."

Sweeny flipped through the atlas in his mind for any other places he'd lived or worked. He'd travelled all over Europe, during the war and after, either as a correspondent or a freelancer, or just as a tourist, getting to some places on his Canadian passport that he mightn't have reached otherwise, but he hadn't worked in every place he'd gone. He'd actually been a correspondent or held a job in all the cities Limousine's suitcase had stickers from—those places in Europe and the States, and Toronto, and here, of course, and Wilkes-Barre, where he'd spent a few months when he and Barbara came back from Europe, freshly married and filled with hopes and plans, just like a couple of kids. That was when he'd gotten a look at the Pennsylvania Dutch country up around King of Prussia and Blue Balls . . .

"Jesus," Sweeny said.

"Hey, are you okay?"

"Yeah, I'm fine. Just a little dizzy, maybe."

"There's a bench over here on the corner."

They sat down at the bus stop, and Sweeny unbuttoned his coat to let the night air in. His breath was coming in short, rapid bursts, as if he had just run up a couple flights of stairs. When he closed his eyes, Charlie Cook's fleshy nose was bobbing in front of him and the mouth beneath it was pronouncing a list of cities someone had telephoned just before dying. "That's London, *England*," Charlie Cook said. "And some place called King of Prussia, Pennsylvania."

Sweeny hadn't ever actually gotten there, but he'd been in another town, not too far from it, that he imagined must be almost the same, the neat frame houses stretched out in identical rows like sailors at inspection, tunics and fingernails filthy with the coal dust that filtered constantly through the bleak sunlight. Barbara had been born there, in that town small enough to put in the palm of your hand, and there was a house, empty since her parents' death, they could have lived in. There was a country weekly there, filled with news about mines and miners, more like a company newsletter than a paper, Sweeny said when she showed it to him. There was a photograph on the first page of a woman with a flowered hat and a mashed potato face holding up a cabbage big as a rabbit she'd snared in her garden.

Barbara wanted them to buy the paper. "You can do what you want with it. Make it into something."

He'd laughed. "And go broke. Or break my back. The only woman who urges her husband to buy a weekly is one who's tired of her husband."

She protested, laughing. "Well, that's not me." She was a big-boned brunette with the kind of bangs the young women were all wearing that year, and she'd brushed them away from her eyes, deep brown eyes he loved to gaze into.

"But mostly," he'd said, "I'd be weighed down by a feeling of deja vu. I've done that. No, hon, it would be pleasant, maybe, but it's not for me."

"We could be happy," Barbara said simply.

Sweeny looked at her. Years later, he could remember the way she looked at that moment as clearly as if he held a photograph in his hands, her dark hair windblown, cheeks red, eyes watering. They were walking across a quarry that lay like a scar on the shoulder beneath that tiny town, trees behind and above them, folding them in, gravel crunching beneath their feet, the wind funnelling through the narrow passage made by trees and rock buffeting them, snatching the words out of their mouths and flinging them into the wild air.

"We're happy now," Sweeny had said.

Barbara leaned toward him, tilting her head. "What?" she shouted.

Being there in Wilkes-Barre had been an accident. Barbara had found him in Europe when he was in a bad way, working when he felt like it but drinking most of the time. He'd come off the tracks somehow. She put things he hadn't even noticed he'd lost back into him and they returned to the States together. He still had his green card and was keen to get to Washington again, but there weren't any jobs there or in New York, either. A guy he'd known in Europe was working as managing editor in Wilkes-Barre and offered him a job. It seemed as good a place as any to hole up till something better came along, and Barbara's eyes lit up when she heard there was a job waiting for him there. But near the end of summer he got a bite from Miami, and there was even a chance he might get sent to Washington. Barbara was still talking about that weekly, didn't want him to take it, but she went with him. He never did get sent to Washington, but after a year something came open on the *Star*, and he was doing well enough that they were willing to take a chance on him. She didn't go with him that time. After the divorce, she went back to Pennsylvania, and could still be there, for all he knew, walking through quarries with some other joker. He'd lost touch.

Lost touch. Like gelatin that hadn't set right, there'd been something wrong with his life that Barbara hadn't been able to fix after all. And he didn't know why. All that killing he saw in the war, that might have been it, part of it, anyway, but that sounded too easy. There wasn't any one moment he could point to and say, "There, that's where things went sour." It wasn't like he hadn't done the things he set out to, some of them, anyway. He'd bought a train ticket to Toronto, and that's where he'd gotten to, just for openers. Later, when he was wandering from job to job, through two marriages, he would think back to his father and mother dying on him, then his grandfather, then Highmountain, and he would nod his head, as if recognizing some cosmic design scrawled in the dust. "Oh yeah, this is why I behave as I do, because of that." Then he'd shake his head, have another drink.

"I'm beginning to think this fucker Limousine has been following me around the world," Sweeny said. His mouth was dry as a snake's skin and he feared his hand would soon start to shake. "No wonder I think I know him. He's been dogging me." He forced a grin. "I don't suppose he's your father, eh?"

She laughed. "No, hardly. Though he reminded me of my father, a little."

"Reminded you? Hold on. You saw Limousine?"

"Sure. I checked him in."

"Now you tell me. Wait a minute, Charlie Cook said *he* checked him in."

"No, I did it. Mr. Limousine asked if he could use his American Express card, and I wasn't sure so I had to ask Mr. Cook. But *I* checked him in."

"All right, don't get huffy. What'd he look like?"

"Well, sort of like my father. And . . ."

"Yeah?"

"Tall, about your height. About your build, too."

"Fat."

"No, not fat. Just big, solid. Like you."

Sweeny edged around on the bench and took hold of her shoulders. She felt so small and soft beneath his big hands, and he realized it was the first time he had touched her. His hands fell awkwardly to his sides.

"What about his face? What did he look like?"

A car drove by and Sweeny could see the green of July's eyes in the lights.

"Well, he looked . . . sort of . . . like you." She put her hand on his cheek, and he shivered. "But it was kinda hard to tell what he looked like under all those whiskers."

Sweeny's cheek twitched under her soft hand. He was glad he had shaved that evening. "Whiskers?"

"Sure. He had a beard. A full beard. Black. Didn't anybody mention that?"

"Nope, nobody did mention that little thing."

He abruptly brushed away her hand and got up. "Not that it matters worth a shit. Jesus, come on. I'd really like to take a look at that map of yours."

She took his arm. "You okay?"

"Sure. Listen, how come you didn't tell me before that you saw Limousine?"

"I don't know. You didn't ask me?"

"Ha ha. Very funny. I don't suppose you have any booze at your place."

"It happens I do."

"Now you're talking. What else are you holding out on me?"

"You'll have to stick around to find out, won't you?"

Sweeny stopped again and looked at her. In the light from the street lamp on the corner, her hair formed a hazy glow around her head. Her chin came to a point, and she was almost beautiful. "What kind of a game is this, anyway?"

"No special game," she said quietly. "Just a game."

VI

Saturday

IT WAS A HELL OF A DAY FOR A FUNERAL, BOTH COLD and warm, depending on the mood of the clouds skittering across the face of the impervious, even-tempered sun. When he'd left July's late the night before, the sky was overcast and later his fitful sleep was broken by bone-rattling thunder overhead and lightning that flared the sky outside his bedroom window. Then hard rain had come, and now the air smelled like it might rain again, soon. As Sweeny sanctified his breath with Colgate's and laced his head together in a corset of aspirins and instant coffee, he listened to the Apollo launch from Cape Kennedy on the radio—even with his head splitting, he was still that much of a news junkie. Everything went off exactly right, and he toasted the astronauts with his coffee cup. He knew better than to drive, so he walked a few blocks to clear his head, then hailed a passing cab. He had the driver make a quick stop at a liquor board store to pick up a pint of vodka.

A man Sweeny didn't recognize was standing in front of the oak door beneath the stone arch incised with the name Benno & Benno. He was a large, kindly looking man with a face as bland as a loaf of white bread and a large roll of fat pressing tightly into his belt. He wore a black suit with a white-on-white shirt and a black tie, as if he had dressed himself following instructions from a correspondence course for funeral attendants. His thick-soled black shoes were highly polished, and his roundish form lumbered forward silently on them as Sweeny's taxi pulled up behind the two Cadillacs parked in front of the mortuary. His breath, in contrast to Sweeny's, reeked of consolation.

"Party?" the man asked. He raised his large, puffy hands slightly, in a gesture of readiness, as if he were expecting his guest to fall.

"Party? You folks having a party here? Must have the wrong address."

The bland man smiled indulgently, not at Sweeny but at his left ear. "Which party will you be joining?" His voice had a crooning quality, implying no guilt, no remorse. "For whom are you mourning?"

"Limousine. I'm a member of the Limousine party," Sweeny said. "Never voted any differently in thirty-nine years. How many parties you folks having today?"

The large man looked discouraged. "Saturdays are usually quite busy for us," he said hopefully. "There are two services this afternoon at two, another at 3:30, and we had three already this morning. We have three chapels," he added, his voice swelling slightly, as if with pride.

"Well, it's a nice day for it," Sweeny said, gesturing up at the heavy sky. A wind was working its way up the street, pushing a tattered newspaper before it. "Looks like rain."

"We certainly could use some," the bland man said.

Before Sweeny could reply, another taxi pulled up and several people emerged from it. The air of self-importance returned to his host's slightly stooped shoulders as he approached them, his hand extended. Sweeny made a getaway.

In the men's room off the lobby, he stripped the foil off the bottle and unscrewed the cap. He saluted his reflection in the wide wall mirror above the wash stands and took a swallow. The face in the mirror frowned at him as he screwed the bottle closed and returned it to his raincoat pocket. He wiped his mouth dry with the back of his hand, shoving the frown away. "Just today," he assured the reflection.

Taking a left as he came out of the men's room, Sweeny encountered the door to a chapel and, beside it, a smoothly polished wooden table, edged with gold, holding a guest register. At the top of the first page, the name "Kissick" had been written in a fine hand, and beneath it several mourners had already signed in. Sweeny bent over and scanned the first few: Robert Colby; Dan Willows; Mr. and Mrs. Anson Kissick, Vancouver; Dick and Doris Anderson, Kamloops. He glanced up at a clock on the wall and saw it was only 1:45, still plenty of time. There was no sign of the large man and the lobby was empty, although he could hear the muffled sound of voices creeping out from under closed doors. Across the hall, beside the second chapel, was an identical table, with a second guest book. It bore the name "Limousine."

Quite a few names were already entered, but he quickly found the one he was looking for: Ormand Harriman, Washington DC. Ormand! What kind of a name was that? He slid his reading glasses onto his nose. There were more names here than in the other book, filling three pages, but, while the guests at the Kissick service had clear, strong writing hands, most of the names on the Limousine list were smudged or illegible. A few stood out more clearly than the rest—William Festerman, Los Angeles; Robert Shanks, Phoenix; and, in an effeminate hand, Walter Wilby, New York City—but most were too much of a challenge for Sweeny's eyes, even with the glasses. One name, indecipherable, took up five lines with its flowing scrawl.

He folded away the glasses and glanced again at the clock. He heard voices approaching and, after a moment, the bland-looking greeter came around a corner with an elderly man and woman dressed in dark clothing in tow. Sweeny waited while they signed the guest book, the white-haired woman smiling at him nervously, then followed them into the chapel.

The room was considerably larger than Sweeny had imagined, and he thought back to other times, years before, when he had been in various corners of the mortuary—his recent visits had been confined to Benno's office—but he could dredge up nothing of these proportions. An addition, most likely. And why not? Everybody else was adding on, everything else was bigger.

Despite its size, though, the room was already half filled, which surprised Sweeny even more. Most of the mourners were seated in the pew-like benches, which were comfortably upholstered with inky purple velvet, but others were cast about in clutches of two or threes in the open area at the rear, in the aisles, and at the front, where the coffin rested on a black-draped platform. A pale, narrow-faced man sat on a straight-backed wooden chair just below and to the left of the coffin, a bulldog on guard at the foot of its master. He wore a tight, dark suit and a pained expression, as if the suit were actually causing discomfort. Across his lap, a tan raincoat was folded and he was using it as a desk for a writing pad upon which he furiously moved a slim black pen. He looked up quickly from his writing, as if he had felt Sweeny's eyes on him, and returned a piercing gaze—even from that distance, a hundred feet or more, Sweeny could feel its heat. Then the man lowered his head, and raised his pen once more.

Benno was at the back of the room, engaged in rapid conversation with two trim, youngish men in grey summer-weight suits and complexions just a shade lighter. Their haircuts were fashionably longish, with sideburns growing almost to the tips of their earlobes and the upper rims of their ears concealed by carefully brushed back hair. Except for a certain earnest stiffness to their lips, they appeared little different from thousands of similar young men Sweeny had dealt with over the years, in business or government. Beside them, Benno seemed shabby.

"Sweeny," Benno called, waving him toward them. "Come over." The poor man looked like he was being hounded. Sweeny took his time making his way across the room, however, elbowing his way through a clot of women with their mouths closed and puckered.

"Sweeny, this is Mr. Harriman, from Maryland, I told you about, and this is Mr. . . . ah . . ." Harriman leaned forward, as if to block the view, and extended his hand, but the second man was suddenly gone. Benno kept his composure, turning to Harriman gracefully. "This is Mr. Sweeny, from the local paper." Sweeny's head was turned, watching the bashful young man pause at the door to look back at them balefully before ducking out, like a man caught staring at a woman adjusting her stocking. There was something familiar looking about the man, something he hadn't noticed until he took flight.

"Ah, the press," Harriman pursed his lips. "I didn't know our Nick's fame had spread this far into the hinterland so as to make him worthy of notice by the press."

Before Sweeny could reply, Benno interjected, "I believe that Mr. Sweeny's interest is purely personal. The death was so . . . well, *mysterious*, if you don't mind my saying so, and Mr. Sweeny was aware of it, professionally, of course, although he didn't write a story. . . ."

Sweeny smiled and put his hand on Benno's sleeve. "I'm an old friend of the deceased." Harriman's jaw dropped just a hair's width, his lips parting to form a crack like that in old alabaster, but Benno's surprise was undisguised.

"So you *did* know him, then, you remembered?"

"Yeah, I remembered all right," Sweeny said caustically. But he had his eyes on Harriman, who was buttoning his lips up again. When he spoke, they barely moved at all.

"I didn't know Nicolas had any friends in this part of the world."

"Mr. Sweeny has travelled quite extensively," Benno gushed, a tic beginning to work its way around his right eye.

"Oh, then you knew Nicolas elsewhere? Washington?"

Sweeny rubbed his nose to cover a small smile. "I don't hang around post offices much." He kept looking at Harriman, who blinked his longish lashes. "No, I knew Nick from these parts, quite a few years ago. Nick is from this area, you know."

"Limousine?" Benno said. "I've never heard that name before around here, Sweeny. Are you sure?"

"No, I didn't," Harriman said. His voice trickled out of his mouth like a chip of ice down the back of Sweeny's neck. He put his hands into his coat pockets and fingered the bottle reassuringly. "Nick always was full of secrets," Harriman went on. Close up, he was older than Sweeny had thought at first, his frame a little more plushly upholstered. "I've known him for years, but I realize now I never have known where he was from. Somehow, though, I never would have suspected . . ."

"Some people seem to come full-blown into the world," Sweeny said, "without ever having soiled their diapers."

"Well, that would clear up some of the mystery," Benno said, turning up the corners of his mouth at the vulgarity.

Harriman turned his eyes slightly in their sockets to take in Benno's face. The eyes were as grey as a battleship and wide as a cat's.

"I mean, it did seem odd, checking into the hotel and dying, just like that."

"You mean Nicolas came here to die?" Harriman asked politely. A light flared up in his eyes, as if candles had been lit there. "Surely you don't think . . ."

"That's not it at all," Sweeny said. "Nick came here to see me. His dying was purely accidental. Now, if you'll excuse me. . . ."

He was on his way before they could answer, and didn't look back. At the door, turning to open it, he glanced toward the front of the chapel, which was now almost full, and again caught the eyes of the man guarding the coffin, raised from his writing, pen poised. The man's nose was upturned and his nostrils were two black points, like reflections of his eyes, in his pasty lower face. Sweeny winked at him and went out. The door to the men's room was just a few feet away.

Sweeny in the men's room. Alone with porcelain tiles, stainless steel, chrome, all the fixtures of convenience, alone with his memory of the night before, alone with his knowledge. In his hand, a bottle. *Down the fucking hatch.* When had he first started carrying a flask? It was a habit grown out of the war, he supposed, like so many of his bad habits. In

France they had carried wineskins around their necks, drinking whenever they were thirsty, whenever the fucking spirit moved them. *That was the way to live, eh? Of course, wine was one thing, booze another. Down the fucking hatch.*

Nicolas Limousine. Nicolas. Old Nick. Who would have suspected you would have come so far, become so widely known? You did a favour for a friend of mine once, now you've got a hassle of your own.

Hey, I think I just made a rhyme. Jesus. Looka me.

Sweeny in the men's room. *Down the fucking hatch.* He is alone. He takes a piss.

❖

"Keep your hands off my bum," July had said.

"I didn't put a finger on it."

"You were thinking, though."

They were climbing the stairs, she ahead of him, his eyes transfixed on the tight brown corduroy motion.

"I keep getting confused," Sweeny said. "I thought that was one of the reasons we were here."

"That's *later*. First," her voice dropped, taking on a menacing tone, "zee document. *Then*, zee payment."

"No tickee, no shirtee."

She stopped on the stairs and looked back at him. "Right. And it's *me* who squeezes *your* ass. Get that straight."

"Like I said, I keep getting confused."

"It's a lifetime of habit you have to overcome. Keep working at it."

"Some lifetime."

She lived above a drugstore four blocks north and east of the Heights Hotel, just a few minutes' walk from the restaurant, though it had taken them almost an hour to get there. Entry to her suite was up a long, steep flight of outside stairs, like a fire escape, and across a wooden balcony. The stairs continued up one more flight to another balcony and suite above.

Below, the drugstore took up two high-ceilinged storeys, so the climb was the equivalent of three flights, and Sweeny was puffing by the time they were at the door. He put his hand on the balcony rail and gazed out over the city while she fumbled with the lock. Timber had made a mistake turning its back on the Heights and growing in other directions, down along the flats of the river valley, he decided. The view from up here was too good. For the sixty or seventy or eighty bucks a month she paid, July had probably the best view in town. "It's okay," she said lightly when he made that observation.

He could see most of the city spread out beneath him, a glistening, twisted blanket with the tower of the Queen's Hotel, its neon light blinking, and, two blocks to the east, the big clock of the *Chronicle* building, standing aloofly above the rest. Sweeny felt his life floating in the space between those two tall structures. He had a vision of Limousine sitting on the edge of his bed in the hotel room, dialling one number after another, eating steak, then lying back on the bed and dying, falling out and making a thud. Who had he called? And what had he said? Goodbye? Sweeny chided himself for not having checked out those telephone numbers. There could be something there. Tomorrow, for sure, he would look into it. He wondered what he had been doing at that moment, the moment Limousine died. Three in the morning—he'd been awoken that night by thunder, he recalled, probably right around that time, and had lain awake listening for some time, in that squeaky bed in his furnished suite in the strange town that was home.

Home. Had Limousine known he was going to die? Had he come here for that? Sweeny could see him standing beside the bed, his hand on the telephone receiver, putting it down, listening. There was something wrong with the picture: it was of a big man, in his shirtsleeves, the cuffs neatly rolled back along powerful, hairy wrists, the collar loose beneath a well-trimmed, dark beard—the face blank.

"You could kill yourself climbing these stairs," he said. July had opened the door, flicked on the light, and sidled up beside him quietly, but he had become aware of her breathing.

"That's funny, it doesn't bother me. Keeps my belly flat."

"Good that something on you is flat."

"That's the *only* thing."

"You know, it's really a pretty city," he said, ignoring her. "See over there? That whole area west of the tracks on the other side of the river, when I left this town it wasn't there. I mean zero. Just rolling hills with cattle munching grass."

July laughed. "And now it's rolling cardboard boxes called houses filled with cow-eyed ladies and gentlemen munching cardboard breakfast cereal. But nature gets its revenge. Already it's a slum, going to seed, and in another hundred years it'll be a forest, completely grown over."

Sweeny looked at her, shaking his head. "You *are* a cynic. Jesus. Was I like you when I was your age, I wonder?"

"Weren't you?"

"I guess."

"You don't remember?"

"Yeah, okay, I was."

"It sounds worse on someone else, though."

"It sounded rotten on *me*."

July laughed. "Aren't you supposed to say now, 'What's made a sweet, pretty young thing like you so cynical?'"

"No, what's made a hard-assed, hard-nosed, foul-mouthed, brown-roots dirty *old* girl like you so cynical?"

She laughed again. "You have to ask?"

"Sure."

"Well, I can't blame it on the Queen's, really, because I was like this before I started there. But that place would make anyone cynical. Like checking in your friend Mr. Limousine."

"My friend, yeah. Whatd'ya mean?"

She put her chin into the hollow between her collarbones and lowered her voice to a childish bass. *"Would you care to join me for a drink in my room later, my dear?"* After a moment's pause, she raised her voice. *"Oh, no, thank you, sir."*

"Limousine tried to put the make on you?"

"You don't have to sound so surprised. I'm not completely without charm and appeal, you know."

Sweeny laughed this time. "I guess I'm more surprised that you turned him down. Wouldn't that have been grist for your mill?"

She mimicked his grin and put her hand on his cheek for the second time that evening. "I don't like beards. They scratch."

He followed her through the door, taking a last look over his shoulder.

"You're too much," she chided him. "You've seen skylines all over the world and you're gaga over a third-rate view of this fourth-rate burg. What's with you?"

He shrugged. "You said something this afternoon about mirror images? Things sometimes turn out to be the opposite of what they seem to be?"

"So?"

He shrugged again and lit a cigarette. "Nice place you've got here." He glanced around the cluttered room for an ashtray.

The suite was not unlike his own. The living room was a chaos of mismatched furniture and piles of books, *Rolling Stones* and other magazines. The frayed blue carpet was littered with balled-up paper and an old Royal standard sat on a rickety writing desk wedged against a wall. A matted reproduction of *The Old Guitarist* hung above it. On the wall opposite was a large Beatles poster with a bright red lipstick X across Paul's face. The room opened out into the kitchen, where he could see dishes stacked in the sink and on the counter beside it. There wasn't anything remotely feminine about the suite that he could see, and his eyes went to a closed door he assumed led to the bedroom.

"Yeah, well, it's home," July said. She took his coat and hung it in a narrow, curtained-off closet behind the door they'd come through. "It has character, I think. Like something in Paris."

"That's exactly what I was thinking." He gestured toward the Beatles poster. "I see you've killed off your boyfriend."

She turned, following his pointing finger. "Oh, him. That's what he gets for deserting. You won't desert me, will you Sweeny?"

"Perish the thought. Say, didn't you say something about having a little something . . ."

"To drink? Sure."

She went to the refrigerator. "The can's through here, if you're interested." She gestured with her chin toward the rear of the kitchen.

In the bathroom, he took pains to urinate against the side of the bowl so the sound of water hitting water wouldn't ricochet through the suite. Washing his hands, he looked at himself in the mirror above the sink and grinned. "Limousine, the hell with you, Nicolas P.," he whispered.

She had cleared off the overstuffed chesterfield and arranged glasses, a chipped blue ceramic bowl filled with ice cubes, a matching pitcher of water, and a bottle of Johnny Walker on a narrow coffee table. "I don't have any soda or anything. I hope you don't mind."

"Are you kidding?" Sweeny sat down next to her and put a couple of ice cubes in a glass. He wanted to just take the bottle and drink but he wasn't going to do that, not in front of her. She poured for him and he waved his hand. "Whoa. Take it easy. It's staying power that counts, not the size of your glass."

"Sure. Staying power. What're we talking about here?"

"I was talking about drinking, but use your imagination." He swallowed half of what was in his glass and felt the fist inside his belly open up, for just a moment, then close again, not quite as tightly as before. "No tickee, no shirtee. Keep your hands off my body and your mind on business, please. Let's see this map, and tell me again exactly how you come to have it."

"Well, nothing has changed since this afternoon, but I'll go through it again if you really like."

"I really like." He took another drink, just a cautious sip this time.

"Wednesday morning, after the police had puttered around in the room and the body's been taken away and all, the maid goes up to clean. By now, it's just another empty room to her. I mean, there isn't blood or bullet holes, the cops haven't even made chalk marks on the floor. So it's an empty room. Someone died in it, but people do all kinds of funny things in hotel rooms, and maids are used to it."

"They're cynics like you."

"Right. Changing sheets does that to you. So anyway, she isn't looking for anything, she's just making the bed. So, naturally, she finds something."

"The map."

"Uh huh. It's in the bed, down by the foot, in between the sheets. Right where the police should have found it if they'd had any eyes in their heads."

"Yeah, but they were looking for things, so naturally they couldn't see."

"Hey, you've seen this movie."

"A number of times."

"Anyway, there it is, all curled up in bed. When Annie pulls out the sheets, it just flutters to the floor, like a falling leaf."

"Annie?"

"That's the maid."

"Okay. It could have been some little girl who came up to join him for a drink." He turned his voice down low, mimicking her.

"No, Annie's very sweet, but nobody would invite her up to their hotel room."

"Okay, anyway."

"Anyway what? That's it. She finds this folded up piece of paper, she looks at it, it doesn't mean anything to her, she folds it up again, and puts it in her pocket. Forgets about it. Goes about her business."

"And?"

"And what?"

"And gives it to you."

"Oh, yeah. On her way off work, she passes through the lobby, where I am now on duty, it now being afternoon and my turn on the desk. You see . . ."

"*July.*"

"Okay, okay, don't get sore. I thought you were interested in details. Anyway, Annie and me are friends." She shrugged. "She thought I might be interested."

"Just like that."

"Well, I bought her a cup of coffee."

Sweeny poured half a glass of Scotch and drank half of that. "Lemme guess. Grist for your mill, right? Here's Annie, just finished cleaning up a room where a man with a beard died during the night—a man who had offered you a drink. The character must be just dripping off her, right?"

July sipped at her own drink and pouted. "Something like that."

"So you head off for the coffee shop, prime her, and get her talking. Okay, fair enough. And she shows you the map and leaves it with you. She has no inclination to give it to the cops?"

"Oh, the cops. Who gives things to the cops?"

"Right. And besides, it's not like there's been any crime, so it's not like it's evidence or anything. Just a piece in a puzzle."

"And Annie doesn't even know there's a puzzle."

"And you do. How *do* you know that?"

"I got a nose." She grinned.

"Yeah." He looked at her nose, which was smooth and shiny with a slight lift at the end. "Annie tell you anything else that might be of interest?"

"Just that your friend Mr. Limousine was burning something."

"Huh?"

"There were ashes in the trash can. Like some paper had been burned up."

"Hmmm." Sweeny's own nose wrinkled, as if he could smell the acrid odour of burning paper. "I don't suppose Annie gave you the ashes."

"Why would she do that, silly? She threw them away."

July went to the desk and opened a drawer. She lightly touched the typewriter with her other hand, the same way Sweeny would, and it sent a shiver along the ridge of his spine. "This is pretty crude, but I think I've got it figured out."

"The great detective."

"Uh huh."

She sat down next to him again, her knee pressing against his, and smoothed a much-folded sheet of paper out on the coffee table. Sweeny leaned forward, trying to ignore the heat alongside his leg, and stared at the drawing, touched it. The paper it was drawn on was newsprint, exactly like the kind the *Chronicle* used, but dry and yellowed with age. Immediately, though he couldn't tell what it signified, the map looked familiar, as if he might have seen it or one like it before. Goosebumps sprang up on his arms, and he felt the back of his neck tighten in the same way it had when he'd first seen Limousine's signature. He took a long swallow, emptying his glass.

"Good idea," July said. "Sharpens the vision."

"Oh, shut up, will ya?" He poured more whisky into his glass but left it sitting on the table, next to the map. "Okay, you're the great detective." He patted her knee, leaving his hand there. "Let's hear your interpretation."

"Okay, wise guy." July leaned forward and her hair slid along her cheek. "This is Timber, right?"

They bent their necks over the map, their heads almost touching, and Sweeny's nostrils were filled with the scent of her, something delicate and faintly sweet, like vanilla in a fruit cake, something you taste with just the back of the tongue. The map was no more than a crude drawing, with no attempt at scale. Directions were indicated by the letters N, S, W, and E in the appropriate places. In the lower right corner, a lopsided circle had been shaded in next to the letters TR, standing, he supposed, for Timber, and a little bit to the north, as a clincher, was a narrow, crescent-shaped form, which had to be the lake that supplied the city with its water. A line meandered south from the crescent and wiggled through the shaded circle, petering out just below it.

"Yeah, I suppose. This is the river, eh?"

"Very good. And this is the mountains. See the bumps?"

The map was dominated by a mountain range drawn in the form of a series of looping arcs. A thick line beginning at the letters TR snaked through them, veering first west, then northward. "Yeah, and the highway," Sweeny said. The map depicted a fairly accurate, if crude, layout of Timber, the valley it lay in and the mountains to the west and north.

"Now look here." July pointed with a slender finger, her hair brushing against his face. Her finger followed the northward line as it wiggled along the foot of a range of mountain arcs, then loped east until it ran into

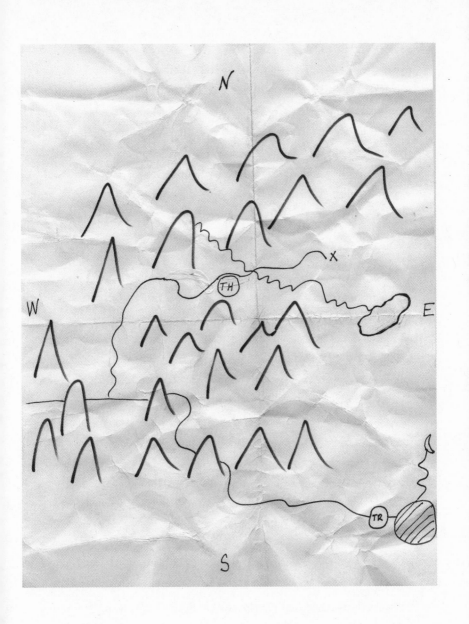

a circle within which were the letters TH. Sweeny's eyes narrowed. Just to the right of the circle, there was another thin line, wriggling southeast, which he knew was a stream leading to a lake, shown on the map as an oval shape. Another line, apparently a road, swung out of the TH circle to the east, crossed the stream, and took a sharp S swing around a mountain arc to the north, then jagged east again and ended in an X. The back of Sweeny's neck was cold, and sweat stood out on his forehead like a message in Braille.

"TH," July said. "True Hope. It's an old ghost town. Used to be a mining camp, back in the days when men were men and women were cattle. I've been there, it's a neat place."

"Yeah, I've been there too." Something was churning in Sweeny's head, beginning to take shape, edging out the massive accumulation of thirty-five years' worth of trivia. Names, faces, places, things, motions, words, feeling, meanings piled one on top of another were swept away as if an arm had brushed through his head, pulling away cobwebs, pulling down a screen upon which a new image could be projected. And on that screen he saw a car toiling up a winding dirt mountain road, an old, open black car—the kind not seen anymore, except at antique rallies—its joints straining over the bumps in the road. Behind the wheel is a young man with a moustache, a cigarette in the corner of his mouth, singing loudly above the roar of the engine, his eyes fixed on the mountain looming up ahead of him as the road bucks and turns—Sweeny, himself, driving through the mountains, in the sunshine.

"And there," July said, pointing to the X mark, "is where the buried treasure is. X marks the spot, just like in the movies. So when do we leave?"

Sweeny was staring at the map, still struggling with the image forming in his mind, a memory elbowing its way out of a pit at the base of his skull.

"I said, when do we leave?"

He looked up with a jerk. "What?"

"Well, we've got the map. And here's the buried treasure. So when do we dig it up and get rich?"

"Oh." He smiled. "What makes you think there's treasure buried there? Maybe the X is for a closet, and there's a skeleton in it."

July shivered. "Brrr. I don't like skeletons. But that's silly. Of course there's treasure. X always marks the spot where the treasure's buried. Let's go and see."

"Yeah." Sweeny dropped the map on the table and leaned back in the chesterfield, glass in hand. He took a sip, lit a cigarette, blew smoke, and stared at a corner of the ceiling. There was a cobweb there and if he squinted he could make out the individual threads that made up its complex form.

"Hey, I don't think you're paying attention." July got up and stretched. "It's time for payment, you know. I delivered zee document, now it's time for my payment of flesh." She stood in front of him, legs spread and hands on her hips, head cocked, like a pirate demanding tribute from a princess. She was smiling, smiling at him. He wanted her very badly, wanted to touch her, to drop on his knees and put his arms around her legs and just hold her, but he had to remember something first, something that was working its way into shape, like ice forming around the rim of a pond.

"In a minute, July. I'm thinking, eh?"

"Thinking? You're supposed to be paying your debt. But, okay, I'll give you a minute or two. An old man like you needs to catch his breath. By the way, if it's thinking you're into, turn that map over."

"What?" Sweeny looked up, distracted.

"Turn it over, like the great detective did. There's something there to think about."

He was staring at her dumbly, his head spinning.

"The map, honey, the map. We'll turn *me* over in a minute."

Sweeny carefully picked up the map. The paper it was drawn on had been folded many times, and it was torn in a dozen tiny spots along the fold lines. He turned it over. In one corner, written in faded pencil, was a series of numbers.

"Holy shit, look at these phone numbers." Sweeny sat up straight. "Why didn't you tell me about these before?"

"I can't do all your detective work for you."

He ran his finger down the list, pausing at the area codes. "Here's New York, and Washington. I'm pretty sure this one is southern California, LA probably. And 416, that's Toronto, right? I don't know these, but these at the bottom are in Europe, this one's London." He looked up. "What were those places Limousine called?"

"New York, Washington, Los Angeles, Chicago, Miami, and some place in Pennsylvania called King of Prussia, those in the States," July recited. "Toronto. And London—that's London, *England*, Mr. Cook would say— and Paris and Geneva in Europe. I already checked the hotel list. These are the numbers he called."

Sweeny looked at her in amazement, his cheeks burning.

"You're some girl, July."

She was grinning. "Glad you think so."

"I don't suppose the great detective has called any of these numbers?"

"That much of a detective I'm not. Besides, like I said, I can't do *all* your snooping for you."

He shook his head. "Geneva. July, you *are* a wonder."

"You ain't kidding, Jack. And that's just an appetizer. And I hope it's gotten your appetite up, because you've had your couple of minutes."

"Who the hell was he calling?" Sweeny was studying the list, the numbers repeating themselves in his eyes like a reproach.

"Only one way to find out. But later, Okay? You have a debt to pay now, remember?"

"What the hell?" Sweeny got up and began to pace around the room. "Geneva, that's a new one. So's LA and, what'd you say? Chicago?"

"You go much for foreplay?" July asked. She flopped down on the chesterfield, putting her legs up on the coffee table. "I guess not."

"Washington, okay. That's his connection to Harriman. New York, London, Toronto, Paris—we know he's been to those places because of the stickers on his suitcase. That doesn't mean all that much in itself, but maybe there's a pattern there because I've worked in those places. King of Prussia, that's something else." He stopped pacing and looked at July. "Now who the hell could he be calling in that little burg in the middle of the night?"

"Call the number yourself and find out." July shrugged her shoulders. "Don't talk about it, *do* it. Doing it, that's what I'm talking about."

"Sure, great," Sweeny said sarcastically, moving again. "I just call up King of Prussia and see who answers. 'Hi, I'm calling from the welcome wagon, just wanted to say a big hello . . .'"

"Just hang up. At least you'll hear what they say when they answer."

"Oh, sure."

"Speaking of hang-ups, I hope you don't have any really *kinky* ones."

"That doesn't always work. It does with companies, offices, that sort of thing, where a receptionist answers."

"Like, I'm not big on hurt."

"But it doesn't always work with people, just plain people, in their homes. Most people just say hello and then you haven't found out anything." He was talking too loudly, he knew, protesting too much. It *was* what he should have done, yesterday.

"So you lose your dime," July said. "How about it?"

"Some dime. To London. How about what?"

"You know, Sweeny. Come on, you owe me."

"Oh, that. In a minute." He went to the window and stared out at the city, its lights burning like stars through a clouding sky. In fact, the sky had curdled with clouds, and there was no light above except for a dull reflected glow. "The fucking guy comes to town, this little hick city, checks into a hotel and bows out. But before he goes, he makes a bunch of calls from a list he's brought with him, written on the back of a map showing a ghost town and an X."

"We can turn out the lights if you'd rather," July said behind him. "I like to see what I'm doing. But, hey, if you're shy, that's okay too. I'm not fussy."

"So what's he here for? Let's go through the possibilities. One, he's legitimate, a businessman on a business trip. A travelling man, been to a lot of places, who makes a lot of phone calls. All the rest is coincidence, and so is his death. We all have to go sometime, and this is his time."

"Light, dark, I don't care, make no nevermind to me. I'm so ready, it really doesn't matter."

"But that's got to be a dud possibility. There's the phony credit cards. So the second logical choice, he's a conman, in town to pass some cheques or run a scam. But why the calls? Travelling, sure, conmen are always on the move. But Europe? No. Still, the calls were on a phony card, so that would be consistent. But, then, how to explain all the other things? The post office box. Harriman. This crazy funeral they're having tomorrow. Why shouldn't he just be left alone, the way he died? There's too much here for a two-bit grifter, as your Charlie Cook would have it."

"On the other hand," July said, her chin scraping her collar bone, "maybe we need something more to drink first. There's a bottle of wine around here somewhere, a little stale maybe, but still drinkable. Help us relax. Maybe you'd like to take off my clothes piece by piece, thread by thread, and lick my body from head to toe, or the other way around." She yawned.

"So that suggests some bigger type of criminal. And that brings me back to the Mafia. Maybe I was right all along." He turned around and looked at her. "I was saying this morning it smelled like Mafia. I didn't really think so, but I said that. Maybe I was right."

"Yeah, something more relaxed. *I* would like it that way. Sounds delicious."

"Then there's this spy business. Friend of mine suggests Limousine has something to do with the CIA or those boys."

"After all, why shouldn't I get it the way *I* want it? I'm the one who's due the payment, not you."

"What's that?" Sweeny said. "What are you talking about, July?"

"Oh, nothing. Don't mind me. What were you saying?" She got up and walked across the room and stood beside him by the window. "Why do you care so much, Sweeny?" she said, serious now. She wasn't smiling, and her eyes had darkened.

"I don't know."

But he was lying, and he was sure she knew it. They faced each other for a moment, and Sweeny knew he should take her in his arms—*now*, before the light came and she vanished like a dream just before waking— but something was stopping him. He had the sense that there was some- one in the room, watching them, disapproving. He took his eyes from her face and scanned the room, searching out the intruder, then quickly let his gaze dart to the window, half expecting to see someone standing on the landing, staring through the glass at them. *Limousine.* He could feel his presence, here, in this room, hovering over them, between them, pre- venting him from touching her, keeping him from going on with his life. *Limousine.* He was in the Scotch, his voice laughing in the ice cubes, his eyes in the window, he was in the air. Sweeny's hands, raised alongside July's arms, dropped to his sides and he turned back to the window to stare into the night. After a while, he felt her move away from him.

Sweeny opened the door and went out onto on the balcony. His head was spinning, his blood racing, and his skin tingled. He felt, suddenly, alive, powerful—but, at the same time, old, vulnerable, impotent. Behind him, in the room, there was a girl who could give him softness, warmth— not love, he didn't fool himself that way, but something of meaning. And out here, in the darkness, out here where people without pasts could die alone in hotel rooms in the middle of the night, there was something, *some one,* pulling at him. He raised his hand but his fingers closed on air, closed in on themselves. He saw himself standing on a platform suspended three stories above the street, looking down on just that—not a life, neither his nor anyone else's, not a past or a future, not a city itself, just streets, dark and empty.

He stayed on the balcony for a long time, gazing above the city lights at the dark sky, tugging at the strands of memory that had become dislodged in his mind, letting them coagulate into form, fall into patterns, lead him. It was dark where he was and he had struck a match, flashing light across his hands like a flood of water. He heard water running, splashing, spray- ing down beside him, and in his nostrils there was the sharp, acrid odour of burning paper.

Something clicked in Sweeny's head, as simple and sharp as a match tip bursting into flame. "Jesus," he said. "Holy shit, holy shit. *Nicolas Limousine!*"

He stepped back into the suite, but the living room was empty. The door he had assumed led to the bedroom was partially open but there was darkness behind it. He took a long drink, straight from the bottle, then went to the door.

"July?"

"Yes." Her voice was small, distant.

The light from the living room illuminated the darkness enough for him to see her motionless shape lying on the bed, under the covers. He took a cautious step closer. She was lying on her back, legs together, hands under her chin. She seemed very small, even smaller than before, as if she were a child. She made no sound and, for a moment, Sweeny's breath caught in his throat.

"Hey, I guess I wasn't a very good date."

She snorted, reassuringly, but said nothing. He thought he saw her eyes move slightly, turning to him.

"Hey, I think I got this cat Limousine figured out."

"That's good, welcher. Good you got something figured."

"Welcher?" His voice faltered, but he took another step. He wanted to go further into the room, sit on the edge of the bed, take her in his arms, slide down. But his legs wouldn't move, his arms were weak. "I guess I'll have to owe you."

July smiled, the whiteness of her teeth illuminating the darkness. "I don't like welchers," she said gruffly. "We got ways of collecting."

He moved to her suddenly, bending down and kissing her forehead the way, he imagined, you might kiss a feverish child. She made a small noise and he thought she stiffened under him, but it was hard to tell, she was so small in the big bed.

"Tomorrow, we'll go treasure hunting, eh? I'll call ya."

He left the bedroom door open but he turned off the lights before he left the suite. He took the bottle with him.

❧

There is water running, a roaring in his ears like the artillery he heard in Sicily so many years before, cold spray on his face. His feet are wet, his legs wet, his hands wet. In his dream, Sweeny is in darkness. His hands are wet and he marvels at this, as if he were lost in a desert, as if it were a miracle. He is in darkness but there is a flash of light and, in his nostrils, a sharp, acrid odour. He leans over and his eyes tear from smoke. There is sunlight filtering through the trees sheltering the road, and he has to peer closely at the young man in the car before he realizes it is himself, his face thin, the moustache a bristling black badge above his lip, smoke curling up against eyes clear as sunlight, and he smiles in his sleep, makes a noise deep in his throat that might be a laugh. He is driving, the road turning, narrowing, trees and bushes pressing, hands of leaves brushing against his face, sun pressing down. Then the branches part, the road has ended, and he is in a clearing, grey ruins loom out of the vivid green bush like the shoulders of disappearing men. There is a roaring.

And he is in darkness, a small light cracking above him like the gap between God's teeth, something hard beneath his shoulders. He is cold, the room spinning, dawn seeping in above him like gas from a tap, greyness spreading, light raining down on him, *light*. And in the centre, his mother's face, every feature distinct as always, the funny brown mole in the shape of a comma on the ridge of her right cheek, just below the eye, her long lashes, the pink lipstick, the pink of her nails, the white flashing of her teeth. He is a boy again, aching and feverish with chicken pox or measles, and she is leaning over him, her cornsilk hair wisping around her head, eyes sparkling, her hand cool on his forehead, lips cool and soft against his cheek, her breath fragrant as peonies, her voice a ribbon wrapping itself around him.

He reaches up, his hand in the silky strands of her hair, melting now like cotton candy. He closes his eyes, *just for a moment*, and when they open she is gone, he is alone, in the apartment in New York, his shoulders aching, a bell ringing in his head, cold darkness. *He is alive*. It is night and he is lying on the kitchen floor, the rough texture of the linoleum buckling beneath him. Some little thing skitters across one bare foot. The window shade is up, the cracked panes of the window staring down at him like the loose smile of an idiot. On the other side of the sooty window is clear black night, clear black winter night, its face smudged with stars. There is a hand on his shoulder, the creak of the rocker on the porch, the smell of the smoke drifting from his grandfather's pipe, the spruce in the distance, clouds tangled in its branches, the sky pressing down.

He lights a match and the damp, rough walls glow, the wick sputters, dims, catches, coal oil sour in his nostrils, the dirty glass breathes with yellow light, shadows flicker in the air around him. He kneels, his rolled up pants legs wet against his skin, gravel rough against his knees, shoulders hunched as he works, another match strikes, a flash of light in the darkness, the sharp, acrid smell again, smoke in his eyes, pages turning in the small flame. The walls glow, dark walls sulking with curve and shadow, hidden places. Rocks in his hands, a pile, a grave. "Ya, boy, ya, it be all right now," his grandfather says, voice rasping, lips barely moving, "it be all right now." Above him, a cracked sooty window, clear black night, smudged with stars, and Sweeny murmurs in his sleep, his mouth dry, turning, turning. Above him, her face appears again, her eyes puffy, mouth set and hard, a thin line like a crack in dry mud, hair lying in ragged sheets against her bony face, obscuring the brown mole, her laboured breathing an intimation of death. Sweeny thrashes in the damp sheets, cries out. In his dream, the boy reaches out, hand trembling, but there is nothing for him to touch, only rain and darkness, and his hand closes in on itself, the nails biting into the palm. Nothing is contained, nothing is found.

Outside his window, lightning turns the sky Broadway bright, thunder rolls through heaven.

VII

Like actors, orators, and ventriloquists, morticians have trained voices, voices that can soothe, sell, manipulate, whisper, and thunder. Not all morticians, perhaps, but Benno had a voice like that, inherited from his father, who had been a founding member of the Timber Toastmasters, district president of the Kiwanis, and possessor of the frustrated soul of a Shakespearean actor. The younger Benno had none of the wit for that sort of ambition but boasted a voice that could soar and whimper nonetheless. Sweeny imagined that when he was selling a casket, that voice was persuasive but soft. Explaining the details of a funeral, it would be sympathetic, but firm. Tendering a bill, it was likely to be apologetic but unyielding. But when Benno stood at the head of a chapel, in front of and just to the right of a casket, and gazed at the mourners, their eyes all focused on him, that's when his voice became more than a mere instrument, like a telephone, and became an *instrument*, like a violin, like a trumpet. Or like a tuba, Sweeny thought as he took a seat in the empty back row.

Coming back from the men's room, fortified, he'd found the chapel almost full. There were seven rows on each side of the aisle, giving the room a capacity of seventy. Sweeny's eyes quickly scanned the heads, and he came up with a professional guess of close to fifty.

"My friends, it is my sad duty to welcome you to this humble chapel, where we are gathered to pay our last respects to Nicolas Limousine."

Benno's voice had dropped like a stone from the level at which he usually talked, half an octave, perhaps more, and it was rich in timbre and resonance. He had the ability to imbue the most inane information with significance.

"We will have a few words first from Mr. Ormand Harriman, a good friend of the deceased, then a short blessing from"—Benno's eyes darted down to a small white card he held cupped in his right palm but his voice didn't falter a beat—"the Reverend James Lightburn of the Nineteenth Avenue Presbyterian Church of Washington, who has come all this way to be with us today, as have many of you, I know, travelled far to be here today with us, to pay final respects to your friend, Nicolas Limousine."

Jesus, Sweeny thought, covering a yawn, what a Hamlet he'd make. No, a Polonius. But he was surprised at the mention of the minister. Hadn't Benno told him Harriman said there wouldn't be one? Maybe he meant Benno didn't have to arrange for one, since they'd be packing their own. This was some outfit. He shook his head and studied the face of the man on the outside of the row just ahead and across the aisle. He was a slight, small man with a thin moustache twenty years out of style, an apparent toupee, a sharp nose that twitched, and a pointed chin. He looked like someone had picked him up as a child and squeezed him hard. He was crossing and uncrossing his legs nervously, rustling his hat and coat in his lap.

"Immediately after the service, cars will leave from the side of the chapel for the cemetery. The hearse containing the casket will lead, followed by a"—Sweeny thought he detected a slight pause here, before Benno's voice intoned smoothly on—"car containing the closest friends, in lieu of family, then all the others, in hired cars."

Benno's voice snapped off, its meagre supply of information used up. A barely perceptible murmur passed through the chapel, floating over the heads of the mourners like a haze. Who, Sweeny wondered, were the clos-est friends? Shouldn't he be in that group?_

He nodded, smiling slightly. When he looked up, he saw Benno backing into the corner, where welcoming drapes would receive him. There was, Sweeny thought, a look of helplessness in his eyes, as if circumstances had gone beyond his control.

Harriman rose from his seat in the first pew and, moving with an effi-ciency of motion that combined speed with an illusion of languor, took up a position at the lectern. Sweeny hadn't noticed him sitting there and he craned his neck now, trying to pick out the other occupants of the pew. To the right of the spot vacated by Harriman sat the pale, narrow-faced man who had earlier been positioned in front of the casket. From the rear, he was so ordinary looking Sweeny wasn't sure it was the same man until he turned his head slightly to the left and his pained expression and black nos-trils became visible. He was whispering in the ear of the slim, sandy-haired young man who had been at Harriman's side earlier, then fled so quickly. He sat very still, his fair head motionless, the back of his neatly combed neck stiff.

"We all know why we are here," Harriman began. He put his hands on the lectern and leaned forward. "Our friend Nick is gone. We've come to say goodbye." He paused, glancing over his audience. "I don't propose, though, that it should be a tearful goodbye. Nick lived well, and reason-ably long, and when he died he left behind him nothing of which he need be ashamed. What more could a man ask than that?" He paused again, his eyes darting from face to face, as if hoping to elicit a response. He was a graceful man, built like a dancer, powerful-looking, with broad shoulders and slim hips and something vaguely effeminate in his posture. He raised his right hand, holding out the spread fingers like an offering of help. "We all knew Nicolas in various ways, for he was many different men." Sweeny sat forward, listening intently. "But, at the same time, he was also only one man—Nicolas. Nicolas Limousine, different men to different people, one man to himself."

Jesus, this guy is good. Harriman's eyes were looking right at Sweeny, straight and cold, as if he were speaking only to him. Then they flickered away.

"To me," Harriman said, "Nicolas was a friend. A business associate, too, of course, but first and foremost a friend. He was . . . I hesitate to say a gentle man, because we tend to judge so much about a person by his size, and Nick was a big man, not the kind you would tend to think of as gentle. He projected an aura, in fact, of, frequently, ferocity. And he could be a ferocious man, as some of you, I'm sure, know." He smiled slightly, a thin, half smile that set his face off-centre. "But, yes, gentle. Perhaps he was not a gentle man, but he was a man who could be gentle, and often was." Harriman pushed himself back from the lectern, stiffening his arms and holding his head back, as if overcome by the convoluted logic of his eulogy. *"But let anyone who mistook that gentleness for weakness beware."*

Sweeny had closed his eyes to shield himself from the onslaught but they sprung open, startled by the severity of tone that knifed its way into Harriman's voice. The graceful man had thrust his arm out and was pointing an accusatory finger at the mourners. Sweeny was sure it was levelled chiefly at him. Harriman was taking up the tempo of an evangelical preacher, beginning slowly, warming to his message, preparing himself for the thunder of bringing down the true word to his listeners, some of whom were true believers already, some of whom were skeptics, and some of whom, no doubt, were outsiders and heretics. Like Sweeny.

"For Nicolas was *not* a weak man." Harriman's voice was hushed and slippery again. "He was a man of purpose and determination. A man who could set a light for himself with assurance that he could reach it. He was a man who reached many lights, who sparked many lights." Harriman paused, his eyes narrowing, a hand drawing close to his chest. "Who extinguished many lights," he whispered.

Sweeny shivered, as if something sharp had slid along his backbone. Across the aisle, the nervous man with the pinched face crossed his legs, his nose twitching as if he had detected a strange odour. In front of Sweeny, a large, middle-aged man stuffed like a sausage into a woolen salt-and-pepper suit scratched at the red, bloated folds of skin on his neck. He turned to the woman beside him, her ostrich-like head bobbing at the end of the long, cylindrical neck that rose out of the white fluted collar of her severe black dress. Although she was silent, there was something about her narrow, bony back that evoked loudness.

"But that, of course, is all behind him now." Harriman sighed, squaring his shoulders. "A gentle man, a powerful man, a man who was many men to different people, *but always only one man to himself*"—Harriman's voice rose, a hawk spinning upwards to the killing height, then rushed down with a murderous whir of wind—"comes down, in the final moment, to no more than this." He half turned to face the casket, directing the mourners' eyes toward it. "The important thing," he said softly, "is not that our friend Nicolas is dead, because death comes to us all, is inevitable, and therefore is neither to be feared nor regretted." He shifted his dancer's body back to the lectern, his grey eyes swinging around and focusing on Sweeny.

"That's right," the bird-like woman whispered to the fat man.

"The important thing is not even the way he died, because dying is a lonely thing, of no interest, really, to anyone but the one who is dying." Harriman's eyes burned into Sweeny, and he skipped a beat, using the silence the way a musician does. He, too, had a voice of value. "No, the important thing is the way a man lives. The important thing for us to ponder about the death of our friend Nicolas is his life. *His life*. Not his death. Not his dying. But the way he lived."

Harriman arched his head back, his hands jumping on the lectern as if an electric shock had coursed through it. Something on the chapel's scrolled ceiling caught his eye and he held the pose for a moment, scrutinizing the plaster. He slowly lowered his head, his eyes raking across the faces of the mourners.

"And we know, we his friends, we know the way Nicolas lived."

For a moment, as Harriman nodded his head in a stylized half bow, Sweeny thought there would be applause—he felt like clapping himself. Instead, there was a faint murmur beginning at the front of the chapel and moving backwards like a wave until it spent itself in the pew in front of his, where the skinny woman bobbed her head soundlessly toward the fat man's red ear and, across the aisle, the man with the pinched face twitched his nose at the new unpleasant odour. Above the grey hum, he heard a soft sob, but he couldn't tell where it came from.

Harriman sat down and the slim young man on his left whispered in his ear. He nodded and glanced over his shoulder, catching Sweeny's eye for a fraction of a second. It seemed that the fire behind Harriman's grey eyes was burning higher, ripe with new fuel. But it was only for a moment, and then the eyes were gone, the carved head turning. A pale man in a black collar and tan suit was easing his way out of the opening in the drapes, coughing discreetly into his fist for attention.

"Let us pray." The minister's voice was as soft as grains of sand trickling from a child's hand.

The bottle in Sweeny's pocket pressed against his leg as a reminder and he took the opportunity, while the heads in the chapel were lowered, to pull it out and drink furtively, his eyes hanging tightly on the man at the lectern. The vodka slid down hot and fierce, like the liquid lead they had used to print the *Chronicle* in his day. *It's not the drunkenness, but the way you drink,* he thought with satisfaction.

"Dearly beloved, we are gathered here today to pray for the soul of our departed companion, Nicolas Limousine, who has gone to join his Saviour."

The Rev. James Lightburn was a somewhat smallish, fragile-looking man in his mid-forties with a calm, pale, settled face and almost pupilless eyes. His tan suit was baggy and seemed, somehow, inappropriate for the occasion, but the black collar pressed a stamp of professionalism around his frail neck, and when he spoke it was as if his voice emanated from the collar. He had the look, Sweeny thought, trying to recall if he'd ever heard of or been by the Nineteenth Avenue Presbyterian Church, of a minister you could hire for almost any occasion.

"Nicolas was a man of many talents, many different callings, a big man in the true sense of the word, a man who gave of himself." Lightburn's voice had an irritating quality, a toneless whine that seemed to lack conviction.

"He was a devoted friend, a trusted employee, a valued associate. He was a man people could rely on. He was a man people knew would not let them down. And yet, some might say now, he *has* let us down, by taking himself away from us, by relinquishing his soul to death." The minister paused to survey his audience, his mouth pursing. "But can this be a correct interpretation of death? Is this final rest a selfish act? Or might it not be better to think of it as the final fulfilment of a deeper, ultimate trust? For in death are we not—has not Nicolas?—completing a contract with God?"

Sweeny yawned, fidgeting in his seat. He was going to do it too, he thought. He was going to eulogize Limousine, pray for him, sermonize over him, but he wasn't going to say anything *about* him.

He rolled his eyes toward the ceiling and thought of another drink. He could taste the harsh booze settling onto his dry tongue like acid on a photo plate, bringing up a picture before his eyes. *Well, what the hell was there to say about Nick, anyway?*

He found himself thinking of his grandfather suddenly, the way the old man would sit stoically in his rocker on the porch, a curl of pipe smoke rising above him, his head nodding stiffly to the cadence of the boy's voice coming from the steps just below. It was a solitary life out there on the farm, the old man creaking silently in his chair, the woman, Greta, humming to herself in the kitchen, the solitary boy given to reading books, daydreaming, hitchhiking into town on Saturday for the movies, burying himself in the hayloft with a pad of lined yellow paper and three pencils sharpened with his jackknife. Sitting at his grandfather's foot after school or in the evening, he would read his stories aloud, pronouncing the big words carefully, pausing after every paragraph to glance upward to make sure the old man hadn't fallen asleep. The stories were often very similar to the plots of movies he'd seen the Saturday before, but the old man hadn't seen them, and no one else got to see or hear the stories, so it didn't matter.

One or two of the stories broke away, put a straw into his head and sucked at his imagination. There was one in particular, that he'd written when he was eleven or twelve, he could still remember well—funny how he could remember that but not so many other things. The story was about a man who had a scarf with a life of its own—the man took the scarf off the neck of a man he killed in a war, then put it around his own neck, and later the scarf tightened and choked the life out of him. When he read the story to his grandfather, the old man chuckled, the lines of his face jerking with the struggle to smile. He raised a hand stiffly from his lap and extended it with pain, letting it rest on the boy's head. When the story was over they sat like that for a minute or more, silent, connected by that once-powerful hand, its shaking stilled. "Ya, that be a gud vun, boy," his grandfather said, and the boy flushed with pleasure. The old man rarely said more than that, but that was enough. Then Sweeny would retreat behind the barn, where he would burn the story, stuffing the torn pages into an old tin can and setting them ablaze with a kitchen match. The flames would shoot up, devouring the pencil marks, then char down to yellow heat and black, flaky ash. When the ashes had cooled, he sifted them through his fingers, as if looking for inspiration for the next story, and buried them in one of what was to become dozens of tiny, unmarked graves in the nearby grove of birch.

Graves. Sweeny had left a lot of them behind him. By the time he was sixteen, the shadowy face of his father, the fragrant breath of his mother, and the creaking rocker of his grandfather had all retreated behind a wall he couldn't follow. And for the rest of his life, he mused now, people had continued to die on him, or let go, which amounted to the same thing, didn't it?

His father was no more than a handful of senses in his memory, a tone of voice without words; a tall frame towering over a small boy's bed; a face coming forward to be kissed, a rough cheek with a day's growth of whiskers, a luxuriant moustache tickling the boy's own lips, but no features, no eyes or nose or mouth in that face, no character; and a smell, antiseptic and medicinal. The one really vibrant impression of his father Sweeny had carried with him for a lifetime was that bittersweet aroma— he could conjure up that smell, but that would be it, of course, it would be medicine he'd remember, not his father.

His mother, she was a different story. His father's face might be a blur, but let Sweeny close his eyes, as he did now, fifty years after her death, and he could summon up her face as clearly as if he'd been talking to her yesterday, the features sharper than any photograph could have preserved them over that length of time, though he didn't have such a photograph: the fine, honey-brown hair, wisping around her face like corn silk; eyes exactly the same colour and invested with a persistent sparkle that has fascinated the boy; hands soft and cool as linen, hands that knew how to work wonders on hot foreheads; lips soft as peonies just after they open in June . . . Sweeny gave his head a sharp shake, as much to clear it of sentimental cobwebs as to dispel that ghost, both pleasant and unsettling at the same time. She hadn't always looked that way, and he had dreamt of her that morning, he suddenly remembered, for the first time in longer than he could recall.

Well, what the hell could he do about them, anyway?

Father had been named Reg, Reginald. Family lore had it he always hated the name, though not enough, apparently, to stop him from inflicting his only son, his only child, with Wilfred, which was just as bad or worse. He came from old Ontario Irish stock, drawn west for adventure and, Sweeny always imagined, to get away from his parents, of whom Sweeny knew nothing. He was a doctor in a place and time when being a doctor meant being a teamster, too, driving his horse and rig through any kind of weather, on any kind of road, except that mostly there was only one kind, dirt and rutted. But he went away to serve in the war and he didn't come back. That was the end of the story.

His mother's story was not much longer but a bit more complex. Nora was the only one of four children of illiterate, Swedish-speaking parents to get any sort of education. She studied to be a nurse and might have gone further had she not met the town's new young doctor and decided to stay where she was, soon becoming a mother. When her husband went off to war, she put her own uniform back on; when word came that he wouldn't be returning, she made herself even busier, spending long hours at the hospital, coming home exhausted and thin, the colour gone from her cheeks. For a long time, Sweeny remembered, she didn't eat, hardly slept, drifted around the house like a ghost, staring out the bedroom window while he clung frightened to her leg. But with cold weather, her colour returned, she seemed to revive and she told him, "It's okay, Mum's going to be okay now. Mum's over it and we'll be happy again, you'll see." But he was happy then, just hearing her say that, even if he didn't understand. Later, the words lodged in his memory like a thread of meat caught in his back teeth. There was a flu epidemic that winter and she spent all her time at the hospital, coming home exhausted but cheerful to tell him stories in his bed and rub his nose with hers the way Eskimos kissed, she said. It was spring and the epidemic was almost over when she caught it herself. Her cheeks behind the mask she wore the last time he saw her burned with fever, her eyes smoking from it.

"Ashes to ashes, dust to dust."

Sweeny jerked his head up, the familiar words jarring him. Lightburn had been droning on, filling the stuffy chapel with dry, grating words. The room hummed with them, bees around the heads of the mourners. The buzz stopped now, and the minister's hands were raised threateningly, his chest puffed, face darkened by some stern exertion. "Ashes to ashes, Nicolas, dust to dust," he repeated, his voice gritty. "Go in peace, back to the arms of our Father." The minister dropped his head and his arms fell to his sides, the darkness draining from his face.

"Ashes," Sweeny echoed silently. He thought again of the birch grove behind his grandfather's house and the unmarked graves there, faint depressions in the ground where tin cans filled with ashes seeped words into the soil. *Ashes.* He had a vision of a liquid orange flame, tipped with blue, smoke curling above it, the dry smell of shrivelling paper in his nostrils, pages turning black and curling as the flames consumed them. He was in a dark place, and the flame formed a centre, a bright halo around which the darkness softened, melted, gave way. Shadows danced on a craggy wall and oxygen was sucked out of the air, leaving the roof of his mouth dry, his lips paper. He moved close to the fire, smelling it, feeling it on his face, pressed close to it, away from the darkness, his eyes transfixed by the liquid dance of colour—orange, black, blue and grey, and the whiteness of the pages, the black of the words marching across the curling sheets like troops of ants, the whiteness of the ash.

Sweeny blinked, shook his head. The chapel was stirring. People were getting to their feet and, at the front, Benno had reappeared beside the casket, gesturing toward the rear doors. Organ music had begun to play, a tuneless dirge. Harriman, his slim young friend and four tall men who had been in the second pew strode to the casket and took their places around it with an ease that suggested they had rehearsed their roles or often served as pallbearers. One of the tall men was completely bald and had the worried, weary look of someone who has attended too many funerals.

The Rev. Mr. Lightburn gestured and the six men lifted the casket with an almost effortless shrug of their shoulders that surprised Sweeny. The minister led the way and the casket was manoeuvred down the narrow aisle bisecting the chapel. Harriman, who was on Sweeny's side, gave him a reassuring half-smile as he went by. One of the tall men, a smooth-looking Negro with greying hair who took up the rear, nodded at him, as if in recognition. Then the mourners poured into the aisle in the casket's wake, trapping Sweeny in his pew as they streamed past. The red-necked man and the bird-necked woman struggled past him, eyeing him coolly. The nervous man hurried by, clutching at his raincoat as if it contained something of great value. A man with a patch over his eye and a tight collar gave Sweeny a searching look. A wiry man with musician's hands smiled at him.

Sweeny put his hip against the pew arm and waited as the mourners filed past, a hum of muffled voices vibrating through the chapel. He peered into the face of a middle-aged woman, stalled beside him in the traffic, who looked as if she must once have been quite pretty. She wore a brown and gold bandanna around her auburn hair, and her eyes were a chocolate brown, specked with light. There was something familiar about that face.

When the last of the mourners had elbowed their way past him, Benno, who took up the rear like a sheepdog worrying the heels of his flock, blocked the end of his pew. "You didn't tell me you *really* knew him," Benno whispered.

"Well, I didn't remember for sure until last night."

"And he came here to see *you?*" Benno's voice had a complaining edge to it. "Something like that," Sweeny said, raising his hands in a gesture of helplessness. He edged around the mortician's slight frame into the aisle and took his elbow, guiding him toward the door.

"*Sweeny.* You mean to tell me this fellow Limousine was from these parts, that you knew him in the old days, but you haven't seen him since? And he came here to see *you?* And died in the process? And you were calling *me* superstitious the other day." Benno made a sour face, like a man told a dirty joke in the presence of his wife.

Sweeny laughed. They were in the doorway, about to emerge into the crowded lobby. The second funeral had also just ended, and a stream of people was pulsing out of the other chapel, adding to the press. The bland-faced man who had accosted Sweeny earlier was standing at the large double doors trying to direct traffic.

"Limousine party to the left," he was saying loudly, "Kissick to the right."

"I'd like to go to the cemetery and wish my old pal Nick bon voyage," Sweeny said. "Think you can get me a seat in one of the cars?"

Benno rolled his eyes and shrugged. "I'll see." He pushed through the crowd to the door and conferred with the bland assistant.

Sweeny edged along the wall to the gilt-edged maple table and bent over the guest book, his glasses on, until the lobby thinned out. "Festerman, Shanks, Wilby." The names still meant nothing to him. Most of the signatures were just scrawls, scribbled marks and nothing more. Outside, a car engine sprang to life, then another. When he looked up, a heavy man was struggling into his overcoat in the doorway.

Outside, Harriman and his two companions were standing beside a car, about to enter it. Harriman had no coat, but the other two had put theirs on. The man with the dark eyes and deep nostrils wore a cocky hat, a porkpie. Harriman looked over his shoulder as he slid into the back seat, catching Sweeny's eye and smiling icily.

Sweeny was almost alone in the lobby. A woman with birdsnest hair was hiccuping softly in a corner. The man in the overcoat was standing by the door, hand on the knob, waiting. They were from the other group.

"It's Wilf Sweeny, ain't it?" the heavy man said. Sweeny turned slowly, his face blank. "I seen your name in the paper." After a moment's hesitation, he added: "Henry Limhouse," and extended his hand.

"Limy!"

The heavy man made a snuffling noise that was part laugh. "*Limy*. Gawd! Been a while since anybody called me that."

"I'll be damned," Sweeny said. "I was just thinking about you the other day."

"Sure, sure." The Chevrolet dealer had grown into a man more than twice as large as the young man Sweeny had known. His cheeks were red and they jiggled as he shook his head.

"No, seriously, I was looking through the files and I . . ." Sweeny's voice trailed off and he felt a momentary panic.

"Shame about Stan, eh?" Limhouse said. Sweeny just stared at him.

"Stan Kissick. Hell of a nice guy." Limhouse's fleshy eyelids narrowed. "Ain't that why you're here?"

Sweeny laughed. "*Kissick*. Sure, Stan Kissick. I wrote his obituary the other day and it didn't even ring a bell. Sure." He laughed, again, shaking his head. "I'm here for the other guy, a cat named Limousine. For a second a few days ago, I thought maybe he was you."

"Me?" Limhouse's lips pursed and his eyes bulged like thick chocolates. "That *would* be a good name for me, Wilf, but I'm still very much alive. What was it Will Rogers said?"

"Twain," Sweeny said. "I think that was Mark Twain." He poked Limhouse's pillowy shoulder. "Hey, listen, good to see you, I'd like to talk but, you know, gotta run." He headed for the men's room, his hand closing in his pocket on the cool, reassuring bottle.

"Let's get together, Wilf," Limhouse called after him. "Hey, you got an automobile? I can make you a good deal. Come see me."

Sweeny didn't answer but he raised his hand in a vague gesture as he ducked through the door. His throat was too dry.

VIII

S WEENY RODE TO THE CEMETERY IN A CHAUFFEURED
black Chrysler Imperial, a '69, long and wide, with three of the tall pallbearers and a man so small he might have been a midget.

The three tall men, all middle-aged, sat in the back, their shoulders
wedged together, almost blocking out the light from the rear window.
Sweeny sat in the front by the window, with the small man between him
and the driver, a bellhop from the Queen's, hired along with the car for
the occasion. He was a boy of eighteen or nineteen, with dirty blonde hair
hanging down to his shoulders, dressed uncomfortably in a tight black suit
he must have borrowed from his father and a chauffeur's cap. Benno &
Benno had at its disposal, in addition to two hearses, a number of sedate
limousines and liveried drivers, but the Limousine funeral had taxed the
mortuary beyond its means. Almost all of the mourners had arrived in the
city by plane, it seemed, and were without transportation. Benno had
quickly rounded up an armada of rented cars—only one was not black—
and he'd managed to find drivers for them all.

"I'd just as soon there was only one body at this funeral," Sweeny said, turning toward the driver.

"Eh? Oh, yeah, I getcha." The kid had been tailgating the car ahead of them, and the speed of the procession was gradually picking up as it swung toward the outskirts of the city. He slowed the Chrysler a fraction. Sweeny could hear the boy's foot clicking rhythmically from the gas pedal to the brake and back again, in time with the snapping of his gum. They were somewhere in the middle of the long procession of ten or a dozen cars, led by the glimmering hearse. Overhead, the sky hung heavily, grey as the hearse and ripe, like the bottom of a watermelon about to crack open. The wind whipped up dust devils in the gutters as they bulldozed through intersections. All men stand aside for marriage and death, Sweeny thought. Both come in long trains of cars, both mean the end of something. And the beginning, perhaps. *But you don't get laid at the end of this.* The image of July lying on her bed, the covers tucked up under her chin, popped into his head, and he closed his eyes tightly to grind it out. The car lurched as the boy hit the brake sharply. "Sorry, eh?"

Eh! Sweeny liked the sound of it. "He was a hell of a guy, eh? Our Nick?" He threw out the opener gingerly, like a swimmer testing the water with his toe. He squinched his weight around, being careful not to crush the small man who sat sullenly beside him, staring straight ahead at the dashboard, shoulders hunched like a wishbone, and surveyed the trio in the back. They were so tall their heads almost brushed against the Chrysler's ceiling, so broad-shouldered you couldn't have slipped the blade of a knife between any of them without drawing blood. The area between the seat and the back of the front seat was a tangle of legs and feet.

"Yes, yes, Nicolas, Nicolas," said the man on the left. He was the Negro who'd nodded to Sweeny earlier. He was gentlemanly looking and dark as a bouncer's glance, with a glistening moustache and a slight British accent. He was wearing a pinstripe suit that probably cost as much as all of Sweeny's clothes put together. One arm was slightly curved, as if clutching an invisible briefcase. "He was a man of humour, good humour."

"You knew him well in Washington?" Sweeny asked. There wasn't any place but Washington that the elegant black man could have been from, that or any of a dozen embassies around the world.

"Yes, yes, there and, of course, London. London. We met in many hallways." His eyes brightened before he lowered them to inspect a fleck of lint on his striped knee. He brushed it away and raised his eyes to study Sweeny with the same sort of interest. The muscles around his mouth tightened, causing his moustache to tremble.

The man in the centre wrenched his elbows loose, making the car all but shake, and blew his nose, a tubular piece of flesh the length of a child's hand. Above the white handkerchief, his green eyes were moist and there were beads of perspiration on the vast expanse of his forehead, which rose smooth as a highway into his U-shaped russet hairline.

"You look warm," Sweeny said.

"Warm, hot, cold, this is the beastliest country for weather I've ever seen," the man said. "I was fine this morning. A few hours in this country and I've got a cold. How the Canadians can stand to live here I don't know."

"We've got thick skin," Sweeny said. He could hear the driver chuckle.

The russet-haired man peered at him, stuffing the handkerchief into the breast pocket of his blue suit. The lapels were as wide as the shoulders of the small man sitting directly in front of him. "Do you really?" he asked mildly. "You're Canadian?"

"Off and on," Sweeny said cheerfully. "On, at the moment. The weather's like the language. It only seems different at first. If you listen hard, it's the same."

The man sniffed, rubbing the bottom of his nose with a finger. "Thick skins. Thick heads, perhaps. No offence."

"Of course not," Sweeny said. He blinked. "You and Nick . . ." He left it hanging, waiting for the sniffing man to fill in the blank.

"School," he said simply. "Nick and I go way back. Rowed together." His eyes brightened, as if some wavering light had shone on them from the past.

Sweeny weighed the sound of the man's words. "Harvard?"

He smiled weakly. "We had a sensational time our third year. Nick and

I and . . . well, there were a number of us. All good ones, strong arms and lungs. I haven't been out on the water in years." He sniffed. "Nick was the strongest."

Sweeny shifted a bit further so he could get a better look at the man directly behind him, but he couldn't do it without decapitating the short man beside him with his elbow. He straightened and shifted to the right, his head resting against the half-open window. They were driving through the edge of the city now, on a street that led to the westward highway and the mountains, looming blue and hazy above them. The clouds concealed the peaks, and the bases seemed smooth and treeless in the grey light, like mounds of metal on solid rock.

The man behind him was completely bald and his features had conspired to make that even more noticeable, with a bulging forehead suggesting a brain twice the standard size had been shoehorned inside. His ears stuck out, large and fleshy, and his bluish-grey eyes popped out in an expression of constant surprise.

"You and Nick . . . were you quite close?" Sweeny asked gently.

"Yes," the bald man said. His mouth hung loosely, the lower lip unhinged, revealing a swatch of pinkish gum below bad teeth. He had the look of a man who'd been badly shocked and had never recovered.

Sweeny waited, his neck beginning to ache. After a moment, when it became clear the bald man intended to say nothing more, he asked: "An old friend, I suppose?"

The bald man seemed to be thinking, and, despite the size of his forehead, it apparently took some effort. "No," he said finally. "Not old, really, in terms of years. But very close, *very close*." The whites of his eyes pulsed, and Sweeny turned away. A raindrop spattered against the windshield, leaving a thin, ragged stain.

The car was silent except for the snapping of the driver's gum and the clicking of his shoe against the pedals, and another sound it took Sweeny a moment to identify. Beside him, the short man had lowered his head so that his chin touched his collarbone, and he was softly crying.

"It's raining at last," the driver said, turning on the windshield wipers.

"Man, we really need this." Sweeny looked at him over the head of the small man. The wipers' soft swishing drowned out the whimpers.

"And what about you?" the ruddy-haired rower asked. "What's your connection to old Nick?"

Sweeny twisted in his seat again, smiling. "Old, very old. We go *way* back, Nick and I. To school days." He was puzzled by the short man, but the trio in the back was amusing him tremendously. "Nick and I grew up together."

"That was in . . . Toledo?" the bald man asked, his ears seeming to wiggle with the effort at concentration.

"Toledo?" Sweeny had to crane his neck. "No, that was right here. In this town. Toledo? Where'd you get that?"

The bald man seemed confused. "I thought Nick said something . . . I must be remembering wrong. He did live there later, though, I'm sure of that."

"Yes," Sweeny said, warming to the game. "They moved away. I remembered it as Cleveland, though. Not Toledo." He watched the bald man carefully.

"I could be mistaken." The startled eyes grew wider. "Perhaps I'm confusing him with someone else." He darted a glance across the car to the black man. "Of course, I know who it is now. *He* was from Toledo. Both in Ohio," he added lamely.

"Of course," Sweeny said. He shifted his eyes to the russet-haired man, easing the pressure on his neck. "I remember it was Cleveland they moved to, because Nick was looking forward to going to university there. Western Reserve."

The rower sniffed, his sea eyes threatening to drip down his fleshy cheeks. "Yes, that's right. Nick didn't start with us, he transferred in, third year. I knew he came from somewhere out west, but I didn't know where exactly. Didn't talk much about his past, Nick."

"The accident," Sweeny said, raising his brows.

"Ah, yes, the accident, the accident," the black man said precisely. He looked at Sweeny appreciatively.

"It was so painful for him, he didn't like to think about it," Sweeny said. "He always loved baseball, you know, even as a little kid. He could have made the majors, I think. He was that good a pitcher."

The man in the middle blinked his runny eyes and withdrew the handkerchief from his breast pocket. He blew his nose noisily.

"After the accident, his throwing arm was ruined," Sweeny said carefully.

The rower blew his nose again, wiped it carefully, thoughtfully, and put the handkerchief away. He spoke with conviction: "Yes, Nick didn't complain, but we could see he was in pain quite often." He lifted his eyes slightly, as if inspiration might be found in the car's dome light. "He wasn't able to finish the season."

"Ah," Sweeny said.

"Yes. He had a strong left arm, but . . . he tired so quickly. He was a great one for getting us started, though. A great man for a sprint, Nick."

Sweeny nodded, smiling, and looked at the black man. "Nick always had trouble with the long haul." He chuckled. "London, for example. That's where Nick and I ran into each other again. During the war. That when you knew him there?"

The black man studied Sweeny carefully, nodding his head. Unlike the others, he seemed to be enjoying himself. "Yes, we were both stationed there. What days those were. What days."

"Same outfit?" Sweeny asked quickly.

"No," the black man said cautiously, "different outfits, but at the same base. The same base. We saw each other often."

Sweeny screwed up his eyes. "That was '42, eh? Or was it '44? I was there on two occasions."

The black man brought his hand to his mouth and stroked his moustache thoughtfully, his eyes bright. "Yes, 1942, that was the year we first met."

"That would have been right after he was grounded then."

The black man's eyes were positively glowing. "Yes, that old arm injury was giving him trouble up there in the cold and they found out about it, even though Nick, the old fox, tried like the dickens to cover it up. They put him in operations."

"That didn't keep Nick out of the air, though," Sweeny said.

"No," the black man said with satisfaction. He chuckled and leaned back into his seat, relaxing. "He was able to find a way back up. I remember now." He waited for Sweeny to move.

"That's what I mean about the long haul. They put him in the air, next thing you know he's grounded. They ground him, next thing you know he's in the air again. A sprinter." Sweeny shifted his eyes to the russet-haired man's face to acknowledge the term. The man's long, fleshy nose was wrinkling, as if it smelled something foul.

"But that didn't last long, either," the black man said. He pronounced "either" the British way, with an *i*. "As you put it, next thing you know, he's back on the ground again."

Sweeny nodded. "Of course, being shot down is somewhat different."

The black man hesitated. "Yes, somewhat different, indeed."

"I don't suppose," Sweeny asked thoughtfully, "you ran into Nick again during the war? Reason I ask, I did, but it was so unexpected. That happened to me a lot over there. The war was a small world. You kept running into people you knew." He smiled. The black man could take the easy way out, but he didn't think he would.

"Well, I did, actually," the black man said. He pronounced "actually" like it was a precision instrument. "I had gone over to Geneva on some diplomatic business, very hush-hush. Nick was the last person on my mind—he was cooling his heels in a stalag then, as far as I knew. The Swiss, of course, were neutral, but I think it was clear which way they liked to lean, as long as they didn't lean too far and we didn't try to pull them over." He and the russet-haired man exchanged meaningful looks, as if they had discussed this peculiar characteristic of the Swiss many times before. "So they did favours for us, and we did the same for them. All very . . ." He gestured with his hands, as if the precise word was eluding him, and raised his eyebrows. The car was just making the turn off the highway and starting up a gradual slope. The black man's eyes darted out his window to inspect the iron gates of the cemetery. "I was in intelligence then, and the Swiss had sent word that something of value had turned up, something that we'd want to see. They didn't say what it was, but they had passed along information to us before, quite discreetly, when they were convinced that we couldn't have acquired it any other way. They'd come through with some good things."

The funeral procession stopped suddenly, as if on cue, the Chrysler jerking up short. "Hey, easy," Sweeny said sharply. The small man beside him lurched forward, bumping his lowered head against the dash.

"You okay?" Sweeny asked, but the small man waved him away. He was sniffing and wiping tears from his cheeks with stubby, dirty-nailed fingers. He looked around, as if startled to find himself where he was.

"Geez," the driver said. "Sorry about that, eh?"

Sweeny, sticking his head out of his window into the drizzle, could see Benno get out of the car behind the hearse and approach a man in a grey uniform who came out of a small outbuilding, clipboard in his hands. "Looks like we'll be here for a minute or two." He shifted around, his elbow on the seat back. "Go ahead." He wasn't going to let the black man off the hook.

"I was, as I said, in intelligence, such as it was. They shipped me off to Geneva in civilian clothes with a diplomatic passport to suss it out. We had some people there, of course, but they were all diplomatic and we thought this was the sort or thing someone from military intelligence should see to. I was thrilled to be chosen. I was young and had fanciful illusions. I day-dreamed on the short flight, I remember, thinking of getting my hands on secret documents, in code, of course, containing information that could bring the war to a hasty end. No one back at London would be able to break the code, but I, thinking over some seemingly casual remark made by a small Swiss official with a moustache and a belly, would suddenly see the light. We'd crack the code, the war would end quickly and I would . . . well, you can see what I mean." He smiled, almost shyly, the brightness return-ing to his eyes, and Sweeny decided he liked him quite a lot. This wasn't really necessary.

"I don't remember the war ending suddenly," Sweeny said with a grin.

The black man's smile broadened. "Daydreams never do come true, do they? No, what the Swiss had for us was something quite different. I was met at the airport by one of our people, and was taken to the consulate. They made me very comfortable, but I don't think I slept a wink all that night, so impatient was I to get on with it. Next day, I was driven to a spot where I was picked up by one of their cars, and I was taken to a minor government facility on the edge of the city. No one in the car would say anything other than to make polite conversation, as if there wasn't a war going on in the world and a specific reason for us all being there together. I was burning with curiosity by now, as you can well imagine." He flashed the rower another of his meaningful glances, a low, cool look accompanied by a tightening of the muscles on the sides of his mouth.

"I was led through a long marble corridor, then down some stairs. Everything was very proper, cordial but silent. They led me to a basement room that was bare of everything but a light bulb, a table, and two chairs. They asked me to sit. I can still remember—my *spine* can remember—the feel of that hard, awkward, wobbly wooden chair, the kind of chair a condemned man might be bound to before being shot."

The black man paused, looked at Sweeny, then, turning his head slowly, at the russet-haired rower and the bald man. He smiled magnificently, his teeth filling the back of the motionless Chrysler with light. "A moment later, they brought another man into the room, a big man wearing the uniform of a German general and a self-satisfied expression."

Sweeny began to laugh, but the two other tall men stared with dumbfounded incomprehension.

"It was Nicolas, of course," the black man said, easing his companions' pain. "He had escaped, wearing that uniform, and had managed to get across the border. His German was so good the Swiss didn't believe him. They thought they really did have a German general on their hands, and someone there thought we'd like to get our hands on him. It was a preposterous idea, of course, to begin with, but not as preposterous as it turned out to be. 'Nick,' I said, 'what are you up to?' 'Henry,' he replied coolly, like a man who meets a former classmate on the street, 'what brings you to Geneva?' Then we embraced like brothers. You should have seen the looks on the faces of those Swiss officials."

Everyone was laughing now except the short man, who had lowered his head again, and the driver, who was cracking his gum and pretending not to listen. The procession began to move again. The Chrysler inched forward jerkily, then rolled smoothly and slowly past the outbuilding and the grey-uniformed man who stood stiffly, almost at attention, beside it, the clipboard under his arm. In the back of the car, the three tall men were talking animatedly, the black man's story having loosened them up, and the russet-haired man was telling one now, a rowing story, about the time Harvard took on Yale. He had forgotten about Limousine's bad arm, and Sweeny didn't bother to pay attention.

The light rain had stopped, but the sky still hung grey and moist. The neatly cut grass was glistening; it seemed brighter, greener, than it should be in mid-April and Sweeny wondered if it was real. Bright circles of flowers decorated many of the graves, and on both sides of the narrow road seas of white markers trailed off to the horizon.

This was Timber's only cemetery, except for two small church plots in town, and it had grown in proportion to the city's living population in the years of Sweeny's absence. In his day, the cemetery had been a mile or more from town and was large but manageable. Now, the city's limits had crept outward and the graveyard was three times its earlier size, almost touching the city limit line. Sweeny thought of the obituaries he wrote every morning, of the thousands of people who had died in *Chronicle*land since the last time he lived here. A whole generation and more. Enough people to populate the city all over again, and then some. All here now, quiet, with no taxes to pay, no newspapers to read, no sewers to worry about. He remembered suddenly that his mother was buried here, next to an empty plot bearing his father's marker. He wondered if he could find the two graves.

The procession stopped, for good now, and Benno got out of the first car, signalling an eruption of mourners from the others. Sweeny stood by the side of the Chrysler as the short man slid across the seat and got out.

He was no more than four and a half feet tall, dressed in baggy brown trousers and a tan chequered sports jacket, with a shiny black bow tie in the collar of his white shirt. His feet were inordinately large and were encased in white socks and big cordovan shoes. As he got out of the car, he pulled the chequered cap he had been holding in his lap onto his neatly combed head. Sweeny hadn't gotten a good look at him before and he peered at his face closely now. The little man seemed familiar, but Sweeny was positive he had never known anyone that small.

"You must have known him quite well," he said gently.

"What's that?" the small man said. His voice was high-pitched and cracked. It too was familiar.

"Limousine. You must have loved him."

The small man looked at him blankly. "Oh, Limousine. The character we're burying. Oh, yeah, him." He sniffed noisily, rubbing at his cheek. "Naw, I just got to thinking about my wife. She died last year. Cancer. I guess I ain't over it yet. She was a wonnerful woman." He mentioned a woman's name. "You ever saw her? She did lots of TV."

"I think I did," Sweeny said.

"Wonnerful," the little man said. "She was wonnerful." He blinked, wrinkling his nose as if he were about to cry again. Then he abruptly moved past Sweeny and hobbled up the small grassy hill to where the other mourners were gathering. He walked through the soggy grass with a slight sailor's roll.

Sweeny felt a big hand fall on his shoulder. "Hey, my man." The black man's face loomed close to his, split side to side by the dazzling smile. One tooth, Sweeny noticed, was capped with gold. "That was great stuff. You are *good*. You must do a lot of improv."

"You're the one who's good," Sweeny said. "I really liked your war story."

The black man stuck out his lower lip in a gesture of modesty. "Anyone can tell a story, man. It takes some talent to draw it out." He nodded his head vigorously. "Enjoyed that, man. I *enjoyed* that."

Sweeny stuck out his hands, palms up, and the black man hit them lightly with his. "Later, baby." He turned and hurried up the hill, shoulders square and dignified.

"Yeah," Sweeny said. He looked around him, then up at the still-threatening sky before ducking behind the Chrysler. The vodka bit into his throat, kicking at him like a squalling child, and landed in his stomach with an angry splash. He took another swallow to keep the first one company. Then he trudged up the hill, last again.

The mourners had gathered in a ragged circle around the freshly dug grave, where two men in grey coveralls were struggling with the mechanism that lowers the casket. Benno was fluttering his hands and making apologetic noises, his face pale and thin. Sweeny winked at him from across the abyss of the grave, and the mortician rolled his eyes helplessly. Without thinking about it, Sweeny said to the woman standing next to him: "Some job."

"It's work," she said dryly.

"But what a way to make a living." Sweeny raised his eyes to study the sky.

"Why?" The woman observed him coolly. She was unusually short, but still half a head taller than the weepy, small man he'd ridden beside. "In a way, it's our craft at its highest level, don't you think? It's certainly realism. Even the Actor's Studio doesn't go this far."

"Too far, you ask me," Sweeny said.

"I disagree. It's the ultimate in naturalism. No stage, no props, no costumes, all those things that stand in the way. No script, even, we get to make up our own lines as we go along with a fairly wide range of limitations." Her grey face brightened, her eyes widening. "We become our own audience, playing for ourselves and each other, in a real environment, without the albatross of a camera or all those eyes, without the strictures of rigidly conceived lines—what we're doing is transmitting the essence of the play, the spirit of it, not merely its form. Don't you agree?" She looked at him earnestly.

The woman was almost Sweeny's age, shapeless in her black dress, with a severe, colourless face. She came up no higher than his chest and they were standing so close to each other that he had to look down to meet her eyes. They were black and sharp, and rolled restlessly across his face, sizing him up professionally. He was sure he had seen her, lots of times. "To a certain point," he said after a moment. "It sounds good as a thesis, but in practice it seems more like pretending than acting."

The woman's gaze cooled again. "I didn't see you at the briefing," she said.

"I came in late, from the coast."

She nodded. "Personally, I find it a tremendous opportunity, one of the most stimulating moments of my career. *Pretending*. I don't think there is a difference. The key is who you're fooling."

"Ah, yes, fooling," Sweeny said, raising his eyebrows. "Excuse me." He patted the woman's elbow and slid away. The mourners had coagulated into little clots of conversation as they waited for the ceremony to begin. Sweeny positioned himself beside one group for a minute, then another. They were talking about Limousine.

"He had the coldest hands," a tall woman said. She was wearing a feathered hat that seemed out of place.

"But his eyes smouldered," her companion said. She was young, almost pretty, dressed in a closely fitting brown suit.

They laughed. "Did you ever?" the woman with the hat asked.

"Are you kidding? While he was living with my best friend?"

"Well, you know . . ."

"And those cold hands." She giggled. Looking up, she caught Sweeny's eye and he moved on.

"He just shot him. Right through the eye. The right one. Damnedest thing I ever saw. Nick didn't even blink. He just wiped the handle of his pistol with a silk handkerchief and put it away. Damnedest thing I ever saw."

The man speaking had a thin, carrot-red nose, and red eyebrows over pale, watery eyes. He was hatless, his flaming hair billowing in the wind. Sweeny tried to visualize him with a cowboy hat, the way he was sure he had seen him.

"Well, all right, I said. If that's the way you want to handle the situation, Nick. But don't expect me to help you get rid of the body. Know what he said? Well, sir, he just turned to me, you know, with that sort of aristocratic air of his, looked at me down his nose like it was the barrel of a rifle, and said: 'Body, what body?' I swear, there were icicles dripping from his voice. Then he walked away, stepping right over that poor bastard, and went out of the room. Cool? I'll tell you."

Sweeny moved on.

"He was the kindest man I've ever known." The thin, effeminate man had a wispy, blonde moustache and no eyebrows to speak of. He was wearing a greatcoat with a fur collar and his shoulders were hunched up, almost burying his slender head.

"He did a lot for me too," his companion said. He was an older, fat man with bluish veins protruding from his black cheeks. There were pink blotches on his hands. "He even lent me money, a great deal of it, once. I was in desperate straits, and I had no one to turn to. I was thinking of, you know, when I happened to run into Nick on the street, in Paris, where I'd been stranded. He could see right away that something was bothering me. 'What is it, Maurice?' he asked immediately, without even the benefit of a hello. I was so startled I just blurted it out. Ordinarily, I wouldn't have dreamed of burdening him with my troubles. Not him. 'How much do you need?' he asked. I told him. His manner was so earnest and sincere that I didn't feel ashamed. He took out his billfold, right there on the boulevard, and counted out the amount I had mentioned. He had a tremendous amount of money in his billfold. The amount he gave me was quite large, I wouldn't even repeat how much it was."

"I understand," the wispy blonde man interrupted.

". . . but it didn't make much of a cavity in what he had with him. He folded the bills, tucked them in the pocket of my shirt and put his fingers above my heart. 'Don't say a word, Maurice,' he told me. Then we went across the boulevard and had a drink at a café. He allowed me to buy."

The fat man waved his spotted hands.

"He was the kindest man I've ever known," the wispy man repeated with conviction. His voice had a tired roll, as if he were speaking in his sleep.

Sweeny stuck his head in between them on an impulse. "He was a son of a bitch, you ask me."

He walked away quickly, ignoring the sputterings that sprayed his back.

The coveralled men were clambering out of the grave and Benno stepped forward, Harriman at his side. "I think we can start now," Benno said.

The clots of mourners dissolved and the group became whole again, unified, closing in slightly, shoulders tightly pressed together, narrowing the circle. In the centre, the Rev. Mr. Lightburn took up a position beside the casket, which was draped in blue velvet.

"Here, under God's sky, we gather for the final time to say goodbye to Nicolas Limousine and wish him on his way to God's side. There is little more that we can say of Nicolas that hasn't already been said, eloquently by his good friend Ormand Harriman, and silently by you all, in your hearts. I, too, was honoured to have known Nicolas, to have called him my friend, and I'd like now to read a section from the Bible that I happen to know was one of his favourites, because we discussed it often. It had special meaning for Nicolas. I hope it will have some meaning for you."

The minister opened the soft-covered book he clutched in his hands and began to read in his flat, toneless voice. "Jesus said unto her, I am the resurrection and the life: he that believeth in me, though he were dead, yet shall he live: And whosoever liveth and believeth in me shall never die. Believest thou this?" Almost as if on cue, it began to rain again, gently, the cold drops slanting down against the lowered faces of the mourners. Sweeny scanned the tops of their heads, their foreheads, the tips of their noses that seemed to project like tongues, the points of their chins. He smiled, sighed, then, after a moment, moved away.

They were on a slight hill and from its crest, a hundred feet beyond where the circle of mourners hunched under the minister's buzzsaw voice, he could see the skyline of the city rising like a bizarre clutch of tombstones above the rolling plain of white markers at his feet. He thought again of his mother and began to walk along a row of small headstones, reading the names. "Walker," "Tyronne," "Paley," "Butt," "Stanley," "Reagan." There was no order to them, no key to guide him, and they all looked alike, despite the difference in size and shape and colour of the stones. They were all rectangles or squares, no more than two feet in any direction, mostly off-whites and light greys. Even the names seemed similar, and the dates and inscriptions. "William Walker, 1879–1953, beloved husband, father, grandfather." "Mary Tyronne, 1895–1962, dear wife and mother." "Samuel Paley, 1909–1965/Margaret Paley, 1912–1965, loving couple, beloved parents." They went on, seemingly for miles, mailboxes on a country road marking the homes of the dead. He shivered, hunched his shoulders against the wind and rain. It was useless to look, there was no way he could find his mother's grave and the empty plot with his father's marker. He promised himself he'd come back soon and have the caretaker locate them for him. He hadn't been allowed to attend his mother's funeral and he never had come to visit her grave, nor his grandfather's on the hill near the farm, though he had been at that funeral. No, that wasn't exactly right. The day before he left town for Toronto he came to the cemetery, but at the last minute he'd changed his mind and turned back. He didn't want to go away with the memory of gravestones in his mind.

He turned back, walking slowly down the hill. The rain had drowned out the Rev. Mr. Lightburn's drone, but now, as he approached the circle of mourners, Sweeny could tell they were silent, their heads bowed in a final prayer. He thought about the spaceship launched that morning and its fearless, helpless occupants tumbling high above through God's sky.

"Amen," the minister said.

"Goodbye, Nick," someone said quietly. Sweeny was sure it was Harriman. The mechanism to lower the casket began to hum.

They walked back to the cars separately, leaning into the rain, hands holding down hats. They scrambled into the closest cars, not paying any attention to which ones they had come in or who they had travelled with before. Motors coughed to life and cars began to pull away, in random order, as they filled. Sweeny found himself in a Cadillac with four other damp bodies, steam rising from their coats. None of them was anyone he knew. As the car pulled away, he saw the little man standing alone in a puddle, his chequered cap soggy, the cuffs of his baggy pants drenched. His face was lifted into the rain as if there might be something there worth seeing. Sweeny leaned his nose against the glass but all he could see was rain.

Believest thou this?

IX

SWEENY CAME IN OUT OF THE RAIN LIKE A LONG-HAIRED
dog, giving himself a good shake. He stood in the doorway for a moment,
adjusting his eyes to the dark newsroom. A faint light glowed behind a partition across the broad room and to the right, and the clatter of the wire
machines made a reassuring sound, as if the news they brought could connect anyone who read it—or even heard the keys—to the rest of the
world, to the great amorphous intellect outside. He groped for the light
switch, but it was one of those fancy, multilight kinds, and it didn't work
that simply. Below the main switch, which he depressed with no effect,
was a bank of buttons that had to be pushed for individual lights. He ran
his fingers over them gently, the way he would over the keys of a typewriter when he sat down to write, before selecting one at random,
prompting a row of lights to spring on over the news desk. He pushed the
button again and the lights went dark. The next one was for the first row
of reporters' desks. He played the buttons in sequence, unleashing a band
of light that pulsed on and off down the length of the newsroom, like an

idea flashing across his mind. He stood in the semi-darkness like an idiot, playing with an electronic toy, his fingers dancing over the light console, conducting a symphony of light and dark. He leaned against the doorjamb, soaked raincoat flung open, one pocket bulging, his dripping hat pushed back over the white bush of his hair, the loose grin of an idiot on his flattish face.

"Oh, it's you, eh? Shouldn't oughta do that."

Sweeny jerked away from the wall, one hand darting to his raincoat pocket. "Jesus, Fred, you scared me."

"Shouldn't oughta do that," the janitor said again. He was as short and slight as a child, with doleful brown eyes and a solemn voice that came without any apparent effort from a tiny mouth that scarcely moved. The efficiency of his grey work uniform was offset by the red running shoes upon which he had glided so silently into the newsroom, and the red and white toque perched precariously on his grey, hairless head. Gene, the copy boy, claimed the little janitor had recently been released from twenty years in a mental hospital, to which he'd been committed for killing his wife. Curious, Sweeny had searched the files but could find nothing to back up the story, and he'd dismissed it. The man was creepy, though. The reporters disliked him because he cleaned off their desks with abandon, throwing away half-done stories and notes. Sweeny, though, felt an affinity for him, another castaway from a distant, best-forgotten past like himself, and he'd made a few feeble attempts to break through the small man's shell, speaking to him as he cleaned around his desk or when he met him in a hallway. The janitor hadn't responded with speech—he could talk, but mostly chose not to—but the glower with which he appraised the world and its inhabitants softened somewhat in Sweeny's presence. Now, he glared up at him with a sulky reproachfulness more like that of an irritated uncle than an angry policeman.

"I was bringing light to the masses," Sweeny said lamely. "I can't work this thing, maybe you can." He walked with purpose to his dimly lit desk and sat down, feeling annoyed with himself for his clumsiness. The janitor examined the light console with suspicion, as if hoping to find some damage he could report. He couldn't and, after a moment, snapped the button which controlled the lights over Sweeny's desk and stood frowning in the doorway.

"We's closed," he said finally, gravely. "Shouldn't oughta be here."

"Working on a big story, Fred," Sweeny said, hauling a wad of notes from the desk's top drawer. He noticed the janitor's eyes brighten at the clutter on the desktop. "Very important stuff. A real big one." He slipped the bottle from his pocket into the drawer and slammed it closed. Then, with an air of importance, he began to sort through the notes, his head down, eyes closed. When he looked up after a moment, the janitor was gone.

Sweeny threw his dripping coat and hat across the next desk and lit a cigarette. He spent a couple of minutes, out of habit, thumbing through a copy of the morning's paper; the banner proclaimed "Look Out Moon, Here We Come Again," above the usual fiery take-off photo and a shot of Swigert, the new kid, smiling hopefully. On Page 3, another death's head shot of Nixon, his malevolent grin. He retrieved the bottle from the drawer and eyed it critically before raising it in a silent salute to the astronauts and taking a long slug. He leaned back, letting his weight settle into the swivel chair with a creak, and gazed at the ceiling. There were no windows in the newsroom, and there were three storeys of mechanical and advertising departments between him and the roof, but he imagined he could hear the steady drumming of rain above the wire machines' clatter, imagined he could hear the whirr of Apollo's engines as it idled far off in distant space. Gradually, the tangle of thoughts in his head slowed its churning, like an electronic puzzle about to click into place.

He took the worn map from his inside breast pocket and carefully unfolded it, laying it gently on the desk. He puffed on his cigarette and blew smoke thoughtfully over the map, as if hoping some chemical reaction would be triggered and invisible ink would suddenly appear. Sweeny sighed, gazing around the deserted newsroom, but there were no clues there, and no one to help him. He closed his eyes for a moment, but the maze of lines that made up the map stayed vivid in his mind. He could have destroyed it now and an hour later, even the next day, sat down and reproduced it almost exactly. But the truth was he didn't really need the map. He knew where it led.

He turned the map over, slipped on his glasses, and studied the telephone numbers. Like a drowning man who waits and waits and finds himself dead without his life ever having flashed before his eyes as advertised, he felt cheated. None of the numbers were familiar and he felt, all other things considered, that they should be. At least one should leap out at him. He read them out loud, thinking the sound might jar something. After repeating them a few times, they did begin to sound familiar, but he knew it was a game his mind was playing. He never had been good with numbers. He remembered one time, when he and Barbara had been living in Wilkes-Barre, he'd been making police checks and called his own number at home by mistake. She laughed about it for days afterwards. Everything had been new for them then; they were always discovering new things about each other and he was forever delighting her with new revelations of his eccentricities. Perhaps things had started to go sour for them when there were no new things for her to discover, when she finally knew him. Sweeny sighed, tapping the paper with the arm of his glasses. *King of Prussia*. He stared at the number he'd noted with the letter P for Pennsylvania. The area code was 412, but that didn't mean anything to him. They didn't even have area codes when he'd lived there. The number was 426-7735. He was sure he didn't know it. He shivered and took another drink before reaching for the phone.

He called the numbers in the order that they'd been written, but skipped over the Pennsylvania number, which was fourth on the list—he'd save that one for last. He didn't know what he was expecting as he dialled the first number, with a New York City area code, but he wouldn't have been surprised to find it disconnected. Instead, it rang three times before it was answered by a flat-sounding woman's voice.

"Good evening, *New York Times*, may I help you?"

Sweeny let out a breath with force, as if he'd been struck in the stomach. "Oh, sorry, wrong number," he blurted, hanging up quickly. He felt foolish. He was too good a phone man to do that. He stared at the phone as if it had stung him.

"*The Times.* Jesus."

An idea began to form, its threads spinning out of the grey edges toward the bright centre whose shape he could not quite make out. He peered again at the numbers, shaking his head. "Uh huh." He had a pretty good idea now that he did know one of them after all, the one in Washington, which was next on the list. He picked up the phone.

"Good evening, *The Washington Post.* Would you hold, please?"

The operator had the same flat, nasal tone as the woman who'd answered at *The Times,* and it could have easily been the same one, sitting at a master control panel, an answering service for all the newspapers in the English-speaking world, endlessly saying the same words, changing only the names of the papers. Sweeny didn't bother to hold—he hung up. With purpose now, wondering how much the long-distance tab would be for all these calls but shaking the thought away, he dialled the rest of the numbers. *The Los Angeles Times, Chicago Tribune, Miami Herald*—why the hell hadn't that last number rung a bell? He'd worked there, even if only for a year. *The Times of London. Globe and Mail.* He was certain the Paris number would be the *International Herald Tribune,* and it was. The Geneva number was for *La Suisse,* where the operator, in the same toneless voice as her sisters, answered in French. He lit another cigarette and stared at the phone. Limousine, only an hour before his death, had called newspapers in major cities of the States and Europe. And Toronto. And one other number, in a small town in Pennsylvania, which Sweeny now was sure would be a newspaper too. In a minute, he'd call and find out. But first he had to think. Why newspapers?

"Ads," he said aloud. There couldn't be any other reason. He scanned the list of numbers, frowning, and glanced up at the clock over the news desk. In the semi-darkness at that end of the newsroom he could see the clock's iridescent hands showing 5:31. That meant it was past 6:30 in Chicago, 7:30 in New York and Washington. On a Saturday night. He shrugged and dialled the Los Angeles number.

"Good afternoon, *Los Angeles Times.* May I help you?"

"You already said that," Sweeny said.

"Excuse me?"

"No, excuse *me*. Classified advertising, please."

"Just one moment, sir, I'll connect you."

Sweeny raised his eyes to the clock.

"Classified, Miss Twain speaking. May I take your ad?"

"Good evening," Sweeny said, straining his voice through his teeth. "My name is Bristol, I'm an attorney calling from Washington, DC. I'm trying to get some information on an advertisement placed several days ago. Could you help me, or should I speak to a supervisor?"

"Just a second, sir."

There was a pause. Sweeny casually blew smoke toward the lights above him.

Another voice came on the line. "This is Miss Dunn. May I help you, sir?"

"I certainly hope so," Sweeny said. He repeated his story. "I represent the estate of Nicolas Limousine, a Washington man who died four days ago. I'm trying to get a fix on some of the bills. A member of the family phoned death notices to several newspapers, it would have been on the evening of the seventh, but he neglected to keep a record of which ones he called or the charges. He thinks he gave the ad to the *Times*, but I'd like to be sure."

"Of course. I'm sure I can check that for you. That was Limousine, like the car, with an L?"

"That's right."

"Will you hold, please?"

"Surely."

It took three puffs on his cigarette before the voice came back.

"Here it is. Nicolas Limousine. It was phoned in Tuesday night, too late for the Wednesday paper. It appeared Thursday and Friday. The instructions were for two days. I see the ad says arrangements will be announced later, but there was no second placement. That often happens when the family attends to these things on their own. They have so many things on their minds, they tend to forget. That's why we prefer dealing with the funeral home."

"Yes," Sweeny said dryly. "There has been some confusion here. I wonder if you'd be so kind as to read the notice to me."

"Certainly, sir. 'Limousine, Nicolas. Wednesday, April 8. Of natural causes, while travelling, in Timber, British Columbia. Arrangements to be announced later.' It's certainly short and to the point. That's odd, though."

"What's that?"

"Mr. Limousine died Wednesday?"

"That's right."

"The placement order indicates it was phoned in Tuesday night."

"Well, that would be correct," Sweeny said. His voice was even but his hair was standing on end. "Mr. Limousine died during the night, Tuesday night. It was past midnight, so it was actually Wednesday morning."

The woman at the other end of the line hesitated for a moment. "Yes, the placement order was made at 2 AM, according to the form. It says Tuesday, but I suppose that was a mistake."

"At three in the morning, it's easy to make a slip," Sweeny said warmly. He let out the breath he'd been holding. "What will the charges be on that?"

The woman told him. "A bill has already been sent. To Washington."

"Ah, yes," Sweeny said. "The post office box."

"Yes," the woman said. She read it off. Sweeny didn't have to check it against the ones in his notes.

"Would you want to list the arrangements now?" the woman asked.

"No, thank you, the services were today. You've been most helpful. Thank you again and good evening." He cradled the phone gently, a shiver zigzagging its way up his spine.

It all made some kind of weird sense. Limousine *had* come here to die. And he'd been efficient enough, or considerate enough, to place the death notices himself, before the fact, so everyone would know. But who? Who were the messages directed to? And who the fuck was Limousine anyway? The man Sweeny knew, after all, didn't really exist. Not really.

He looked at the numbers, then thumbed through his notes. There were two lists of cities, basically the same but with some major discrepancies. First there was the list of stickers on Limousine's suitcase, at least the way

Charlie Cook and July remembered them. Now this list, of the places Limousine called the night he died. Sweeny placed the two lists side by side on his desk, put on his glasses and studied them carefully. The suitcase list had New York, Washington, London, and Paris, for sure; Miami and Toronto, maybe, best as July could remember—all cities Sweeny had lived and worked in. And Madrid and Berlin. He'd been there, had functioned as a reporter in Berlin, lived briefly in Madrid, as a freelancer a little bit, hanger-on mostly. There must have been other stickers on the suitcase, too, and he cursed himself for having let it slip through his fingers. On Wednesday afternoon, it had been sitting in Cook's office, just waiting for him to poke through it. But on Wednesday afternoon, of course, he hadn't known what he was getting into.

"Damn." Sweeny reached for the phone. It rang for a long time before it was answered, an impatient voice snapping: "Detectives."

"Sweeny, at the *Chronicle* here. I don't suppose Stanfield is there, by any chance?"

There was a pause, uncomfortably long, as if the person at the other end of the line was considering options. "Well, you suppose wrong, as usual, Sweeny, this is Stanfield talkin' at ya," he said finally, his voice flat and emotionless.

"Hey, you're working late, Stan. Don't you guys get the weekend off?"

"No rest for the wicked. I was just on my way out. What's on your mind?"

"Oh, just that Limousine thing," Sweeny said casually, "you know, the cat that cashed in at the Queen's the other night. There's still some things bothering me."

"Yeah, I noticed that."

Sweeny decided to let that pass. "You still workin' on that case, Stan?"

The voice at the other end of the line sighed. "No, Sweeny, we closed the book on that one."

"That means you ruled out foul play?"

"Never thought there was any."

"Okay, okay, let's not get into that again. There was something about that death you people thought was funny, am I safe in saying that?"

"Something? Yeah, okay, that's a good word."

"And I don't suppose you're gonna tell me what that something is."

"Nope. I mean, yup. Shit, I can't handle those double negatives, that what you call them? Anyway, nope, I'm not gonna tell you."

Sweeny rubbed his eyes with his left hand. "Okay, whatever that something was, I guess you're satisfied about it now or you wouldn't have closed the case, am I right about that?"

Again there was a pause and Sweeny let a picture of the detective form itself in his mind: he was probably a big man with a muscular frame but a beer belly, a flat, emotionless face, thin lips, eyes that had seen everything, an unrepentant crewcut. He was born here, probably, and had spent all his life here, too, too young for the big war, Sweeny's war, maybe too old for Korea, had a wife and two kids and a station wagon and a mortgage, was wondering what to do when he retired, not all that many years away now. He wasn't dumb. "I wouldn't exactly say that either, Mr. Sweeny," he said slowly, the words putting themselves down with careful deliberation.

"Jesus," Sweeny said. "Hey, listen, Stan, sometime, I mean some *other* time, not next week but next month, maybe, or the month after that, maybe I can buy you a beer, eh? And we can just rap, you know, a couple of working stiffs together for a couple draughts, and maybe, just maybe, you can tell me, off the record, of course, what the hell the big mystery was over this case. Maybe we can do that, eh?"

The cop laughed softly into the phone. "I don't think so, Mr. Sweeny. Sounds good, but I don't think so."

Sweeny shook his head. "One other thing before I let you get back to the parking tickets, Stan. That suitcase Limousine had? You got it from the hotel? Any chance my taking a look at it? I don't mean the contents, just the case itself?"

"No chance at all. We don't have it any more. Family picked it up this morning."

"The family?"

"Fella named Harriman."

"Oh, yeah, him," Sweeny said. "That cat really gets around."

"Why don't you ask him? I hear you're a friend of the family too."

"You hear right, Stan. Maybe I'll just do that."

After he hung up, Sweeny sat staring at the phone, running the conversation through his mind. "Damn, even the cops are on the payroll," he said aloud, addressing his typewriter. "That Harriman is some sweet dude."

He returned to his lists, shrugging off what he couldn't understand in favour of what he might. On the suitcase list, he underlined New York, Washington, London, and Paris and drew dark question marks on both sides of Miami and Toronto. They were major cities that meant something to him, but *that* didn't mean anything. They were major cities of the world, places where any businessman might go. Or big-time criminal. Or spy. The phone list was the same, except for that damn number in Pennsylvania. New York, Washington, London, and Paris, they were repeats, and so were Toronto and Miami if those cities really belonged on the first list. Then LA and Chicago. And Geneva. Different cities, but the same in that other way. Major ports of call. Anybody could go there. Even Sweeny had.

It kept coming back to that, didn't it? All of those cities in Limousine's life meant something to Sweeny too: Toronto, New York, Washington, London, Paris, Miami, back to Washington and New York, that was the map of his professional resume across North America and Europe. Throw in those other places in Europe and you had filled in the pieces, with the exception of Geneva, of his personal jigsaw puzzle. Geneva, damn it. What the fuck was that there for? And LA and Chicago? And King of Fucking Prussia. He'd never been in those places, either. They didn't fit.

He took a swallow from the bottle and appraised what was left. One long pull or two short ones. He made a face over the vodka's taste and kicked the drawer closed. He'd have to remember to take the bottle with him when he left the office, get rid of it where he wouldn't be seen. And no more, he promised himself. This was just a lapse, an intermission in a life of dryness begun four months ago, just a blink of an eye in the rest of his life. It didn't mean anything. And it wasn't even doing anything— except for a slight ringing in his ears and a warmth in his cheeks and neck, he was sober now as he'd been at the graveside or Benno's chapel.

Thoughts spun through his head in different directions, like gears of separate machines, spinning in identical circles but within their own frameworks, alone, not touching. The two lists of cities marched in straight columns down the pages in front of him:

SUITCASE	PHONED
New York	New York
Washington	Washington
London	London
Paris	Paris
? Miami ?	Miami
? Toronto ?	Toronto
Madrid	LA
Berlin (W)	Chicago
Geneva	King of P, Pa. ????

Toronto was where it had begun for him. He'd sold the *Chronicle*, after working himself to exhaustion, to a man with the improbable name of Buckstar, and made enough out of it to pay off all his debts, including some personal ones, like the little matter of a girl who'd gotten into some trouble, and buy himself a train ticket to Toronto and keep himself eating and with a roof over his head in that wondrous city for the three months it took before a spot opened up for him on the *Telegraph*. He was a hick, still green as to the ways of the larger world, but he did have an actual masthead with his name on it to show off; and, more than that, he was good, good enough to propel him not only through that city for three years, first on the *Telly*, then the *Star*, which wooed him away, but out into the even larger world. There'd been some good times there, in Toronto, some damn good ones, Depression or not, but mostly it was a blur now, with just one small scar for him to carry with him for the rest of his life, Louise, who he'd married with the same sort of casualness, it seemed to him now, that, less than a year later, he left her. She had dark eyes and long, curly hair the colour of crackerjacks, he could remember that, but not the actual features of her face; he could remember, with his eyes closed, the feel of her small, tight body pressing against him, but he couldn't have said how tall she was or how many pounds she had in her, not for the life of him, not now. What they had between them had been good but it hadn't set, somehow, just didn't take, no one to blame. The *Star* wanted to send him to Washington and there hadn't really been anything to keep him from going. She didn't go along.

Sweeny pencilled out the question marks around Toronto. What was the doubt? The pencil moved on down the column—Madrid: That was the city where he'd met Barbara. The war had been over more than five years but Sweeny was still hanging on, Europe a jagged roadmap of cities and jobs behind him. He'd been working in Paris for the *Trib*, off and on, and in London for a couple of papers, and he'd been travelling, burning up savings, selling the odd piece back to the *Star*, but he was running out of places to go, running out of reasons to keep going. He was drinking a lot then, his life spinning out of control. But maybe that looseness attracted Barbara to him—she a slender college girl, doing her junior year abroad, with eyes that hadn't seen much and showed it; he thick as a beefsteak with a tan that went straight through the skin to the bone and eyes that seemed to have seen everything. "You're the most beautiful thing I've ever seen," she told him after they made love for the first time, lying naked in a hotel room overlooking a square the name of which Sweeny couldn't remember even then. Sweeny had suddenly felt old, although he was far from it, and, simultaneously, inexplicably, young again. There was something about her that made his body feel young, though he was a bit far from that too. He was stuck in the middle somewhere—that was it, damn it, stuck.

Madrid—Limousine had gone there too, lugged his fancy leather suitcase down the narrow cobblestone streets, past the hotel with the fluttering curtains behind which Sweeny and Barbara lay smoking and rebuilding his life, picked up a sticker with a matador and a red cape. But he hadn't phoned that city, he hadn't let anyone there know. Sweeny's pencil moved to the other list and tapped off Geneva, Chicago, LA, Geneva again. And King of Prussia, Pennsylvania. A sour smile spread itself across his wide face at that thought. He hadn't been to any of those places, though he'd come awfully close to King of Prussia, and if Limousine had made it, he didn't have any stickers on his bag to prove it. Not that July had noticed, anyway. That was no good. "Damn it," he said out loud.

The pencil broke as he drove its point hard against the desk, and it came to him with the same sudden sharpness of a splinter sneaking under the skin of his consciousness. Geneva. *La Suisse*, like the *Herald Trib*, was the kind of paper read all over Europe. It was the *paper* that counted, not the city at all. Limousine had been spreading the word, letting the whole fucking world know about his imminent death. Put something in the *Times*, the *Trib*, and *La Suisse* and all of Europe would know about it. Sweeny nodded with satisfaction. There was method here, after all. Maybe.

He tapped at LA with the broken pencil. He'd never worked there, never been there. He had no attachments of any kind, emotional or otherwise. Sweeny wiped his big hand over his face, rubbing his jaw with his fingers. He needed a shave and his skin felt raw. All right, maybe there was no pattern. Maybe Limousine liked to get off on his own once in a while and have a blast, sneak off someplace where it wasn't necessary to keep dogging Sweeny's own footsteps. Sure. He lit a cigarette and watched the smoke rise toward the lighting panel in the ceiling. He couldn't think of anyone he knew on the coast, but surely there must be people he'd worked with on the papers there, at the *Times* and what was the other one called, the *Herald-Examiner*? Yeah, sure, he'd been around so long, knew so many people. And there was . . . Sweeny sat up stiff in his chair and the cigarette fell from his lips, cascading ashes onto his shirt. There was Louise.

She'd had relatives there and after the breakup that was where she went. She had been fooling around with little theatre work in Toronto before he met her, and she had some idea maybe she'd try her hand at the movies. Sweeny laughed quietly at that thought. An actress, yeah, that's what she was, all right. He'd sent the alimony cheques to her there, in Los Angeles, long enough, to an address he could almost visualize on an envelope, until she'd remarried. He hadn't heard from her since, hadn't thought about her in years, except in passing, with about as much interest as he gave to tying his shoelaces. He closed his eyes and could almost see the address, scrawled in his jumbled handwriting, across the face of an envelope. Palm something street, maybe. Palmleaf Avenue? Shit, it was useless. Even if he could remember it, that address was thirty years old. He had no idea what her married name might be, if she were even still alive. And his cheeks flushed at the thought that he couldn't even remember her maiden name. *Louise.* There was no way he could trace her, but the odds were good as any that she was still there, in LA. She hated Toronto, was always talking about going to LA and making it big, now that he thought about it. "Good luck to you, kid." Or was that just the way it seemed to him? But Jesus, so what? What the fuck did it mean, anyway?

He retrieved the still-live cigarette from the floor and crushed it out in the ashtray on the desk. He stared at the phone, then got to his feet. Chicago, he felt sharply, was a blind, meaningless, just a place in the middle of the continent, but there was still one more call to make and he was reluctant, almost afraid, to make it—the answer at the end of the line might be more than he could bear.

He walked through the windowless newsroom and down a hallway to the executive offices. This was an addition to the old building, and he felt unfamiliar in the hallway, lined with oak doors of advertising and business managers, editorial writers, men he barely knew. When the *Chronicle* had been his paper, he'd done all those jobs himself, just as Highmountain had before him. Now Bill Buckstar, the son of the man he'd sold the paper too, had a crew of people taking orders from him.

Buckstar's office was at the end of the corridor, with curtained glass panels flanking the door, which, to Sweeny's surprise, was unlocked. He went in, holding his breath. The office was dominated by a massive walnut desk, but Sweeny had no desire to pry through it, the windows were what he was after. He stood in front of them, his fingers separating the wooden slats of the old fashioned blinds, and peered out at the rain and the gathering darkness.

The windows faced west, and Sweeny could just make out the blue smudges of mountains lumbering beyond the city like dying prehistoric beasts. There was something out there, too, waiting for him, beckoning to him. Some piece of the puzzle. Sweeny stared at the grey rain, trying, like a child, to count the drops, but they fell too quickly, there were too many, and there wasn't any way it could be done. He stood there, counting mindlessly, until the other side of the window was insulated with darkness. It was a puzzle he wanted no part of now, and he cursed himself— cursed his instincts—for having stuck his nose into it in the first place. The man who called himself Nicolas Limousine could have died quietly; Harriman could have put on his show for a less critical audience; and Sweeny could have turned to the next obit, the next sewer story, the next woman who raised daffodils, whatever the hell there was. The world would have kept turning and no one would have been the wiser. He sighed, smiling dryly at his reflection in the glass. But that's not the way things happen, eh? Not if they don't want to happen that way.

He could hear Highmountain saying that, in a voice like water breaking over rocks in a creek, and he smiled, as he always did when the old man came to haunt him. He'd written half a story before going out to doze through a boring town council meeting, then come back to disgustedly tear up what he'd written. "They didn't follow their own damned agenda," he complained, rolling a sheet of paper into the ancient Underwood. "Things roll out the way they want to," Highmountain said. "Not the way people want them to." The old man cackled, turning back to his pipe and proofs. More than forty years later, Sweeny could still see his high shoulder-blades pressing their knifelike ridges against the blue stripes of his railroad shirt.

That had been his first view of the old man, too, a swirl of white hair and that ominous back. The sixteen-year-old Sweeny had stood in the doorway, sweaty hands clutched around the newspaper, mesmerized by the motion of those shoulder-blades. When he'd finally betrayed his presence with a cough, the editor raised his white head and turned a craggy face toward him, a face all leather and sharp angles, the eyes as piercingly blue as anything the boy had ever seen. It was a face so much like his grandfather's that it broke his heart, and yet so completely different, the familiar face of a stranger. "What you want, boy?" the old man eventually said. He looked stern, but there may have been the faintest suggestion of a smile on those severe lips.

Sweeny held out his sweaty hand with the paper clutched in it, turned to the sports page. "I can do better than this," he blurted out. He was in Grade 10 then, already in control of the language, and he knew something about sports, as much as any boy his age, maybe a bit more. He was big for his age and already showing the tendency to spread that would make him a big man, a tall, thickset kid with muddy brown hair that wouldn't comb, eyes pretty much the same colour, a sour look to his mouth, as if he'd been sucking lemons all morning, his grandfather used to say. He'd never tasted a drop of liquor, not even his grandfather's medicinal brandy, but Highmountain probably would have said he had the look of a drinker. Even then.

What he did say, in a voice that betrayed no surprise, was, "I wouldn't doubt that you could." He was a printer by trade, "a lead man, not a word man," he liked to say, with not much of a head for business but enough savvy to know the difference between good writing and bad, even a good debt and bad. He'd driven two other weeklies into the dirt behind him on his trek west, one in Ontario, in the north bush country, the other in Manitoba. He had managed to survive their founderings, had pushed on and fallen into the *Chronicle*, which itself had managed to survive the founderings of its former owners, the last of whom had been killed by the pistol of a prospector who had taken offence at something the paper said about the King.

"That particular story," Highmountain said, peering at the page where Sweeny's thumb was clamped like a vice over a headline, "was written by an illiterate who moves his lips when he painfully prints words, having first injected himself with a small dose of lead poisoning by licking the end of his pencil, much the way you, boy, might lick an ice cream cone. And, to boot, this particular defamer of the purity of the language we're discussing thinks that sport is something that goes on in a sporting house."

Instantly, he'd loved the old man. His grandfather had died, leaving him to fend for himself, but here was a piece of him again, alive in those hawk eyes. He was someone the boy might have created himself, in one of those short stories he used to write in his grandfather's barn.

"You go to school, boy?"

"Yes sir," Sweeny said, unsure which way the question would lead.

"Then you know him."

"Sir?"

"The man who wrote this drivel." Highmountain curled his lip. "One of the teachers at the school. He moonlights for me. I won't mention his name for fear of bringing ridicule upon his head. I pay him a little something for the service and it works out well for both of us. He gets paid so poorly for trying to bring education to you heathens that even the meagre something I give him brightens him up. And I, well, I wouldn't want to have to print a page with blank space on it, and he helps me fill it up. The quality doesn't matter all that much. It's the type, the black lines running horizontally across the white page, that impresses most people, makes them feel the world is unfolding as it should. Leave it out and they howl. But, no, I wouldn't be surprised that you could do as well. If you can write your own name, you're this fellow's literary equal. And I can see by the way your mouth stays closed when I talk to you that you've got more smarts."

Sweeny blinked. He didn't want to say a word, didn't want to break the spell. He wanted the old man's words to keep lying undisturbed on the surface of his memory for as long as possible.

"Sit down, boy, let's see what you can do," Highmountain said, and the feeling of delicious delight that rippled through the boy was unlike anything he'd ever felt before, would rarely feel again. The old man cleared a space for him on the desk among the rubble of papers, galley proofs, pencils, and ashtrays, already starting to spiel off a list of facts and names and figures. The boy scribbled them down as fast as he could, then shifted to the chair in front of the black Underwood bristling with keys and promise. He had to teach himself to type as he went along, and the copy he rolled out of the typewriter after a painful half hour was a smudged roadmap of X'd-out lines and mis-starts, but he had managed to write a story, a news story.

Highmountain came in from the print shop when Sweeny called and, watching him nod his head as he read the story, the pipe bobbing between his teeth, the boy thought again of his grandfather, his mouth smiling in pain, sitting in his rocker on the front porch, taking time off from his endless search of the horizon to listen to the latest piece of fantasy scribbled with a pencil stub on lined yellow paper. But that isn't why the boy loved this new old man—that had more to do with the black Underwood than the white hair; it was the sort of thing his grandfather himself might have understood, perhaps, but Greta or Uncle Tomas or Aunt Alice wouldn't. Highmountain himself understood it well enough, or seemed to. That's why he let the boy write for him as much as he could, but wouldn't let him quit school to do it, swore he would never let another word Sweeny wrote appear in the *Chronicle* and would do all he could to make sure nobody else throughout the west hired him if he dropped out of school before graduation. But he took him on when that time came, giving him a title—assistant editor—and a salary—$20 a week—and the gas to run the second-hand Model A he bought himself. And that's why, too, probably, when the old man died four years after that, from something to do with his liver, with no heirs to speak of and the town and the paper both thin from the hard times beginning to sweep around them, he left everything to the boy, now twenty-two. Not a boy at all.

Everything. That meant the *Chronicle*—the rattling press, the buckets of lead, and boxes of type, the ageing Linotype machine, the engraver, an ink-blackened two-storey building with a mortgage worth more than everything else put together but a building just the same, a place to house all the creaking machinery and the cramped office where the stories were written, the advertisements pieced together, the paper itself conceived and designed and put together, life breathed into it, once a week, every week. The *Chronicle*—that's all there was, and in late 1930, it was like getting a tin-can cat in a country where the cows have all gone dry. "If he can do anything with it," Highmountain had written in his will, a characteristic piece of prose hand-written on a scrap of newsprint and found in an envelope in his top desk drawer, "then by all means let him do it. If he can make it prosper, he deserves all the rewards that will bring. God knows, no one else does. If he can make it even survive, he deserves the satisfaction that will produce. And if he can't—well, despite all I've taught him, he can still use a lesson or two."

Sweeny the grown man laughed at that memory, smiling out the slatted window at the dark rain. Yeah, he'd had a lesson or two. Somehow, he had managed to do something with the paper—hang on, survive. He didn't make the paper prosper, nobody could have in those years, but he kept it alive when other little papers in the country were going under, when this one—everyone said—should have. He did it pretty much himself, letting go the half-senile old woman who had been banging together the social news and cooking columns and gossip for years and the solemn-faced young war widow who kept the books and helped sell the ads, taking those jobs on himself, keeping only the black-handed man with green teeth who ran the print shop, talking to the lead the way some housewives talk to plants, urging it on, "melt, harden, melt, harden, melt, harden," in a never-ending cycle. There wasn't enough business or money that first year or the year after for him to do it any other way. But this was one damned thing that wasn't going to die on him.

The *Chronicle* had the same sort of mixed blood Highmountain must have had. It had been started more than thirty years before, when Timber was no more than a camp for gold-seekers and other miners moving toward or coming back from the higher country to the west. But as the town caught on and grew, so did the paper, slipping from the hands of the merchant who had started it, thinking it would be good for business, which it turned out to be, all right, into legitimate hands—that is, those of printers and newsmen, people who knew something of what they were doing. Despite that, the paper was still good for business, the town's and its own, and it prospered. By the time Highmountain had come to have it, the paper was as entrenched in the life of the town as the Queen's Hotel, two blocks west on Mountain Avenue.

But times were hard now. *Chronicle* was a good name for a newspaper because Sweeny used it to chronicle the town's struggle, and he used it well, in those years when a fist had the town and its people around the belly, squeezing. You couldn't see the pattern in any one issue of the paper—then it was just a hodgepodge of stories about, in the early years, farmers going under the dust, stores being boarded up, dead cattle, empty bellies; and, a little later on, people coming back, doing what the paper was doing, surviving, and more than that, not just hanging on but actually getting a little bit more of a grip on the tree limb they were all hanging from, maybe enough of a grip that, eventually, they could climb right back up onto the limb itself. Then they could start thinking about coming down from the tree. To see that pattern, you had to read the papers, one at a time, over a long period of time, the period of almost four years in which Wilf Sweeny, like it said on the masthead, was the owner, publisher and editor of *The Timber Chronicle*, est. 1896, published every Wednesday.

He was it, he *was* the *Chronicle*—just the way Highmountain had been, and he often thought, late at night as he sat hunched over the typewriter in the drafty office above the print shop, a curl of smoke drifting from the cigarette between his fingers, the muscles in his neck and shoulders aching, his eyes burning, that no one before had ever given him anything of value; anything at all, really, except the bare necessities and politenesses of life, like passing the potatoes, like a new shirt and a pair of pants at Christmas, like a bed to sleep in. No, those weren't gifts—in some ways, they were burdens, because they kept life flowing in you; at any rate, they were no more than were due. If you were going to pump life into somebody in the first place, then you had an obligation to keep him going, he thought, and that included relatives like his grandfather and uncle, who'd inherited the responsibility from his parents. So he didn't owe them anything, Sweeny felt; they hadn't given him anything he hadn't been promised. But the paper was something else. It was a real gift.

Lightning streaked across the sky, followed by a clap of thunder, and Sweeny let the slats of the window blind fall together with a sharp echoing clap. He wondered if the morose, pear-shaped man named Buckstar who occupied this office ever stood for long breathless stretches of time at the window, gazing out at mountains and rain and ghosts thumbing their noses through the streaked glass. His father had seemed decent enough, and had big plans for the paper and the money to back them up. He was a businessman who had managed to hold onto his money through the Depression and was looking around for places to put it—all of which had seemed good to Sweeny at the time. Thirty-five years later, his judgment seemed to have been right. But the truth was the man's name appealed to him—"Buckstar is the kind of name that should be on a masthead that used to sport Highmountain," he'd told Delancy when he decided to sell. "Don't know how something as common as Sweeny got in there."

"Sure, sure," Delancy said. "You don't have to convince me. The old man never said it had to be a stone around your neck. He never said you had to build him a monument."

Would his life have turned out a whole lot different, he wondered, if, when he'd come quaking into the grubby old office above the print shop, the palms of his hands sweating as he faced those intense blue eyes, the old bastard had just told him to bugger off and leave men's work to men? Different, maybe. Better? He wasn't sure about that.

Sometimes it seemed to Sweeny as simple as this: that the train he'd boarded to Toronto all those years ago had changed tracks somewhere, and he'd wound up someplace else, inside his life but outside of it at the same time. But things were never that simple, he knew that.

July's pouting little-girl face, the bedcovers coming up to her chin, flashed across his eyes; for the second time that day, he berated himself for his failure the night before. Whatever else may have happened last night, "failure" was the only word for what had transpired between the two of them. His impotence was hardly physical—was it moral then? Emotional?

What was the logic of that? He shook his head, feeling baffled, helpless—truly impotent. But was his inexplicable reaction to July's mock seductiveness any more mysterious than her behaviour itself? What was *that* all about? He suddenly remembered that he had promised to call her today. "Shit, it's getting late," he said aloud. And there was that other call to make.

He was almost out of the office when something on Buckstar's desk pulled him back. There were two baskets, one marked "in," the other "out," on the corner of the smooth walnut desk. Something akin to instinct, something like smell, guided Sweeny's hand to the "in" basket. He hadn't switched the light on when he came in earlier and didn't want to now, and he'd left his glasses on his desk, but enough dim light from the hallway bent in through the half open door to allow him to make out words on the papers he shuffled through if he squinted. His ears were alert for footsteps in the hall.

He wasn't really looking for anything in particular, but it took him only a minute to find it. He could make out Jim Callan's name on the top of the memo, and his own in its body.

He walked almost stealthily to the door, holding the sheet of paper gingerly, and bent his head to read in the light. "I've been reasonably impressed with Wilf Sweeny, and have discussed him with some others in the newsroom and gotten favourable responses," it read. "My feeling is he's somewhat gun-shy but is by no means burnt out, and after he's more comfortable here he'll be a good addition to the staff. He's a hard nut to get to know, but so far he's shown no sign of drinking, at least not on the job, and he's been in every day, always punctual. No problem at all. Unless you say no, I'll tell him next week he's passed his probation and is on. Maybe that'll loosen him up." The memo was signed "Jim."

"Gun-shy," Sweeny whispered. He read the memo through again, frowning, before carefully replacing it, making sure the papers in the basket were as he'd found them. Buckstar would get to it Monday probably, and on Tuesday or Wednesday Callan would come over to Sweeny's desk, his moustache bristling, shake his hand and give him an awkward

"Welcome aboard" and a ten-or-fifteen-dollar-a-week raise. He would be able to breathe easier then, though never really easy. There wasn't any union and probation was just a nicety, really. They could fire you any time they wanted to, though they weren't likely to if you did your work well and behaved yourself. Carney, the desker who moved his lips, was a lush, Sweeny knew, but he managed to get to work every morning at six, and didn't make waves. He smiled at that thought. It didn't surprise him that they knew about his drinking. Surely they'd have done a little checking. Couldn't have checked too hard, though, or they wouldn't have hired him at all. Probably didn't know his age—he'd told them he was only fifty-nine. *Keep your nose clean, Sweeny, and you're home free, all the way*. He thought of the bottle in his desk drawer and made a face. "Gun-shy," he said again, out loud. "Shit."

Closing Buckstar's door, he almost bumped into the janitor. "Shouldn't oughta be in there," the little man said solemnly. There was something about him that reminded Sweeny of a turnip, with his wide middle and spindly shoulders, his tiny head topped by the red and white toque planted squarely above his out-turned ears. He didn't look like he could kill anything but time, and even that without much precision.

"Getting some air," Sweeny said lamely. "No windows in there." He gestured down the hall, toward the newsroom. "Gets stuffy." He felt ridiculous explaining himself and realized he was shouting, as if talking to a deaf man.

The janitor looked at him stupidly but didn't answer. Sweeny fought down an impulse to take him by the arm and ask him straight out: "Did you really kill your wife? Why did you do it, man? Couldn't you control yourself? And how can you live with yourself now?" But he was afraid to hear the answers. He brushed the little man's shoulder lightly with his hand as he walked past him down the corridor toward the newsroom and his desk, the telephone, the number waiting to be tried. The janitor trailed sourly behind, and Sweeny could feel his disapproving eyes on him as he dialled the phone. The electronic static crackled in his ears like distant thunder. He let it ring ten times, but there was no answer. When he recradled the receiver, he was alone in the newsroom again, the ringing of the phone still echoing in his ear.

The clock over the news desk said 7:15. Saturday night, and it was past nine, maybe even past ten, in Pennsylvania—he wasn't sure where the time-zone division was. He hadn't really expected anyone to be at the other end. He dialled the area code again, then the number for long-distance information.

"Directory assistance. What city?"

"Operator, I'm calling King of Prussia, I think that's in your area, near Wilkes-Barre."

"Yes, it is, sir." The operator's voice sounded thick, with sleep or annoyance.

"I'm trying to reach the newspaper there, it's a weekly. I don't know what it's called, but I do have the number." He gave it to her. "There's no answer, though, and I was wondering if there was another number listed, a night number. It's very important, operator."

The voice sighed. "I'll check, sir." Sweeny tapped his finger against his notebook as he waited. Gun-shy! That made him sore. What the hell did they expect from a relic like him on his way back? A human dynamo?

"I have a listing for the King of Prussia *Eagle*," the operator drawled. "There's only the one number listed, the one you have." Sweeny clicked his teeth with satisfaction. But what else could it have been but a newspaper?

"Operator, this is an imposition, I know, but it really is important. Do you suppose you could check it in the Yellow Pages? Maybe it lists the editor's name. Or perhaps you even know him, if you're from that area."

"I'll check, sir," the operator said icily.

Sweeny smiled. There was a slight southern inflection to the edge of the woman's voice and he doubted she was from King of Prussia or anywhere near it. He doubted, too, that she'd come up with anything for him. Not that it mattered. It seemed a safe bet that Limousine's call to the tiny weekly had been to place a death notice, as he had at the other papers. He didn't really have to call the King of Fucking Prussia *Eagle* himself to confirm that. He was about to hang up when the operator came back.

"I have a T.T. Timmons listed as editor," she said blandly. "I have a home number for him." She gave him the number and he scribbled it down.

"Thank you, operator. Very good of you." She answered by clicking off. Sweeny frowned at the number. What the hell was he supposed to do with that?

"My feeling is he's somewhat gun-shy but is by no means burnt out," Callan had written. *Gun-shy.* He had a flash, inexplicably—the word gun, perhaps—of the face of a dying man he had seen once, during the war, a soldier hit in the throat by a sniper's bullet just outside the tent in Italy where Sweeny was sitting, pecking away at a typewriter on a folding table, out of the blazing sun. There had been shooting in the distance, tiny explosions that were almost drowned out by the fiercer racket of his typewriter, but this shot was louder, and was followed by a sound not unlike the forcible expulsion of air, the kind of sound a man makes when he's slapped hard on the back. The two sounds brought Sweeny out of the tent. The soldier was lying there, almost at his feet. "Jesus, this fellow's been shot," he shouted, and part of the memory he carried around with him for the rest of his life was the feeling of foolishness he felt later, when he had time to think over the details, about using the word "fellow." It wasn't a word he ordinarily used, that wasn't what he called men, but he was travelling with a British outfit—the wounded man was the Limey corporal who only minutes before had stuck his reddish face in the tent flap and asked Sweeny if he'd care for a cuppa tea—and that might have been the influence. At any rate, that's what he'd said, shouted out, "Jesus, this fellow's been shot." And then, because he was there and no one else was, he bent down and lifted the man by the shoulders to see what was the matter, and got his hands wet. He noticed that before he saw the blood—that his hands were wet. Then he looked closer and saw the thick, almost black liquid staining his hands, and when he pulled the man back to cradle him in his arms he saw the bright wet explosion in his neck. The gesture, Sweeny thought later, after they had pried the man out of his arms and someone led him back into the tent and sat him down at the folding table, the gesture was almost instinctive, the gesture he had seen men and women on

two continents, in war and peace, make to comfort the dying—take them into their arms like a sleeping baby and rock them to death, murmuring that all's well. Sweeny didn't do that—didn't murmur anything—but he did rock the man in his arms, his eyes shifting from the pulsing red wound to the grey, twisted face above it. It was that greyness that, minutes later, sitting at his typewriter, and years later, his hand resting on the telephone, he recalled most vividly. After a few minutes, someone brought him a cup of tea, he sipped at it and went back to the story he had been writing.

Sweeny shook his head and chased the memory away, that ten-second memory that swooped down on him at odd times, when he was most unprepared. "Gun-shy," he said aloud. "Bullshit." He took a drink from the bottle. There was just a swallow left, so he downed that too, then carefully screwed the bottle closed and put it in his raincoat pocket. Then he dialed T. T. Timmons's home number.

A woman answered. "Hello," she said simply.

"Is Mr. Timmons at home?" Sweeny asked, darkening his voice a shade.

"May I ask who is calling?" The woman had a pleasant, warm voice, something very different from the sounds that came spinning smoothly from the mouths of telephone operators. It was the kind of voice real people had, real women, and it evoked in Sweeny's mind the image of a woman he once knew.

"Yes, my name is Bristol. I'm an attorney calling from Washington, and I'm trying to get some information on an advertisement I believe one of my clients placed with Mr. Timmons's newspaper several days ago. I'm sorry to be calling at his home, and at this hour, but it's rather important."

The woman laughed, and it was a good, clean, honest laugh, Sweeny thought, the kind of laugh that meant the woman who made it was really amused and didn't mind anyone else knowing it. There was richness to it, feeling. "You're in luck," she said. "My husband doesn't know anything about the ads, but I happen to be the advertising manager, if I may use so big a title, as well as circulation manager, business manager, and personnel director. That means I'm in charge of both of us, and the paper boys." Her voice had taken on a beautifully balanced tone of self-mockery that sent a shiver through Sweeny, it was so like that of the woman he'd known. The voice was so nice, so familiar. "Now, how can I help you, Mr. Bristol?"

Sweeny was silent. He felt dizzy, and his head was throbbing. The woman's voice rattled in his ear like a gust of wind.

"Mr. Bristol? Are you still there?"

"Barbara," Sweeny said with effort. "It's Barbara, isn't it?"

"Yes, my name is Barbara," the woman said, puzzled. "Do we know each other, Mr. Bristol?"

"Barbara," Sweeny stammered. He couldn't think of anything else to say.

There must have been something in his voice, too, when the impersonation ended, that set off something in her. "Wilf," she said suddenly. "Is that you, Wilf? What on earth?"

Sweeny sat slumped at his desk, the telephone receiver clenched in his white hand, the other hand gripping the edge of the desk, staring at the clock over the news desk without seeing the movement of the hands, or the hands themselves.

"Wilf? For goodness sake, Wilf Sweeny, what are you up to now?" The woman's voice kept tugging at him through the telephone, from two thousand miles away, and after a while it became grating to listen to it. The receiver was like a stone in his hand and it took a great effort to move it, but he did manage to hang up.

❧

In his dream, Sweeny is walking with a girl in a park high above the city, its skyline draped at their feet. The sun beats down on them, birds sing, green leafy canopies sway above. Their hands are entwined and Sweeny's eyes are on that sweet joining; he sees the graceful curve of her fingers alongside the stubby bends of his own. Below the clasped hands, he can see the sleek brown corduroy of her thighs, and he can feel her breast against his arm, feel the warmth of her beside him, smell the faint flower sweetness of her, but when he raises his eyes and turns to her, her face is blank, totally without features, like the head of a costume dummy in a shop window, and he bruises his lip against the hard ridge of her teeth. Clouds darken the sun and he is alone, adrift in a sea of ruin. All around him is rubble and devastation, empty hulls of burned-out buildings, the street pockmarked with craters, jagged concrete, and glass. Somewhere in the distance, he hears a cry that could be that of a baby or a woman, perhaps even an animal, and he jerks his head up to search the desolate horizon but there is no one in sight, only greyness, emptiness, a crystal stillness in the air that calms him, leads him on.

He comes to the ruin of a house, the door blown away, the walls blackened and ruptured, but flowers still grow in a curiously shaped patch beneath what once must have been a bay window, daffodils and gladiolas and wild roses, impossible combinations that perplex him. He reaches for a rose but something in the corner of his eye brings his head up. There is a shadow in the cavity of the doorway, motionless, then, almost imperceptibly, a movement quick as the flutter of a bird's wing, then another, then Louise is emerging from the ruin, her hand extended, golden hair tumbling in ringlets along the sleek curve of her neck to her bare polished shoulders. "Wilf, please help me," she says, very matter-of-factly, her voice smooth and even, like honey dripping from a spoon, but there is no alarm in her eyes.

Sweeny gives his head a shake. "Why should I? What am I to you?"

Her black eyes flash, cinders in a dying fire. "I don't mean like that," she says, beginning to laugh. "I don't mean it that way."

The laughter tumbles from her mouth like rain, enveloping him with its liquid sound and he turns away, reaches for something to steady himself, and when he looks again he notices her dress is torn, her arms smudged with dirt, her face smeared with blood. "Oh, God," Sweeny says, reaching for her. "I'm sorry, Louise, I'm sorry." She turns her face to him, nodding, but all he sees is her mouth, the lips parting, the glint of sunlight on her teeth.

"Don't you remember what I said?"

Sweeny is confused. "No, I don't . . . what do you . . ." In the distance, the child cries again, or perhaps it is an animal, and he turns to look but there is only emptiness.

In his dream, he walks on, following a path that leads him into a countryside, toward the sound of water splashing against rock. Bush presses in around him, and he is sweating, branches tear at his shirt, scratch his arms, mosquitoes whip around his head, darting toward his eyes, his throat is dry, parched. He stops to rest in the grass, the sun pressing down on him like a weight, his breath coming fast and short. An ant crawls up his leg and he brushes it away, watching as it tumbles into the grass. A cloud rolls across the sun, casting him into darkness. He scrambles to his knees, fumbling for matches, but the pockets of his shirt have been torn away. He shivers in the cold and waits, without desire, without hope, listening to the wind. High above him, stars flash like sparks, cheerless bursts of light that promise nothing. Finally, the voice he has known would come makes itself heard.

"I'm glad you've come," the voice whispers, and Sweeny spins around on his heels. Across the fire, deep in shadows, a man is kneeling, his shoulders hunched against the wind.

"What did you say?" Sweeny calls, wrapping himself in his arms.

"You heard me." The figure moves closer, and Sweeny can see the strength in those shoulders, the upper arms, in the thick cords of his neck.

"It doesn't really matter," Sweeny says, but he knows it does, and a moment later he adds: "You're him, aren't you?" The man laughs softly, firelight splashing on his beard. But when he leans forward to stoke the embers Sweeny sees his face is a blank, just a smiling mouth, the lips thick and cruel, like worms twisted in sand. They open, as if to speak, but no sound comes from them, just a rushing of wind that sends the flames leaping, scattering ashes into the darkness. Sweeny is alone in the wind, grasping for sparks.

X

Sunday

SWEENY HADN'T BEEN ON THE HIGHWAY FOR THIRTY-FIVE years but it looked the same to him, as if the successive layers of blacktop had served more to cement the road's character and identity than to change it.

The city was three quarters of an hour behind them, back in the haze of the valley, and they were approaching high country now, the lodgepole pines thick on both sides of the road, tall and slender.

The morning had broken as grey as the band of pain pressing across Sweeny's forehead when he woke up, sprawled on the soggy rug in his living room, an empty Scotch bottle lying beside him like a co-conspirator and the weight of rain had still hung overhead as he lurched across town, from his place to July's, in a taxi. He shivered as he stood in the alley, in chinos, a sports shirt, and a windbreaker, watching her nurse the ancient pickup truck reluctantly to life. "That thing really going to get us across town, let alone all the way into the mountains and back?"

July grinned. "Oh, yeah, plenty of life left in this beast."

He kept a watchful eye on the sky as they rattled westward, certain it would open up again. But the clouds soon began to break up and now, as they went deeper into the mountains, the dark masses above them were splintering into blotches of grey and white against a milky backdrop that was slowly filtering into a pale blue. The sun shone haphazardly through the debris of clouds.

Sweeny's legs were cramped and his stomach, lined with lead, surged heavily with the roll of the truck. He would have liked to let his head loll back against the rear window and shut his eyes, but he kept them open, on the brush lining the road, watching for the mouth of the dirt road. He knew he'd recognize it.

"Slow down a bit, it should be up around here soon."

"Sweeny, I know where the road is, believe me," July said. She turned to him, light radiating from her face. She seemed comfortably at home in the pickup, and, despite his sarcasm, he had been only mildly surprised when she led him down her stairs to the alley behind the drugstore. The old Chevy seemed to fit her, as if it had sought her out as someone whose spirit could do justice to the fitful breathing of its plugs and jets. A model from somewhere in the forties, it had been painted red once. Now it was mostly rust and weather-baked dirt. The shock absorbers had long since dissolved to dust, but July was right, the engine was strong, and it carried them forward with force and purpose, faster than Sweeny would have liked. July drove as if the highway were a field, with no borders to confine her, her left arm resting on the open window, the sleeves of her red plaid shirt rolled up, and her right hand resting easily on the gear shift handle, a finger tapping out a ragged rhythm. Her blue jean legs were slightly apart, cowboy boots on the pedals, her hair pulled back and up under a rolled-brim hat. Her face was drained and intense, almost sexless, her mouth set, the lower lip protruding like a slice of apple.

"I've been up this way a bit more recently than you," she said after a pause.

Sweeny smiled, his eyes widening. "That's great, sweetheart, but would you like to turn around? You just passed it."

"I know," she said, sniffing. She didn't slow down. They looked at each other, then Sweeny twisted his head around and looked out the rear window. The dark car was less than a quarter of a mile behind them, rays of sun reflecting off its windshield. It had been there, never out or sight, since they left the outskirts of the city, but Sweeny hadn't mentioned it, hoping that July wouldn't notice.

"I thought maybe we should ditch them first," she said. "There's a campground just up ahead. I'll pull in there. "

"They're just touristas, out for a Sunday ride in the country," Sweeny said, but his voice lacked conviction.

"Right," July said. "Just like us, eh?"

There were no turn signals on the truck, and July stuck her arm out the window and motioned for a right turn as they passed a park sign indicating a campground in a quarter of a mile. Looking over his shoulder, Sweeny could see the car behind them slowing.

"Touristas, sure, more likely treasure hunters," July said.

"Treasure?"

"Sure, you know. At the X."

Sweeny laughed. "There's no treasure at that X."

"How do you know?"

They were bumping across gravel now, and Sweeny's head was caught again in the vice he'd thought had given up.

"Oh, I know what's at the X."

"What?" The truck lurched, almost stalling.

"Easy, damn it," he said sharply.

"Sorry." She rolled the truck to a stop and they both watched the black car behind them slow as it pulled abreast of the campground. It was a sleek new Chrysler, like the one Sweeny had ridden in to the cemetery the day before, and it had the look of a rented car, its chrome glistening. It seemed to hesitate for a moment, as if it were going to stop, then sped up. There were two men in the front seat and Sweeny had a good view of the face of the man on the passenger side, whom he was sure he hadn't seen before, but only a partial view of the driver. His neatly combed sandy hair was familiar, and the furtive way he turned his face behind his companion's shoulder made Sweeny's mouth tighten. He didn't say anything until the Chrysler had disappeared around a curve.

"Just gawking at this ridiculous crate," he said finally, with distaste.

"At the crate, eh? Sure they weren't gawking at me?"

Sweeny smiled and tugged the brim of her hat down over her eyes. "Why would anybody be gawking at a tomboy like you?"

"Maybe they're queer." She pulled off the hat and shook her head so the blonde hair swirled like a cloud of cotton candy above the intense green of her eyes. She stuck out the slice of her lower lip.

They sat in awkward silence for a minute, looking at each other. Then Sweeny reached over and put his finger against her lip. It was moist and warm.

"What is it?" she asked softly.

"I guess I . . ."

"No, I mean, what's at the X?"

"Oh, Christ." He took his hand away. "Come on, let's get going, you're so anxious to find out."

"Hey, Sweeny, don't be that way." She looked at him severely. "I know what you mean."

He looked at her again and stroked her face. He could feel the smooth softness of her skin all the way up to his shoulder. After a moment, she took his hand in hers and kissed his fingers, one at a time.

"Okay, enough of that." She swiveled around on the seat and put the truck in gear. "You didn't know those guys, eh?"

"Never saw 'em before. Just a couple of salesmen out for a drive, looking at the scenery."

"Sure," July said.

The dirt road on the north side of the highway was marked by a faded wooden sign saying "True Hope Road" and that was all, but Sweeny remembered it was less than ten miles to the abandoned mine town—ten narrow, winding rocky miles going mostly up. Before they'd gone in a quarter of a mile, they came to a spot where the narrow, rutted road dipped and was coated with mud glistening like an oil slick in the sun. There were tire tracks, clear and distinct as stone carvings, in the mud.

"Somebody's been on this road," July said.

"It's a public road," Sweeny said. He was beginning to wonder, though, if he had been smart to bring July along. But the way his head had felt that morning, he couldn't have made the drive by himself, he was sure of that. And he had promised her. Besides, he was being ridiculous. It *was* a public road. The driver of the Chrysler on the highway could have been anybody. Limousine was buried and Harriman and his gang were back in Washington and New York and Hollywood or wherever they came from. He shrugged off the feeling of dread gnawing at his belly and concentrated on the dull throbbing at his temples, trying to will it away.

The dirt road climbed and bucked along the shoulder of a pine- and aspen-choked mountain. Grey snow drifts still clogged the roadside gullies, and the aspens, though covered in a light-green haze, had yet to fill out with leaf, but wildflowers grew riotously along the sun-dappled flanks of mountain slope rising sharply on their right. Engorged streams crashed through culverts under the road with the din of city traffic and once they heard a cracking like the sound of rifle shots and turned their heads to watch a small herd of elk leaping away down the slope and into the trees below them like the picture on a television screen dying out in jerks.

It took more than twenty minutes to go the eight miles to the unmarked summit of the pass. Sweeny sat forward as they began the descent; in a couple of minutes the truck went around a sharp curve that opened up to a sloping view of a valley with a cluster of weathered shacks tucked into a curve of a creek running along the bottom, a mile or so away. Squinting, he thought he could see the sun glint off the metal bridge that would take them over that creek after they passed through the ghost town.

"There she is," July said hopefully. Sweeny didn't reply.

The view of the valley floor was hidden by trees again, but they continued to get flashes of it as they descended the last mile. The road widened slightly as it levelled out, and July was able to put the truck into third gear and keep it there. "Oh-oh," she said, pointing her chin at the rear-view mirror. Sweeny edged around to look back. Now that they were on level ground, there was a clear view of the winding mountain road they had come down, and a cloud of dust moving along it. He couldn't see what was raising the dust.

"So it's another car. Don't be so nervous." He shrugged, but his blood quickened and he wished, not for the first time that day, that he had a drink.

"I know, it's a public road."

They passed some desolate buildings at the edge of the ghost town, stripped of everything of value by at least three generations of souvenir and antique hunters; what was left eroded by time and weather, shattered by vandals. Windows gaped open like the mouths of idiots, every piece of glass gone; doors flapped listlessly, like the tongues of dead cattle, their knobs and hinges ripped out or rusted away. One building appeared to have been a prospector's cabin, another the structure of a mine itself, built against a hill with a water trough leading to the roof and a primitive mill wheel groaning in the wind beside it.

"It hasn't changed much since the last time I was here," Sweeny said. "It was pretty much in ruin then."

"You'd think it would just blow away," July said solemnly.

"That's what it's doing."

The road took a jag to the left and they were in the abandoned town where several thousand people had once toiled in pursuit of silver and the pleasures that came from it: a dozen or so buildings in various stages of ruin, rusty nails and inertia all there was holding the rotten grey boards together. Trees were growing through holes in sagging roofs; brush filled the porches; and signs faded beyond reading could be seen on warped walls. The skeleton of what once had been a splendid wooden sidewalk skirted the foaming stream.

Beside one of the buildings, the wreck of a two-storey hotel, was parked a sleek grey car.

"Fuck," July said. "It's a hearse."

"I see it, " Sweeny said, his heart pounding. "Keep going."

He stuck his head through his window. The dust cloud was hovering over the turn in the road, a quarter of a mile back, and a car was emerging from it. He couldn't be certain, but it looked like the Chrysler that had been following them earlier.

"Fuck, there's somebody up there," July said.

He hadn't heard her voice so frightened before and he jerked his head around, following the direction of her pointing hand. They were abreast of the hotel now and July had slowed the pickup almost to a crawl. Looking past her, he didn't see anything at first, just the battered false front of the hotel, its gaping windows, a sign protruding from the roof proclaiming, in just barely readable print, "True Hope Hotel, est. 1882." The hotel, like all the other buildings, was a deathly grey, all colour long stripped from the boards.

"Where?" he cried in frustration. "You're seeing things."

"Up there, in the window."

Then he did see something, what appeared to be a face in a window on the second floor, but they were already too far past for him to be able to tell for sure.

"Back up."

July braked the truck to a halt and rammed the gear stick into reverse. The sudden change in direction threw Sweeny against the dash and he was only righting himself when they came abreast of the hotel again. The truck jerked to a stop again and they peered out, Sweeny leaning over July's shoulder. There wasn't any mistaking it now. There was a face in the window, a thin, dark man staring gloomily down at them. It was Benno, he was sure of it.

"Jesus," he whispered. Then he yelled, "Get going!" yelling it again as July struggled with the gears, which balked before grinding noisily into first. The truck spurted forward just as the black Chrysler pulled up behind it. Sweeny was looking back, but the sun was shining on the car's windshield and he couldn't see who was behind it.

Sweeny fought to keep the panic mounting in him under control. Now

Benno? What the hell did he have to do with all this? He had buried Limousine and should be out of it. But they should all be out of it, it was over. Except it wasn't, obviously. The image of the grey hearse parked beside the ruined hotel flashed into his mind. *Benno.* Of course. Maybe it did make some crazy sense, after all.

"Just keep going and don't stop for anything," he said. "Keep going till I tell you to stop."

July had kicked the pickup into fourth and was speeding along at almost fifty now, laying down a carpet of dust on the ghost town. There was a clear, straight stretch now for half a mile to the point where the road turned right at the rusted metal bridge that crossed the frothy creek, and she put her foot down hard on the gas pedal. She was going so fast when she came to the bridge that she didn't see the car parked on the other side until she was almost on it, but Sweeny did.

"Keep going!" he shouted. "Ram the fuckers."

The car was a black Chrysler just like the one that had pursued them over the mountain, but it was too clean to have just made that dusty trip. It was parked at the bridge's edge, on the side of the road, but the shoulder was so narrow the Chrysler's rear end stuck out into their path. Harriman was standing beside the front passenger door, in the same smoothly tailored suit he had worn at the funeral. He had his hands in his pants pockets and was gazing casually across the bridge railings at the oncoming truck, his cold grey eyes on Sweeny's face. Behind him, at the edge of the stream, the thin man with the razor eyes and deep nostrils was standing on a rock, urinating into the fast-moving, roiling water. He looked up, his hands at his fly, but there was no expression on his face, neither surprise nor embarrassment nor anger nor fear. He turned his face toward the roaring truck with the same bland, dispirited interest he might have given to a bird on the branch of a tree above his head. His dark eyes fell on Sweeny's face and gave him away. He blinked.

Sweeny saw all this in a frozen moment: the faces of the two men hanging in space before him for an interminable length of stopped time; the rear end of the Chrysler, the sleek, shining black of its fenders, the glittering chrome upon which rays of sun shattered into splinters of pure light; the water rushing wildly under the bridge; the swaying of the groaning boards beneath the truck's trembling charge; the long, slender arch of piss connecting the man with the hot eyes to the stream, like a thread of silver. Then the picture was shattered by the crunching impact of the pickup's front bumper grazing the right rear fender of the Chrysler.

"Hold on!" he heard July yell, but he wasn't sure if he heard it before the impact or after. All these sounds were floating in his head at once: her shrill cry, the groaning of the boards, the engine's sputtering roar, the gurgling laughter of the water moving beneath them—he fancied he could even hear the tinkling bell of the thin man's piss hitting the stream—and then the sharp, dry snap of metal breaking metal. He saw the chrome crumple up like the aluminum foil in a cigarette package and chips of shining black paint big as birds career into the air, and the Chrysler jump inches from the ground, then settle back down with a whine of springs. Sweeny was thrown against the windshield, his head cracking lightly against the glass, then thrust back into his seat. His head was swimming, the thin band of pain that had been pressing against his temples all morning broken open now by something far sharper and fiercer. His stomach heaved against his ribs with turgid determination. He was conscious of movement, speed, wind taking his hair and sucking it up into the air like arms reaching for help.

"You okay?" July shouted.

"Yeah. Keep going, don't stop."

"Stopping hadn't crossed my mind."

He peered out of his window but they had already gone around a curve and the Chrysler, the two men, the trembling bridge, all were blocked from view by towering pines and thick brush. The dirt road was no narrower here than it had been on the pass heading up the mountain and into the valley, but it was in worse condition, pitted with deep ruts slick with snow and mud. It ran in a fairly level but winding course along the base of rock that jutted straight up on their left, its smooth brown face glistening in the sun. To their right, there was high mountain meadow, dense with grasses and pocked with orange and yellow wildflowers struggling out of pools of snow. July drove fast, with one eye on the mirror, but no one was pursuing them.

"Sweeny?" she said quietly. "I think I'm a little scared."

Sweeny, who had been rubbing his eyes with the fingers of his cupped hands, looked up and forced a grin. "Scared? Whatcha scared about, kid?"

"Don't kid me, buster. I'm scared because you are."

"It shows, eh? I don't suppose you have a bottle under the seat?"

"Sorry, fresh out. Besides, you said never again."

"That's what I said this morning." He rubbed his forehead where the span of pain was receding to a small circle. If he concentrated on that, on that small, intense circle of bright light, he could keep his fear under control.

"What's going on, Sweeny? Who are those people?"

"Those people, honey, are the friends and associates of Nicolas Limousine."

"That makes you mutual friends."

"No, that makes him a mutual . . ." He stopped and looked at her intently. "You really want a grammar lesson, eh?"

"No, I want to know what's going on, Sweeny. I really do."

"So do I, babe. That's what this has all been about, the past four days, trying to figure out what's going on. But I guess I shouldn't have dragged you into it. I was stupid. I thought the game was over yesterday and every-body'd gone home. Today I thought we were just going for a drive in the mountains. I didn't know the woods were going to be full of tourists."

July snorted: "Tourists! I didn't see any Brownies hanging around their necks, but I had a feeling the guy with his cock in his hands was going to pull out something even nastier."

Sweeny had been listening to July talk dirty for three days, but the sound of the word "cock" coming out of her mouth made him laugh now, and shook away the image of the man she was talking about. He lit a ciga-rette and sucked the smoke in, so hard he began to cough. He could feel the smoke ricocheting off the back of his lungs. He felt its heat coursing through him.

They took a sharp left turn and the rock wall disappeared. The road began to climb and narrowed to little more than a trail through the pine forest pressing in on them. The tree cover was too thick for much sun to filter through, and the road was still clogged with snow. It was clear no other vehicle had passed this way.

Sweeny sat forward and peered out of his window. His memory of the lay of the road for the rest of its short run was as vivid as if he had last been on it within a year. He knew that, in a minute, they would come to an indentation on the right, a lane that led to a cabin that even thirty-five years before had been a weather-defeated wreck. If only it was still there.

"Stop here," he said suddenly. He looked at July intensely. "We can turn around here, head back."

"Are you kidding? Go across that bridge and through that creepy town again?"

Sweeny smiled. He would have liked to take her into his arms and hold her tight to his chest, but there wasn't time. Anything could be catching up with them, and he had a growing certainty that the answer to the puzzle lay up ahead, in a dark cave, where he had left it thirty-five years before. He had to get there and see for himself.

He gestured to the right. "Pull in this lane here. No, wait a second, maybe it'd be better to back in. Let me out." He scrambled out of the truck and guided July into the lane. She backed the truck a hundred feet or so until the track was too choked with brush to go further. The cabin, Sweeny could see, was completely gone, young trees growing robustly where it had once stood. "Turn it off and get out."

July climbed down and came up beside him. Together, they listened to the silence of the deep woods. Gradually, the normal sounds of insects and birds seeped back, but that was all—no sounds of engines or footsteps, no pursuit.

Sweeny surveyed the brush in which the truck was nestled, a tangle of stunted aspen, pine, chokecherry, and berry bush. Even though there were no leaves, the growth was so thick he was sure the truck couldn't be seen from the road. "Stay here," he told July, and walked cautiously down the lane. Looking back, he could make out the cab of the truck if he searched for it. He went back, frowning, remembering something he'd seen in France, during the war.

"I'm going to cover our tracks a bit. You stay here, and don't worry. I'll tell you all about it when I get back. Two minutes."

July started to protest but he put his finger to her mouth and shook his head. He hopped into the truck and turned it on. Something made him look down at July and he saw she was about to cry. He got back out of the cab.

"Hey, what's this?"

He put his arms around her and they stood stock still, like animals caught in the sights of a hunter's gun, frozen against the landscape, tight against each other. He expected the tears to come, to feel the rattling of her sobs against his chest, but that didn't happen. All she did was make herself very small and press tightly against him, her head leaning against his shoulder, her hand on his hip. After a minute, she said: "I'm okay," and he let her loose. She smiled and he saw her eyes were dry.

"Right back."

He drove cautiously down the lane and onto the road, edging forward in first gear. He manoeuvred the wheels into parallel ruts and drove forward for a quarter of a mile like a train locked onto tracks. When he came to a large triangular-shaped boulder on the side of the road, he cut off the engine and listened hard. Still nothing. He started the truck again and put it into reverse. He drove backwards slowly, trying to keep the wheels in the ruts. He stopped several times to study the road ahead, getting out of the cab once to stand on a rock and peer down at the tire tracks. Unless you looked closely, you couldn't tell the truck had backtracked. From inside a vehicle, all you'd be able to see was one set of tracks. Satisfied, he backed into the lane. July was standing where he had left her, bent over, her hands to her face.

"Hey, I thought the crying was over."

"It is." She raised her head, smiling, eyes bright. They were a pure, startling blue, eyes the colour of an August sky. Sweeny hadn't seen eyes that blue since Highmountain had closed his for the last time. "They were killing me," she said simply, extending her hand and displaying two contact lenses, almost invisible in the shadows. She placed them carefully into a small case, clicked it shut, and slipped it into her shirt pocket above her breast.

Sweeny shook his head. "Isn't anything about you real?"

July laughed. "Sure. *I'm* real." She stuck out the slice of lower lip. "Where to now?"

He gestured to the east, into the woods past where the cabin had been. "There's a mine up that way, and a cave and a waterfall. That's where we're headed."

"Sounds romantic."

He looked at her sharply, then smiled. "Yeah, it is. I was a romantic once, believe it or not." Her eyes, Sweeny thought, were even more beautiful now.

"Oh, I believe it. Once, eh?"

July found a rusty old axe in the back of the truck and Sweeny used it to hack down some dead tree limbs while she gathered brush. They piled it all on the hood of the truck, and Sweeny scoured the lane with a pine branch in an attempt to rub out the truck's tracks. The ground beneath their feet was hard with gravel, but the forest had all but completely reclaimed the clearing where a man had sought to defy it; it was easy to hide their presence. When he was satisfied, they pushed into the woods as quietly as they could, Sweeny still carrying the axe.

After a few minutes they came to an open glen and stopped to get their bearings. It was cool in the trees, but out in the sun sweat sprang out on their faces and they opened their jackets. Somewhere nearby was the sound of water, bubbling and rushing. Above them, up a steep grade, was a jutting crag rimmed with lean, scrawny pines, and then a crest beyond which they couldn't see.

"That's the direction, so let's go," Sweeny said. "Can you make it?"

She didn't answer but set off across the glen and, plunging into the trees, led the way up the grade. It took them fifteen minutes to get to the top of the crag; their clothes were bristling with burrs and twigs, their faces bathed with sweat. They stripped off their jackets and sat on the rock, getting their breath. July left him there, puffing, and went on to the crest. Sweeny watched the tight blue sway of her hips as she worked her way up the final stretch, gravel clattering beneath her boots down the slope toward him. His heart was thumping at an alarming rate. He felt drained, exhausted, but his stomach had settled down and he was almost hungry. And his head was clear, the small circle of pain having narrowed down to a pinprick before dissolving entirely.

"Hey, terrific view up here."

She was waving, and he pulled himself to his feet. He was thirsty, but just for water. The craving he'd felt earlier had passed, like the pain and the panic. He had to keep his head clear, he knew, had to keep thinking. He was on the threshold of knowing what it was all about—the charade over the death of a man who never was. The answer, he was certain, was in the cave above the mine, where he had thought he'd put an end to it once before. But he had to be cautious—maybe it was all a charade, but that had been real metal the truck hit as they came off the bridge, real men standing there watching them in their flight, and Harriman was dangerous, that was equally certain.

From the crest of the rise above the crag, they could see a great distance in several directions. To the east, Sweeny was sure he could make out the towering beams of the mine, all but completely camouflaged by the dense timber in which it had been built. To the southwest, through all-but-impenetrable bush, they could see brief patches of the narrow road upon which they had come. They couldn't see the truck, and there was no sign of anyone in pursuit.

"That's where we're heading," he said, pointing to the grey tower.

"Well, let's go," July said, grabbing his hand.

"Take it easy, there's plenty of time. I'd kind of like to see if anybody comes along the road."

"Okay. I hear water over there, I'll go see if I can get us a drink. Maybe you can explain some of what's going on. You know, simple things like where we're going, and why."

Sweeny rolled up the sleeves of his plaid shirt and slouched against a tree. The sun was simmering away the last traces of cloud, and he shielded his eyes with his pale forearm and gazed down the slope. He could see bare flashes of road, and would surely be able to see anything moving along it. And hear. Any car, that is. If they came on foot, that would be something else. He didn't let himself think about that. He felt strong, sure. These were city men he was dealing with. He was too, of course, but he knew this country. His ankles and calves ached from the climb, but he relished the dull pain. It made him feel alive, sharper than he had felt in . . . he couldn't remember how long.

July brought cool stream water in a rusty tin can, and he drank from it in long, noisy gulps, sucking in the flecks of rust like grains of nourishment. Damn, but he felt good all of a sudden.

"You remember you were telling me the other day something about looking in mirrors," Sweeny said. "Life is supposed to unfold in a certain orderly way, but sometimes things happen exactly the opposite from the way they're supposed to?"

"Yeah, I think I said something like that. It sounds like the kind of pretentious crap I come up with."

He laughed. "Well you're dead on, you know? It's like those flyboys up there, Lovey-Dovey Lovell and the other Apollo-ites, spinning serenely through space, everything nicely charted out for them, second by second, the universe unfolding as it should. Six-fifteen, time to wake up; six-sixteen, brush teeth; six-eighteen, take a piss. Twelve-twenty, make slight recalculation of orbit . . . on and on it goes."

"And?"

"And sometimes the best laid plans blow up in your face. You start out for the moon and you wind up on Pluto. Sometimes the universe *doesn't* unfold as it should."

"Now who's being pretentious?"

"Yeah, well. But, anyway, I want to tell you a little story that proves the point. Want to hear a story?"

"Sure." July took a drink from the rusty can and wiped her mouth with her sleeve.

"Okay. Back in the twenties, a couple of years before the Depression started, there was a fella named Raymond who had a bad start one day when he looked in the mirror. Raymond was his last name. I don't remember his first name so I'll call him that. He was a newspaperman, I blush to say, and not a bad one. Worked for a small town paper around these parts, a weekly, but he'd worked for some bigger ones, too." Sweeny paused, frowning. "What's the matter with you?"

"Nothing, just listening hard."

"You looked like you were startled by something I said."

"It must have been about you blushing. Go ahead."

Sweeny sighed. "Anyway, this Raymond had worked on a number of papers, dailies, in bigger towns, but he didn't like that much so he came back to this small town, which was near where he'd been born and grew up. Damn." He shook his head, scratching at his ear. "I haven't thought about this story for a long time. It hadn't occurred to me, until just now, how much like Raymond I've become. That wasn't supposed to happen. Another one of those mirror jobbies of yours."

"They're on just about every wall," July said quietly.

"Yeah. Hey, you're a regular philosopher." He waved his hand, as if brushing away a cobweb, or a memory. "Anyway, enough of me. Back to Raymond. He was in his early fifties, no, late forties. He'd been in the racket for twenty-five years or more, had what you might call savvy.

"So he comes back to this small town, gets a job on a small paper and everything is hunky dory. After a while, he buys out the owner, an old-timer who'd started the paper and is worn out now, and Raymond makes the paper prosper. He's a smart newsman, and he also happens to be a small-town boy, so he knows just the right blend to make his paper work right. It's not easy, you know, because you've got fact, fiction, classified ads, and lead weights to juggle all at the same time and that's why so many small-town papers are so lousy, because most of the people who run them can't juggle, no matter what else they might be good at. Raymond *was* a good juggler, and his paper was successful, and so was he. He was a bachelor, but he met a woman, a teacher, I think, quite a bit younger than him, and the usual sort of stuff happened—not like you and me, I mean normal development of a normal relationship, and stop smirking—and they got married. I don't remember her name."

"It was probably Mary or something," July said.

"Right, Mary. Now stop interrupting. Anyway, Raymond and Mary get married and settle down. They have a house built for them on a hill at the edge of town, looking toward the mountains, and they have a baby, a girl, I think, and everything's just great. They're happy."

"Here's where the trouble starts," July said.

"Hey, who's telling this story, me or you?"

"Sorry." She scrunched her head down between her shoulders and looked small and soft.

"Well, I know this story is a bit predictable, but bear with me, it gets better. You're right, of course, here's where the trouble starts. When people are happy, they tempt the devil and this was one of those classic situations that sets the devil's nose twitching—a man in deep water, just about to go over his head."

He waited for July to say something but she didn't. Her lips were pursed in a caricature of silence. He lit a cigarette, taking care to make sure the match was out before burying it in the loose gravel by his feet.

"Our friend Raymond was, as I say, in his late forties, early fifties, and he's got a young family, a new home, and a job that takes a lot out of him. It's great, except that it's the kind of situation a man usually has when he's a lot younger. Raymond has come to this late, and for a variety of reasons, physical and emotional, some of it is hard to take. It starts to wear on him, even though he's happy. And, after a while, it wears on him enough that it's hard for him to still be happy. He's not *unhappy* yet, but he can sense it coming. That's something maybe you don't understand, but believe me, you do develop that kind of sense."

July didn't say anything and he went on.

"But, you know, the myth is all wrong. People don't say out loud, or even to themselves, 'I would do anything to reverse fate, to turn back time, I would even sell my soul.' It doesn't work that way. People don't expect

miracles or bargains, so they don't ask for them or even think of them con-
sciously. What does happen is sometimes a man will look at himself in the
mirror, see wrinkles and grey, and say to himself, almost unconsciously,
'Ah, what I wouldn't give to be young again, to turn back the hands.' He
doesn't mean it, it's just something he says, like a kid will say 'Rain, rain,
go away, come again another day.' You don't think of the consequences of
what you're saying, because you don't really mean it. So what happened
here is that Raymond looked in the mirror, was troubled by the grey he'd
started to see, and he said a few things to his reflection about being young
again, but never really thought of it seriously, never really *wished* for it. And
never promised his soul, or anything else."

"Ho, boy," July said. He looked at her but her eyes were lowered.

"So what happened was, one day Raymond was looking in the mirror
and he noticed something funny, that there was a little less grey than he'd
thought."

July looked up suddenly, looked at him sharply, as if to make sure the
person speaking was someone she knew, then lowered her head again.

"He didn't think much of it, just smiled and shrugged. He figured it was
just the way he was combing his hair that day, or the way the light caught
it. He forgot about it. But the next day he noticed it again, and then the
next day and the day after, and when he washed his hair. It *wasn't* the way
he was combing it, or the light, he *really* was a little less grey. Still, he
shrugged. He remembered that while hair itself is dead, the follicles it
grows out of are alive, and they can do funny things, like maybe some grey
hairs can fall out and be replaced by young black ones. In nature, anything
can happen."

July looked up again and this time she smiled, as if he had told a joke.
He gazed over her shoulder at the patches of road visible through the trees,
but there was still no sign of a car, or anything else. He was beginning to
wonder if there would be anything. He hadn't imagined what he'd seen in
the ghost town, though. The hearse parked beside the abandoned hotel,
Benno's face in the window. *Benno*. And Harriman and his creepy buddy by
the stream, their car partially blocking the bridge. No, that wasn't his

imagination. And it didn't seem likely that Harriman was merely out for a pleasure drive in the country, not with a hearse and a mortician in tow. No, somehow they had managed to follow him, get ahead. Or, more likely, managed to figure out where he was going. Maybe they had a map too. Maybe they had been as surprised to see him as he had been to see them.

"Anyway," he said, "it didn't bother him much. But he was sort of curious, so he kept his eyes open, and sure enough, after a bit, he noticed some more grey gone. Other people began to notice it, too. Someone he met on the street remarked how young he was looking. His wife, she kidded him about dying his hair and being so secretive and vain. *No, no*, he protested, *it's happening on its own. How can that be*, she asked him, *that's ridiculous. I know*, he told her.

"So it wasn't just his imagination, it really was happening. But what? And it wasn't just his hair. The wrinkles on his face were starting to smooth out. His wife noticed it first, and she said something. *You're looking younger*. She loved him and maybe she thought love itself was making him young. If a man is very happy, she thought, it can make him feel young again, and if he feels young maybe he can look young again, too. But she didn't think about it very hard, because, like him, she didn't really take it very seriously."

Sweeny paused, listening. "Sometimes, people don't take things seriously even when they're right under their noses," he said after a moment. "They wait till the tips of their noses get bitten off. Yeah, Raymond was feeling younger, all right, but it wasn't just the kind of feeling younger you get from being in love." He smiled at July and she smiled back. "He was *really* feeling younger. He had more energy, his bones didn't ache quite as badly when he got up on rainy days. He . . . well, you don't know what it's like to feel old, July, but Raymond felt *less* of it. All the time. At first, he thought something along the reverse lines of what his wife was thinking, that maybe because he *looked* younger it was a natural consequence that he should *feel* younger. Of course, that didn't explain why he looked younger. And he could see there was no logic to it, anyway, because looking younger might improve your attitude, but it wouldn't do anything to your bones, couldn't. He was thinking about it harder now, because he was starting to get worried. It was six months since he'd first noticed the grey disappearing and now his hair was as black as it'd been when he was a young man. His skin was smooth, his aches and pains were gone, he'd lost weight, his flesh and skin were firmer. He looked like he was thirty-five, and when he went to see his doctor, that's what *he* said, *Raymond, you look like a man who's thirty-five. How can that be?* Raymond asked him. *I don't know*, the doctor said. *Well, you know, Raymond, youth is wasted on the young*, the doctor said. *Enjoy yourself.*

"But Raymond was getting scared. Some days, he would wake up feeling like a million bucks, and then start thinking about *why* he felt so good and he'd get depressed and wouldn't feel so good at all. It was a two-sided coin, this getting younger, and the tails side kept coming up more often. He was looking younger all the time now, seeming to lose a year every week or so. He was going to the doctor regularly, and in three months the doctor was saying Raymond had the body of a man of twenty-one. It was impossible, it *couldn't* be happening, but it was. Anybody and everybody, from his wife on down to the delivery boy from the grocer's, could see it. And there it was in black and white on the doctor's charts. And more. The faded old appendectomy scar on his belly grew bright red and tender— then disappeared. The dentist had to take out Raymond's false teeth to make room for new ones growing in. His ageing process had completely reversed. He was getting younger and there didn't seem to be any end to it. He had a vision of himself telescoping back through time into a pimply faced teenager, then a high-voiced boy, a bratty child, a crawling infant, and finally curling up into a fetus and evaporating into the air."

Sweeny paused to let the story sink in. July's face was neutral and blank, like a child mesmerized by a fantastic bedtime story. There was a spider crawling up Sweeny's leg and he watched its progress with interest, his hand cocked on his hip to brush it away if it climbed too high.

"Time for the plot to thicken." He winked. "There was a man in this town, a blacksmith, who was reputed to have some knowledge of mystery, you know, witchcraft, black magic, things like that. Raymond had interviewed him a number of times. For example, a few years before, there had been a long drought that was a topic of considerable interest for the paper. Raymond did a story on this fellow's speculation about the drought. It was loony tune, but the most interesting thing was his prediction of when the drought would end. He named a month and a day, and sure enough, it began to rain, not exactly on that date but close to it.

"This blacksmith was the son of a prospector from Quebec who had worked the mountains around the town for years and a local Indian woman. The gossip was that one night, as the prospector lay before his campfire, she had appeared, naked and sleek as a wildcat, gliding in out of the dark woods silently and unannounced. They made love like animals, wild and noisy, scratching at each other's bodies with their fingernails and teeth, howling together. Then, as the prospector lay panting by the fire, the woman drew away, disappeared. He didn't see her again until, about nine months later, she came walking into camp, barefoot but dressed, carrying a newborn infant. She handed him the baby and, without a word, set about cleaning up the place, fetching water, tending to the evening meal. They lived like that, silent and untouching for several years, until the child was old enough to get along without a mother's care. Then the woman went to fetch water one day and never came back." Sweeny shrugged. "That's what people around there said about this fellow's origins."

"Good story," July said. "Isn't that the way all men want their women?" She was grinning.

"Yeah," Sweeny said. He couldn't help a little grin either. "And, true or not, the stuff about the mother, it apparently was true that he'd been raised in the mountains by his father, the prospector, living all by themselves. So he'd grown up a little wild and strange. Then, apparently, when he was in his late teens or early twenties, the old fellow, who'd been scratching at the rock most of his life without any kind of success, hit a vein and, bingo, there was a bundle of money. The old man died soon after and the young fellow took off and nobody heard a word of him for something like ten years. He apparently travelled all over the world, and studied mystery wherever he went. Black magic, alchemy, witchcraft, the stars, herbs, all that sort of stuff. He also picked up a pretty good general education somewhere along the line because by the time I'm telling you about he was a soft-spoken, refined, well-read man, thoughtful and literate. And he'd accumulated a massive library, books on all sorts of subjects but mostly the occult, and in all sorts of languages. He'd also picked up the blacksmith's art, and when he came back to town he set himself up in a shop. There was still plenty of call for a blacksmith in a small town in the mountains in those days, so he did all right. He was a big man, a friendly, likable fellow who minded his own business unless he was asked, and he had this reputation for knowing a lot about the dark side of life."

Sweeny brushed at the spider, which had begun to crawl up his shirt. It landed on his leg and began the upward climb again without hesitation.

"I guess you can figure out where this is leading," Sweeny said. "Raymond had already been to all sorts of specialists, but they were just as baffled as his regular doctor, so he had nothing to lose. He went to visit the blacksmith, who'd sort of been expecting him. Whenever anything odd happened around those parts, he was usually consulted. Raymond told the blacksmith the whole story. *And here I am now*, he said, *hell-bent for destruction. What do you make of it?*

"The blacksmith didn't know, right off, what to make of Raymond's situation, but he said he thought it maybe rang a little bell with him. He'd have to do a little reading and some thinking and he'd get back to Raymond.

"He set to. His studies were extensive, and he did a bit of meditation and soul-searching too. And, sure enough, he came up with something he thought might help. And not a second too soon, either. Raymond, who now looked for all the world like a gangly seventeen-year-old, was beside himself, practically paralyzed with fear as he felt his life spinning away from him. He couldn't live with his wife anymore, he was so wrought up, so he'd moved into his office, where he slept on a couch. But he couldn't work, either, and they'd hired someone to run the paper. Even if he could have functioned, he'd lost his old savvy. As he got younger, he kept forgetting things, even simple skills. He was losing his experience."

He paused to let July make the crack he thought would be coming but she was silent, so he went on.

"The blacksmith came to the newspaper office and found Raymond cowering there. He was a boy now, and totally incapable of coping with the situation that had befallen him. He put himself completely in the black-smith's hands."

The spider had gotten caught in a fold of Sweeny's pants. Gently, he smoothed the cloth, and the spider scurried free.

"He took Raymond into the mountains that night, onto a high peak, and built a roaring fire. It could be seen for miles around and people were puzzled because there was so little smoke and it was in so small an area but seemed to be so intense. There was a lot of hocus-pocus. Raymond had to repeat some incantations and anoint his body with oils and ointments. The blacksmith had brought an anvil along, and a thin black chain. He wrapped this chain around Raymond and placed him and the anvil close to the fire. Then he raised his head and shouted to the dark sky, "Set this man free," shouting it first in English, then in French, Spanish, Greek, Latin, and all sorts of other languages, including some that couldn't be recognized. And then, with one blow of his hammer, he broke the chain and threw it into the fire."

"Fuck," July said.

"Damn straight."

"Bit melodramatic, perhaps."

"Perhaps." Sweeny's smile faded. He thought he heard a sound coming from down the slope and he raised a finger and leaned forward, but there was no movement and he heard nothing more, just the singing of birds, the swaying of branches.

"You can guess what happened next, I suppose."

"Raymond stopped getting younger," July said.

"Right. Very sharp. The blacksmith lifted Raymond, who had fainted, in his arms and carried him down the mountain to his own home and his wife. Raymond slept for a week—he was in a coma, actually—and when he came out of it he looked older. Tired and older. He was calm and could think rationally. Some of the things he had forgotten began to come back. And, gradually, he was able to pick up his life where he had left it. He didn't revert to normal just like that, but the reverse ageing process had stopped and the usual ageing process was accelerated. In a few weeks, he was a man of thirty. A few weeks after that, he was up to forty. The doctor kept a close watch and he could practically see the changes as they occurred—muscles turning to flab, hair starting to grey, reflexes slowing. The appendectomy scar came back, first red and raw and painful, then quickly receding. The aches came back. There were endless dental visits. Raymond slowed down. He was himself again."

July smiled. "Happy ending?"

"No, not quite. One day, Raymond looked in the mirror and thought, *I am myself again*. It was more than a year since that day he'd first noticed the grey fading, and he was, of course, chronologically, a year older. That struck him and he thought, *If I am now, today, who I was then, a year ago, when this nightmare began, then I am not really myself again yet, I still have a year to go*. He thought about that for a while, and he mentioned it to the blacksmith, who he was visiting regularly.

"The blacksmith frowned. *You want to catch up*, he said, annoyed. *You're not satisfied*. But Raymond protested, *I just want to be where I was, I want to be normal*. The blacksmith shook his head. *You can't be normal*, he said. *You've undergone an experience perhaps unique in creation. How can you even speak of being normal?* But Raymond was adamant. *I won't feel right*, he insisted, *until I'm back in the right time, in my* own *time, where I would have been if that* thing *hadn't happened to me*.

"The blacksmith was reluctant to fool around any more, but Raymond pleaded with him. So he went back to his books, and brewed up a drink from all sorts of godawful ingredients I can't even imagine. He had Raymond say some more hocus-pocus and drink it down. Immediately, Raymond turned all variety of shades of red and collapsed. At first they thought he was dead but there was still a bit of life in him, so they put him to bed, and the attack, whatever it was, quickly passed. He was up on his feet the next day and claimed to feel good, except for a strange sensation of movement. He would stand or sit very still, and yet have the strongest feeling that he was in motion."

Sweeny shrugged. "Well, in a way he was. He was ageing. You can't usually gauge something as subtle as the passing of a year, it doesn't show up on the doctor's charts, but Raymond himself was sure he could feel the bottled-up year slipping away. He was pleased, and was sure he'd be able to tell when the whole year was used up. He thought there'd be a kind of click he could actually hear or feel when his body slipped back into the proper groove of time, and he felt sure he'd be satisfied then, that he'd never complain or even wish for anything different in his life. He'd had, after all, a good life, so why should he complain? He'd be back in his groove of time, he'd grow old gracefully and die happily, when the time came, grateful for a full, rewarding life." Sweeny stopped to light another cigarette.

"Sounds too pat," July said.

"Uh huh, right again." The spider had crawled again to his waist and was now on his shirt, moving up his chest. He brushed it away with an impatient gesture, crushing it with the force of his hand. He didn't notice where the spider's twitching body landed, but he regretted striking so hard.

"What happened, in fact," Sweeny said, "is that Raymond kept ageing and never did click back into his groove. For a few weeks, everything seemed to be normal and he experienced nothing unusual except for the strange sense of motion. Then, without warning, like a spell taking hold, he began to age rapidly. His hair turned snow white and started to fall out. His skin shrivelled and he lost weight. In a few weeks, he was like a man in his eighties, and it kept going, like a roller coaster car out of control, dragging Raymond along by the heels. The doctor and the specialists stood by helplessly and his wife was in shock and had to be sedated. Raymond took to his bed. He was a weak, sick old man. He was old. And, of course, he was dying.

"He asked that the blacksmith be summoned. The man came into the room where Raymond lay, minutes away from being a corpse. He was a big man, the blacksmith, a big man with a dark beard, and he filled the doorway, blocking out the light and casting his shadow on Raymond. *You should have been satisfied*, he told him. *You shouldn't have tried to catch up*. Raymond gasped for breath and beckoned for the blacksmith to draw close. The big man sat on the edge of the bed and leaned over, and Raymond whispered to him: *No, I was right, you always have to try to catch up.* And, with that, he died."

Sweeny blew smoke into the air and watched its aimless drift in the sunlight. There was a bank of clouds in the southeast, fluffy as dumplings but lined with sullen grey. There'll be more rain yet, he thought.

"And?" July asked. She looked pale again, and her eyes, somehow, were deeper, like blue gobs of paint on a white canvas.

"And nothing. And the end. That's the story."

They were silent, looking at each other, smoking, listening for sounds from below that didn't come.

"Great story," she said finally. "Is there a point to it?"

Sweeny shrugged defensively. "You wanted to know what was going on."

She didn't say anything but she kept gazing at him, eyes cool and level.

"The blacksmith was Limousine. Nicolas Limousine was his name."

He thought she smiled slightly, the corners of her lips moving up almost imperceptibly. "I kind of knew that, or guessed it. And it was a very good story, Sweeny. Don't get me wrong, I'm not complaining. For spur-of-the-moment story-telling, it was excellent."

Sweeny laughed. "That's just it, July. It's not excellent, it's shit. It's corny and melodramatic, as you pointed out at one point, and the characters are stereotypes. *And* it's predictable. *And* . . . well, it's shit. But I didn't just make it up here. That's the point, too. I made it up thirty-five, thirty-six years ago, in a novel I wrote then."

He got to his feet, brushing grass and twigs from his pants. He stood over July, looking at her. Her eyes were like deep pools of seawater into which he would gladly plunge—plunge and allow himself to sink forever.

"Don't you see? That's the whole point. It's all a story, a story *I* wrote, centuries ago. Nicolas Limousine doesn't exist at all, he's just a character in a book burned to ashes over thirty-five years ago. We've been chasing after the corpse of someone who doesn't even exist."

He felt the panic that had been tugging at him earlier surge up again, like hot vomit boiling out of his stomach into his throat. He swallowed to keep it down and turned away, gazing east toward the towers of the mine. The stark grey beams seemed to call to him, naked arms stretched out in welcome.

"Burned?" The cool tone of July's voice brought him back. He could feel the panic recede, the way coffee in a percolator calms out of its black, bubbling rage when the heat beneath it is lowered.

"Yeah." He laughed lightly. "The book was called either *The Man Who Grew Young* or *The Man Who Caught Up*. I had both those titles on the first page, and I never did decide which one I liked better. But it didn't matter because I never did anything with it—except burn it. I was twenty-six then, twenty-seven, I don't know. Still pretty young. People were younger in those days than they are today, you know. And I was a romantic. I had put a lot of work into that book, stealing time for a page here and there while running the *Chronicle* single-handed, working sixteen, eighteen hours a day. And a lot of dreaming, too. I thought it was going to make my name and my career. But when I finished it and read it over, I realized it was shit, that it wasn't worth the paper it was typed on." He laughed again. "It didn't sound too bad, just then, the way I told it, but reading it was something else. Or maybe I just had higher standards then. Anyway, I thought it was shit and I wouldn't have dared to show it to anyone. So I didn't get any conflicting opinions."

"Sweeny," July said, exasperated, "you're a newspaperman. Your stories are read by people every day."

"I know, I know. I've always been like that. I'm public as hell with my newspaper stuff, but, hell, that's the nature of the game. You put your stuff in a newspaper with your name on it and the whole world peers at it, and at you. But I'd been writing stories, fiction, I mean, since I was a kid and I'd always been private with them. There was only one person I'd ever showed any of them to, my grandfather, and he'd been dead for years. I'd write these stories, read them over, and burn them. It was just for fun, after all. The novel, of course . . ." He shrugged. "It was for more than fun, but that's what I did with it, too. I burned it. Right over there." He pointed across the slope to the east.

"I don't think I understand," July said. She was looking up, her chin pointing at him, her white throat exposed.

"I didn't either," Sweeny said. "Until you showed me the map and bells started going off. You have to remember, this was thirty-five years ago, more, and there's been a lot of stuff in my life since then. My memory's not the greatest anyway. I *knew* that I knew the name Limousine from somewhere, and I was pretty sure it was connected to this part of the world. A hunch, a very strong one. Well, it *was* connected." He gestured toward the south, where Timber lay at the foot of the mountains. "He was a character *I* created, in a book I wrote in this town. It was a name *I* made up, God only knows how I came to it. But damn if I hadn't forgotten all about it, all about him, the character, the name, the book. It was as if I'd never written it, as if it'd never happened. It was just gone completely out of my mind. But the name was there, dangling in front of me, bugging me, tugging at my memory. Then, when you showed me the map, it all came together in my head, bits and pieces of a puzzle falling together. As soon as I saw the map, I remembered this place. I've been here a couple of times. I grew up in Timber, don't forget, and I know this country around here pretty well. Or did. And when I started remembering being here, natural-ly I remembered what I'd done the last time I was here."

He took a step away and pointed to the east. "If you look hard, you can see the beams from here. There's a mine down there, an abandoned prospector's digs, and the superstructure of the waterworks for the mine. A kid I knew who was half Indian used to come out here hunting, and he stumbled on it. There's a mineshaft opening, but it doesn't go back very far. In fact, it's a phony, a blind. If you go under the waterworks, there's a cave behind a little waterfall, and the cave opens up into the real mine. This kid was cooling off in the pond when he saw something glint behind the waterfall and investigated. It was something metal, an old pick or a shov-el, and it led him to the cave and the mine. Anyway, I'd been out there once or twice with him to explore. It was a grand place. There had been a nat-ural cavern there to begin with, and the prospector, whoever he was, had dug it out even more. Don't know if he struck it rich or not, don't know *anything* about him, but he'd created a marvelous chamber, with a maze of passageways leading off it and looping around, coming right back to the main chamber. He must have been insane, as many of those old coots were, I guess, digging himself a rats' maze to hide in, in case of claim jumpers. There wasn't much chance of them finding the mine but if they did, he could run them ragged in that cave, take them by surprise, do whatever he wanted. Didn't find any bones in there, so I don't think he died there. But there were lanterns, dry and rusted, and we cleaned a couple up and brought some kerosene. The place was real cozy. We came out on horseback, camping, and it was a great place to spend the night. Spooky. The kind of thing teenaged boys love."

July had gotten to her feet. She took Sweeny's hand, and he sighed. "I told you I was a romantic. I took my manuscript and drove up here in an old Ford I had then. It was rough going, but you could get through. It was spring, around this time of year. I remember there were patches of snow on the ground and wildflowers growing around them, just like now. I went into the cavern, lit a lantern, and, like Limousine on the mountaintop chanting for Raymond's soul, I said a little incantation."

He looked at July, surprised to find himself blushing. She squeezed his hand.

"Hocus-pocus. Then I burned the fucking thing in a big pottery bowl I found there, page by page, until there was nothing but a bowl of ashes."

He shook his head. "Jesus, I was a romantic. I can hardly believe it now, can hardly believe that was me I'm talking about, but it was. After the ashes cooled down, I found a nice smooth rock that was just the right size and put it into the bowl to sort of seal it, and I buried the works, there in the cavern, under a pile of rocks. I guess you could say that was Limousine's grave."

He looked up, shivering. The panic was on him again, like a small, dark animal leaping up his leg. He pulled his hand free and moved away to shake it off.

"But it was me, all right. I did it. A couple of months later, I sold the paper, left town, and never looked back. In a year's time, the whole thing had probably slipped from my head. Once I got to Toronto, I didn't stay a romantic for long."

They were silent again, standing shoulder to shoulder, holding hands. He concentrated on the feel of her hand in his, the weight of it, its warmth, the curve of the fingers. After a while, the panic slipped back into the darkness.

"And the man who died in the hotel," July said, "all those other men, the map—what does all *that* mean?"

"I don't know. It could be anything. If it weren't for the map, it could be nothing more than coincidence, the name, anyway, and the rest . . ." Sweeny shrugged. "Maybe I've precipitated some of the rest myself, by snooping into other people's business. I don't know. Things like this shouldn't happen. It's all nuts. Everything, from the word go, it's an insane maze, with me caught in the middle." He let go of her hand. "I don't mean to sound like I'm feeling sorry for myself, that's not what it's about, but there's some other things that you don't know about, too."

"Tell me," July said. "I want to . . ."

"No." He shook his head. "It has to do with me and nobody else." He took a step down the slope. "The answer's down there. I'm more sure of that all the time. In that cave, that's where the X on that fucking map is. And I guess our friends aren't following us, so maybe I should mosey on down there and see what's to be seen."

"*We*," July said. "*We* should mosey on down there."

"No, you'd better stay here. I don't know *what's* down there. It's not very far. I won't be long."

"I'm going," July said firmly. "But . . ." She hesitated. "But you know something else?"

"What's that?"

"Remember I told you about my father?" She bit her lip and looked down.

Sweeny nodded. "Yeah, he was a newspaperman and maybe I knew him but you wouldn't tell me where or his name or . . ." The words slowed down, petered out.

"Yes." She looked up and a shiver seemed to pulse across her face, twisting the features. Then it was still again. "You don't know my last name, do you?"

"I guess not. You probably never told me."

"It's Raymond."

Sweeny digested that for a minute. It was a common enough name.

"And . . . and your father is still alive?" he said cautiously.

"No. He died, about two months ago, just before I came to Timber and went to work for the hotel. He was healthy, although he wasn't young. He just got sick and died in the winter. The doctor said it couldn't be helped, it was just old age."

Sweeny put his hands on her shoulders and gripped her tightly but gently. His head was beginning to swim again and he held onto her as much to keep himself from falling as to impress himself upon her, his strength and will.

"You know, someone's lying," he said after a while.

"I know," July said quietly. "But it isn't me."

"I know that," he said without hesitation. "It isn't me either. But someone is."

Sweeny put his arms around her and she put hers around him. They sank to their knees but their embrace didn't falter. They held onto each other tightly. They didn't kiss but their faces were pressed together, cheek against cheek, his mouth against her throat, hers against his. He could feel her hot wet tears on his face, and, after a moment, his own joined them. All his strength was in his arms, and he held onto her for all he was worth, as if he would never let her go. "I'm sorry I don't have the strength to make love to you," he whispered. "I'm sorry if I let you down." He didn't think she would answer, because he could think of none that was suitable, but she did:

"You are making love to me. Right now. Now."

XI

IT WAS LATE AFTERNOON WHEN THEY MADE THEIR WAY down the bluff to the mine, and the sky was turning dark with the renewed threat of rain. Sweeny felt calm, his stomach quiet, head clear. He felt strong and sure, as if he were actually perched somewhere just above and to the left of the shoulder of the body resembling his that trudged sure-footed through the thick brush growing stubbornly along the slope. He was watching it all, watching this anxious fool blunder his way to a climax that Sweeny himself, safe and cool above his shoulder, had figured out long before.

There weren't to be any surprises this afternoon, not any more. Thirty-five years was a long time; many hunters and hikers had probably stumbled on the old mine, camped by the stream, cooled off in the pond. Some may even have, just like that Indian boy, followed the glint of metal behind the waterfall curtain to the hidden cave and its dug-out chamber and tunnels. There was a chance the pile of rocks under which he had left the pottery bowl filled with ashes had been disturbed, the bowl shattered into sharp-edged splinters, the ashes scattered, but he didn't think so. He had a strong feeling—the sense of certainty he'd had sitting in a darkened theatre watching the unfolding end of a movie he'd seen before—that they would find the rock cairn as he had left it, the bowl still intact, the ashes cool and indifferent.

It would mean, of course, that there was no connection between him and the characters in the absurd play that had been swirling around him the past few days, that it was all coincidence, chance. Well, that was okay, Sweeny was willing to let it all end that way, happy to. The big bearded man called Nicolas Limousine who died at the Queen's Hotel was an agent of some kind, sure, a spy like Pat and his friends in Washington had guessed, or something else that required false identity, masks, secrecy—a special agent of the president of the United States, say, preparing for a secret rendezvous with representatives of a foreign power, maybe even an alien race from a far-off planet. It was no more preposterous than the broth-thin plot of a dozen thrillers he'd read or movies he'd seen flickering on his midnight TV. And Harriman was an agent, too, sent here to cover the tracks to protect national security or prevent the kind of panic that would likely sweep the earth should the truth come out, or perhaps merely to reconnoitre, to see who else was sniffing around, just like that Mafia funeral Sweeny had covered, where you couldn't tell the mourners from the cops there to watch the mourners, where you couldn't tell the players from the critics.

That time, Sweeny had been a watcher with a purpose, mingling with both sides without disrupting the rhythm. But this time, he'd been an unscheduled erratic, getting in the way, throwing Harriman and any other real players off the track, confusing things with his obstinacy, forcing them to play to *him*. He'd committed the worst sin a newspaperman is capable of by getting involved, by injecting himself into the story, by becoming a *player*. And all, he was becoming sure, because of a simple coincidence, because of a lousy name, and his need to make something of it, to turn nothing into a story that would impress his new bosses, to make something of *himself*.

Straws, that's what he'd been grasping at, straws and a coincidence that, at some other time of his life, he would have just chuckled over and shrugged off. Nicolas Limousine—did he really think he'd invented that name, that he had a copyright on it? There were millions of people in the world, billions, and only so many names, so many combinations and variations. It had just worked out that way, damn it. And everything else that had seemed to be connected, that had seemed to be falling into place like the spinning pieces of some gigantic galactic puzzle—July and Barbara, the suitcase stickers that had appeared to plot a course along Sweeny's own lifeline, the telephone calls, everything else—they didn't mean anything, damn it; that is, they meant something to *Limousine*, whoever the fuck he was, Limousine with his walletful of credit cards, his folded and refolded map, his list of numbers to be called; they meant something to Harriman, whoever the fuck *he* was, Harriman with his post office boxes, his fleet of rented Chryslers, his cast of thousands at beck and call; but not to *him*, they didn't mean piss-all to Sweeny except what he wanted to make of them. He wasn't the centre of the fucking universe, after all, with everything revolving around him, he was just one chip of matter floating in an infinite sea of space and time, along with billions of other chips, and if, from time to time, some of their circuitry got crossed, their electrical impulses tangled, and the wake of one person's universe crossed that of another's, their atoms mingling like ashes and dust, well, so be it, who was Sweeny to object? Men who stumbled in the dark floated effortlessly in space now, and there were more things revealed under the sun than he ever imagined back when he was a boy lying on bales of hay in the barn with a pencil and pad, tapping the universe for its wonders, creating little worlds of his own.

The important thing to remember, he told himself now, as he watched the feet below him pick their way down the rocky slope, was that it didn't all *have* to make sense, there wasn't any law, natural or made by man, that said *everything* has to fit. It had to be that way, because there were only two other possibilities, and both were too fearsome to consider. Sweeny didn't believe in a god of vengeance and wrath, or a god of any sort, for that matter; didn't believe in the kind of universe where good and evil wrestled for control, the latter manifesting itself in a myriad array of sharp-teethed, horrific forms, disrupting the natural rhythms of life and death; didn't believe, in short, in the kind of world where the Nicolas Limousine he'd created lived. And he was sure—sure as anyone ever can be—that he wasn't going mad.

The proof was in the cave, a bowl filled with ashes buried beneath rocks he had piled himself years ago. If it was there, intact and undisturbed, then he'd know all this had been little more than a bad dream sent to torment a bone-weary old drunk trying to make a little light for himself near the end of his road, just as July was a wondrous dream sent to dispel the darkness; that's all, a bad dream that had worked its way into his waking because it seemed to hold so many possibilities and he had grasped at it, wrenched it from sleep's dark gate. In that bowl was all that was left of the Nicolas Limousine *he* had created, crumbled fine ashes of pages burned one at a time into curling, brittle carbon, crushed in his hands to dust. He could almost see the bowl—it was cream with a blue chicken pattern, and badly chipped, cracked—and the acrid smell of the ashes waved over him, bringing stinging tears to his eyes.

He would kneel in that cave like a supplicant and dip his hands into the ashes, let them run through his fingers, rub the dust between his palms smooth and slippery as graphite. He and July would laugh, mock their overheated imaginations and scatter ashes in the cave and into the stream, letting the water pulverize and dissolve any last vestige of life in that grey dust—that's what he should have done in the first place, denying it the right to grow with sullen mushroom magic into something that could threaten him. They'd laugh, dispel ghosts, frighten away darkness. Then they'd splash back through the waterfall and across the pond, and trudge through the rutted trail—openly now, singing, not looking over their shoulders—to where they'd left the truck, meeting no one, then drive home over the narrow bridge, seeing no one, through the deserted ghost town, over the mountain pass, meeting no one, pursued by no clouds of dust, into town, and fall into bed and into each other's arms. They'd have the rest of their lives ahead of them, if Sweeny was really lucky, and they wouldn't have to look over their shoulders to see if anyone was following.

At the base of the bluff, there was an apron-like clearing perhaps twenty yards wide. At its back, there was the bluff itself, thick with brush and jackpines; on its sides and front, the woods continued the downward plunge. The stream came rushing down the bluff, cascading over a final cluster of boulders to form a waterfall six or seven feet high and no more than three feet wide, then meandered bubbling along the foot of the bluff before plunging back into the pine and aspen and down the slope. Shrubs and wildflowers grew in the clearing, along with stunted orphan pines. It was a place where deer came to drink, where bear rolled in the sun, digging gouges of black dirt with their shoulders.

It was an ideal spot to set up camp, and that's what someone had done, eighty or ninety years before, a prospector who'd pushed on beyond True Hope, and stumbled on what must have seemed like a sign from heaven. Aside from the pleasantness of the clearing and stream, and the way the bluff formed a shield against the wind, the waterfall the stream created as it danced down the bluff's flanks was a marvel—and the cave behind it surely a miracle. The opening wasn't visible, but anyone brave enough to stand under the icy water for a shower might stumble on it—the warm, dark mouth lying safe and secret behind the silver flashes of water. There was something more than merely secret about the place, though—it was holy in the way small boys know dark pockets of the woods are, places where the light filtering through the dense branches above creates the same quality as in churches, places where it is always quiet. That's what had drawn Sweeny to it.

The prospector had put up a cabin, just a shell now, and built a dam to force a pond in the basin beneath the waterfall. Above it, he'd erected a trough to direct part of the stream out of its natural path and through an intricate waterworks leading to a trap and a mill groaning with motion. And beside the cabin he'd dug a pit in the face of the bluff. It was gold he'd been after, panning for it in the stream and the trough, digging for it in the mine. There was no way of knowing how successful he'd been, or if there'd even been any gold to find. The gaping scar dug into the bluff didn't go very far and may have never been more than something to fool anyone bent on jumping a claim. Anyone wandering into the clearing would see the pit, and be drawn to it, see the hard, barren rock, chipped out no more than three feet wide and a dozen deep. They'd shake their heads ruefully and move on. A silent man would be standing on the other side of the waterfall, inside the cave, where his real mine, and perhaps his riches, lay, his secret safe within him and the earth.

All of that was gone now, and all that remained were skeletons—the bare rotting bones of jerry-built structures, grating like teeth against the wind's rustling; the patient bubbling of the stream, tirelessly working its way through the wooden troughs. As Sweeny and July came down the final curve of the slope, a curtain of trees still stood between them and the clearing and Sweeny could not see any of this, but he could hear the stream roiling in its artificial channel, splashing against stones as it broke free, hissing against itself in sheets as it cascaded from one level of ground to another. But nothing else. There were no birds, no insect sounds, even the wind was still, and the aching beams held their breath.

Sweeny stopped and cocked his head, listening.

"Nothing," July whispered.

"Uh huh. Nothing." He held one hand shoulder high, fingers splayed as if feeling for vibrations, and crept forward. He could see the waterworks, flat and grey against the sky behind the naked branches of the trees. He took another step and the whole clearing opened up. There was the gaping dark mouth of the pit. There was the sagging remains of the cabin. There the waterworks; there the pond and the waterfall.

And there, in the centre of the clearing, gleaming in the sun, was a hearse.

"Jesus." Sweeny's breath rattled as he stepped back suddenly, colliding with July. He would have fallen if she hadn't slipped in behind him.

"Holy mackerel," she breathed softly. If there was fear in her voice, Sweeny didn't hear it, but he was busy with his eyes.

The sleek grey and black and chrome body of the hearse caught the rays of sun and sent them spinning back into the air like flies buzzing around roadkill. A man in a dark suit was leaning over the hood, polishing the windshield with a cloth, his back to them. There was something immediately familiar about the slant of his narrow shoulder-blades that made Sweeny gasp in surprise. This wasn't the way it was supposed to end; there wasn't any room in the rolling picture he had painted in his mind for either of these shapes, the car's or the man's. As he stepped into the clearing, he tightened his grip on the axe he'd been carrying. As if on cue, the head of the man cleaning the hearse lifted. His eyes raked across Sweeny and his nostrils flared, the four spots of black giving his narrow, pasty face the sort of mean cunning a coyote brings to the side of the carrion.

"Hey, he's got his pants zipped up," July said, putting her hand lightly on Sweeny's arm. Again, if she was frightened, it didn't show.

Sweeny took a deep breath and bounded across the ten yards or so separating them, brandishing the axe. He moved with a sureness and grace that surprised him and startled the thin man, who made a motion to reach inside his jacket but hesitated.

"Put your hands down on the car or I'll knock your head off like a golf-ball," Sweeny said. "Don't think I won't."

The thin man studied the raised axe attentively, as if taking note of its design, then swung his fierce bird's eyes to Sweeny's face. His own face was smaller and softer than Sweeny had thought, with a nose like a work-ingman's knuckle and dark hollows in his cheeks. Black hair curled up along his neck and his thin lips were red and cracked. He opened them to speak, and his tongue darted pink as a lizard's over tobacco-stained teeth.

"You can't have it," he said languidly.

His voice was as cracked as the lips through which it slipped, dipping in the air like a moth. It was an old man's voice, high, broken, with a shade of whine to it.

Sweeny and July looked at each other.

"Can't have it," the thin man said again. He let his eyes drop to his hands, which held the dirty white cloth with which he'd been wiping the hearse. He stared at it stupidly, as if mystified by its presence there in his bony, gnarled fingers.

Sweeny lowered the axe and rested it against his foot. "Can't have what?"

The thin man looked up and his shoulders jerked, making his jacket rustle like a sack on a stick. "The gold," he said in his cracking voice. "The riches. They're mine and they're gonna stay that way." He looked down and shuffled his feet, which were encased in huge boots, the toes square and solid, beneath the sharp crease of his suit pants. "All gone, anyways, all gone and ain't no more. You won't find it." He raised his eyes and swung them around to July. They went narrow and sly. "Never was nothin', anyways." He jerked his thumb behind him to the open pit. "Nothin' in there, sister, jest a lot of sweat and blood, mine mostly, and some piss, too." He cackled. "Nothin' in there but hard work." He began to laugh hard, his thin shoulders quaking, his face colouring, and at the same time, Sweeny thought, he began to twist out of focus, his mouth going slack, the muscles of his neck sagging. He was laughing so hard Sweeny thought he might tumble over, and he took a step toward him.

"Don't you touch me," the thin man hissed, recoiling. He seemed to be smaller, thinner, the suit hanging loose on his shoulders. A dribble of spit trailed from the corner of his mouth down his chin. His eyes were formless smudges of charcoal on a crumpled sheet of white paper. "You won't find it and neither will they. Told 'em so, too." His voice was defiant, but the whine was growing stronger.

"They? Who's they?" Sweeny asked sharply. He looked around, but there was no one but him and July and the puny man in the clearing, along with the ruined buildings and the gleaming hearse. "How'd you get here with this thing?" Sweeny asked, pointing with his chin. "Where's Harriman?"

"Dunno," the thin man whined. He looked tired and confused, nervously wiping his hands with the cloth. "I'd be pleased to offer ya some coffee and beans and have ya sit a spell, but I'm fresh out." His sly eyes scanned the sky, as if looking for a message written in the tangle of treetops. "Looks like evenin's comin' on, so maybe you'd best be gettin' back, eh?"

"Sounds like good advice," July said cheerfully. "It's kind of creepy here. This guy is not what I . . ."

"How the hell did you get here?" Sweeny said impatiently. He took a step toward the man, hefting the axe. "Come on, now, don't play dumb with me."

The black eyes widened with fear. "Honest, mister, there ain't nothin' here, ain't no gold, nothin' but rocks and dust and somethin' for an old fool like me to . . ."

Sweeny dropped the axe, and grabbed the thin man by the lapels of his jacket and forced him back a step. "Don't bullshit me, now. How'd you get here?"

"Get here? Ya damn fool, I live here," he cackled, his face reddening.

"Jesus," Sweeny said. "How'd that fucking hearse get here." He gestured over his shoulder with his chin. "Not on that road, it didn't."

"Hearse?" The word squeaked out of the man's mouth like a jet of air forced through rubber.

"This goddamn car you were jerking off over a minute ago."

A glimmer of light flickered into the black eyes. "Oh, the limozeen. That what ya call it, a horse?"

Sweeny stepped back with repulsion, dropping his hands. After a moment, he said softly: "How the hell did the fucking hearse get here, old man?"

The thin man shrugged. "They came the back way." He jerked his thumb over his shoulder.

"There is no fucking back way," Sweeny said.

The narrow face turned toward July. "The back way," he whined.

Sweeny grabbed him by the front of his shirt with his left hand and scooped up the axe with his right. "Listen, you little scumbag," he hissed, "there ain't no fucking back way and you know it. Tell me how you got that fucking hearse in here, and what you're doing here with it, or I'll split your head open like a watermelon."

"Sweeny," July scolded, but he ignored her, tightening his grip on the man's shirt, twisting. He could feel a button snap loose, and then the little man began to cry. "There ain't nothin', nothin'," he blubbered. He put his bony hands around Sweeny's and pressed but he had no strength.

"Sweeny," July said again. "You're hurting him."

"I'm going to kill the little fuck if he doesn't give me some straight talk."

She put her hand on his arm and, as always, he could feel it all the way up to his shoulder. He looked at her, her blonde hair in a haze around her face, her blue eyes wide. Jesus, she was beautiful. *What the hell are we doing here? We could be . . .*

"Can't you see there's something wrong with this guy?" she said softly.

It was true, and he knew it. "With him? There's something wrong with everything around here." He gave the thin man a disgusted shove, dropped the axe and wiped his hands on his pants. The man teetered for a moment, then righted himself and gazed about aimlessly. From the relative safety of the five feet that now separated him from Sweeny, he observed his attacker with studied disinterest. "You can't have it, " he said after a moment, defiantly, the whine hovering at the edge of his voice.

"Hey, man, whaddya know?"

Sweeny spun around at the sound of the new voice. The tall black man he had ridden to the cemetery with was standing by the open pit of the false mine, his face beaming with pleasure. He wore a flowing brown robe that covered him from neck to feet and a matching skullcap was perched atop his bristling hair.

"Hey, look who's here," he said over his shoulder, then strode forward, the skirts of the robe flapping against his shins. Behind him, the other two tall men who'd been in the funeral car stepped out of the mine entrance, dressed in identical robes and skullcaps. The russet-haired man was blowing his nose with a dirty handkerchief trailing from his billowing sleeve.

"You here for this, too?" the black man said, coming up to Sweeny. "You're late, though, it's all over."

"Harriman always likes someone to be late," the bald man with the huge forehead said. "It makes a good impression."

"What's over?" Sweeny said. He clasped the black man by the shoulders, unsure if he was glad to see him or not, and whispered: "What's going on here, man?"

The black man twisted his mouth in amusement and looked sideways at his two companions, who were approaching. The bald man was wiping his bulging forehead with his sleeve. There were dirty rivulets of sweat in the lines of his cheeks. "Why, the funeral, man. What else? We just buried Nick."

"Damn it," Sweeny yelled, banging his fist against his thigh so hard it hurt for a moment. "I knew it, I knew it," he said aloud, but speaking to himself.

"Hey, knew what, man?"

"Sweeny," July said quietly. She had edged up beside him and took hold of his arm, nervously looking at the tall men as they formed a semi-circle around them.

"A fake," Sweeny said, ignoring them. "I knew it but I didn't let myself know it. I should have . . ."

"The funeral? Is that what you're talking about, man?"

"The goddamn funeral," Sweeny spit out. "Everything else, sure, I was wise to *that*, but I didn't think the actual . . ." He pinned his eyes on the black man's face. "*You* knew, though, didn't you?"

"Well, sure, man, we all knew." He looked at his companions. "Didn't we? It was just for show, we all knew that." His voice trailed off and he stared at Sweeny.

"Who the fuck was buried?"

"Oh." The black man shrugged. "It wasn't Nick. I thought you knew." He peered closely at Sweeny now, his eyes darkening, as if he had suddenly recognized him, or, more likely, realized that he *didn't* recognize him, that he didn't know this man at all. "Hey, are you all right, man?"

"Sure," Sweeny said. "I'm fine." But he felt his legs liquefying beneath him and saw the horizon tilting. Strong hands grasped his arms and he found himself sitting on a rock, his ears ringing. He could hear the steady drone of voices but couldn't make out the words. There was a strange sensation on his neck, as if a spider was crawling there, and he concentrated hard on it, making out the feel of fingers, easing the muscles, and he knew they were July's.

"How about taking a little of this, man," he heard a voice say. There were actual words, coming into his ears one at a time, with meanings beneath them like crawly insects under rocks. If he lifted each word, the meanings would come slithering out and he would know what it was all about. Sweeny lifted the words carefully, one at a time, and looked under them. Little black things, bugs, wriggled and took shape. There was something else, too—a smell, right under his nose.

Brandy.

The flask came into focus and Sweeny lifted his hands weakly to take it from the black hand, which steadied it as he raised it to his lips. He drank, spilling some of the smooth, burning stuff. A charge the size of a fist went careering down his throat, exploding against his stomach walls like the thousands of time pills he had seen in an animated TV commercial for cold medicine. He took another swallow, feeling his guts take hold, his legs solidify, his vision snap into focus. He shook his head, gulping air. "I'm okay, I'm okay." Blood was racing through a vein in his forehead like water in a trough, but he *was* okay. He looked up into the black man's beaming face, eyebrows arched like birds on a telegraph wire, about to take flight.

"You had us worried there for a minute, my friend. Thought this might turn out to be a double funeral." All traces of British elegance had drained from the black man's voice and he spoke in a matter-of-fact tone, a radio announcer's. He smiled broadly, displaying even, white teeth, more than should be able to fit in any jaw.

"No, no chance of that," Sweeny said. "Just a little too much heat. Little dizzy, that's all. Do you mind if I . . ." He reached for the flask in the black man's hand, his fingers brushing against the flapping sleeve of the robe.

"No, go ahead, help yourself, help yourself." The black man straightened up and watched Sweeny drink, then turned to his companions. "You know, I don't think our friend here is one of us."

"No," the russet-haired man said, shaking his head. "Definitely not."

The bald man muttered something in what might have been Latin, then added: "Harriman will be very unhappy." He looked sadder than ever, as if he still had some unpleasant task to perform.

"Where *is* Ormand?" the black man asked of no one in particular. He turned and scowled at the thin man, who had inched his way backwards to the hearse and was busy again with his polishing cloth. "Where's Harriman?"

The thin man ignored him, his arm a furious piston moving along the hearse's gleaming hood.

"Hey, you, dummy," the black man called sharply, but the man with the cloth continued his polishing, his jaw fixed with determination.

"Shit." The black man raised his arm in frustration and the robe flapped, creating the impression of a huge brown bird about to ascend.

"This is all a terrible mistake," July said. Her voice startled Sweeny— there wasn't anything *July* in it, nothing small or fragile or playful—and he swung his head to look at her. Her face was shining, as if the skin was on too tight. "We didn't realize this was a private thing, you know. We'll leave right away, you needn't trouble your friends. C'mon, Sweeny, let's go now." She tugged at his arm, frowning at him.

The black man's big hand stopped him before he could stand up. "That's all right, young lady." The gleaming white teeth radiated at July. "There's no trouble at all. Our friend will be interested in seeing your friend again, I'm sure. Mr. Sweeny, is it?" He peered down at Sweeny, who was lifting the flask to his lips again. "Feeling better now, Mr. Sweeny? I'd better take the flask. Wouldn't want you to overdo."

"Thanks." Sweeny handed over the flask. The brandy had done the trick, like a transfusion of blood, and his mind was working clearly again. The quality of the light in the clearing had changed subtly and everything was in sharper focus. In the pause between words, he could hear the soft *whish* of the thin man's cloth, the fluttering of leaves high above them, the silvery rush of water. July's hand was on his shoulder and he squeezed it with his own and smiled up at her. She was on his right, the three tall men in their ludicrous robes ringed around him, frowning down like schoolmasters. Their shoulders were so close, they blocked the view behind them, but Sweeny could hear the thin man toiling over the hearse, the wordless whine that had begun to seep out of his mouth like water from behind a stone. They had better get the hell out of there. *If we still can.*

Another sound was buzzing in his ears and he looked up. The three tall men had closed their eyes, clasped hands, and begun to softly chant in an unfamiliar language. A chalk-stroke chill ran down Sweeny's back. The tall men's faces were serene and closed. In a moment, when his strength returned, he would shove one and they'd all fall, still chanting. Then he and July could flee, run through the brush back to where the truck was hidden and be gone. There wasn't any fucking way they could get that fat hearse down the dirt track, he knew that, so there was no way they could pursue. But he knew, too, even as he thought all that, that there was no flight, no chance for it, and no will. What he had to do was here, ahead of him, not behind.

"Well, Mr. Sweeny, you again?"

He lifted his head and looked across a distance of a hundred feet or more into the glacial eyes of Harriman, who was standing just outside the mine entrance, brushing dust from his suit. Two other men were emerging from the pit behind him. One was the bashful young man who had been at Harriman's side at the funeral the day before; the other was Benno.

"Sweeny!"

The three tall men who had ringed him opened their circle with the sure-footed grace of angels spreading their wings. Sweeny stood up and July's hand slipped off his shoulder, leaving him with the sensation of her fingers trailing down his back sleek as a flow of butter into a bowl.

"Hey, Harold. Right on the job, eh? Personalized service, that's nice."

Benno sucked in his sallow cheeks and fixed his eyes on the tip of his left shoe. He might have teetered over had not the young man with the sandy hair wedged his shoulder against his. There was nothing pleasant-looking about the young man now and he seemed heftier, more muscular than Sweeny had earlier thought. He had smooth, stony cheeks, a straight, knife-cut mouth and a nose thin and menacing as a mosquito's snorkel.

"You do seem determined to pay your last respects to Nick," Harriman said. His voice was so cold and brittle it struck at Sweeny's ears like bits of hail slanting down from a sudden storm.

"We're old friends," Sweeny said.

"Yes, so you say," Harriman said dryly. "You're becoming quite a nuisance. And you've brought a charming friend with you, I see." His grey eyes shifted to July, who cocked her head and grinned fiercely back at him.

"How do you do?" she said in an aloof voice.

"Not very well, I'm afraid. Your friend, Mr. Sweeny, has been quite determined to spoil a very precious moment for me."

"Precious!" Sweeny snorted. The brandy had warmed him, filling him up like a balloon shot through with hot air.

"Yes, precious, damn it." Harriman, Benno, and the sandy-haired man had been walking forward and were beside the hearse now. Sweeny could see Harriman's cheeks reddening. "We're burying a dear friend, not carrying on a circus."

"Friend? He's *my* goddamn friend, not yours."

Harriman shook his head, a faint smile creeping along the corners of his thin mouth. "Oh, my poor dear Mr. Sweeny, Nicolas hasn't been *your* friend for years." There was a touch of warmth along the edges of his voice.

"Maybe we should leave," July said cheerfully. "We had no idea we were intruding." She took Sweeny's hand and tugged, but he held his ground.

"You bastard, Harriman, you robbed me," he said fiercely.

"Robbed you? Me?" Harriman's laugh was more a snort of disgust. "You threw it away."

"That doesn't make any difference," Sweeny said miserably. "It was mine to do with as I pleased." He could feel the vein in his forehead throbbing.

Harriman smiled indulgently. This close, Sweeny could see lines and wrinkles he hadn't noticed before, dark bags under the soft grey eyes, and a sheen, like frost, on his lips.

"You threw it away, my friend. You signified you had no more need for it. I merely came along and appropriated it, like someone picking up a discarded candy wrapper. Recycled is the word they use these days. It's considered quite proper."

"You robbed me, you fucking bastard!"

Behind Sweeny, the three tall men resumed their chant, their voices blending into one singsong drone, the rasping of a file against metal.

"Mr. Sweeny, please, there's no need to shout." Harriman turned his head slightly toward Benno: "Is he always like this?"

The drone behind Sweeny rose a notch and one voice broke for a moment to utter an indecipherable oath.

"He's usually very reasonable," Benno said woodenly. He looked up at Sweeny like a dog caught soiling the rug.

"Harold, Harold, why you?" Sweeny took a deep breath. "How did you get the hearse here?"

"The hearse?" Benno looked at Harriman nervously, then fixed his eyes at a point just above Sweeny's left shoulder. "We came the back way," he said stiffly.

"'THERE AIN'T NO FUCKING BACK WAY!" Sweeny lunged forward and grabbed the mortician by the neck, shaking him. Benno was tall but slender, and Sweeny's weight and force of rage buckled him. "There ain't no fucking back way," Sweeny yelled again. Benno's eyes were popping and his leathery face was going dark red, almost purple, like the rouge he applied to the cheeks of his clients. There was a flurry of arms around them, voices bouncing in all directions, something tugging at Sweeny's shoulders. He could hear the droning chant of the tall men rise to a shriek, blending into the whine of the thin man with the deep nostrils. Then he heard July's voice cutting through: "Sweeny, for God's sake, you'll kill him."

He let go and Benno dropped to his knees, a sound like an infant's cry bursting from his swollen lips. Sweeny hunched over him, his head lowered, panting, eyes fixed on Harriman, who stood no more than three feet away, watching him coolly with those imperturbable grey eyes, his mouth a thin, smooth black line across the bottom of his smooth, pink face. "You robbed me, you fucking bastard," Sweeny said through gritted teeth. He charged.

All his anger and frustration, building in him over the past few days like the pressure generated by alcohol in a still, exploded now as he rammed Harriman. He was a big man and still strong. Harriman, while considerably younger, was built with the grace and economy of a ballet dancer, and, despite all the warning signals Sweeny had given him, he was taken off guard. Sweeny's head thunked into his chest with the force of a wind raking a dead tree, sending him flying, crumpling. There was a dry sound of something snapping. Then the tumult of voices, which had stilled when he'd let go of Benno, erupted again, a melange of voices calling his name, cursing, invoking God and Jesus. He heard the black man's deep baritone and July's clear, high alto, and the chorus of tenors the two tall men provided, their chant abandoned, and the whining falsetto of the thin man crouching behind the hearse's fender, his blunted eyes blazing with fear. "I never, I never," he kept crying aloud, as if certain that the burst of violence would sweep him under next. The one voice Sweeny didn't hear was that of the bashful, athletic man with the sandy hair who was standing at the edge of the fray, a pistol in his hand. He was extending his arm uncertainly when July leaped on his back, her arms around his throat, feet kicking at his groin.

Sweeny was straddling Harriman, his knees on the groaning man's arms, fists smashing into his face, arms moving smoothly up and down with a comforting, reassuring smoothness of muscles, nerve, and bone. His arms were independent weapons, attached only vaguely to Sweeny, intent, on their own, to reducing Harriman's face to a sack of crushed bone and pulp. Sweeny watched this process with detached fascination, but something made him raise his head just as the sandy-haired man broke his arm free from July's grip and brought the gun down, its muzzle coming level with Sweeny's eyes.

He lunged forward just as the gun made its firecracker report and something whizzed past his head with a hiss like steam from the radiator in his apartment in New York. The force of his sudden move carried him over Harriman's head and onto the feet of the man with the pistol. He wrapped his arms around the legs, toppling over the body above them, which fell with a crash and a tangle of legs—the sandy-haired man's, July's, and Sweeny's. July was on top of the tangle and she rolled over, and Sweeny scrambled to his feet before the other man, the wind knocked out of him, could move. He moved quickly, doing a two-step: one foot came down hard on the man's gun hand, snapping the wrist; the other foot came back, then sprang forward sharply, cracking into the man's jaw. The sandy-haired man groaned, tried to roll over, then lay still as a spray of blood from his mouth began to irrigate the beaten ground. Sweeny bent down and grabbed the pistol, whirling around as the bald man and the russet-haired man, their robes flapping, surrounded him.

"Uh uh," Sweeny said, shaking his head and waving the pistol. The two tall men regarded him coolly, bowed their heads, stuffed their hands into their sleeves, and resumed their low, monotonous chant. He heard another sound and turned toward the pond, where the black man stood facing the waterfall, his back to Sweeny. He had taken off his robe and was naked, his arms upstretched; his shoulders were surprisingly thin, the skin on his scrawny shanks loose and wrinkled. The black man's head was thrown back and a ceaseless rush of unfamiliar words poured out of him toward the sky, which had been growing clearer and brighter.

"Wilf, for God's sake," Benno croaked. "What's the matter with you?" He was on his knees, a sorrowful frown on his reddened face, messaging his neck.

"With me? *You're* asking *me* what's the matter? I thought you were my friend, Harold."

"I *am* your friend, Wilf." Benno got to his feet and stood shakily, facing him. "I didn't want any of this to happen." He gestured down toward Harriman. Sweeny's eyes followed his hand to the two men in now-crumpled suits, red smears on their faces and the starched collars of their pastel shirts. They lay in odd positions more like those of broken dolls than of men. "I *told* him this was insane."

"You told him? Harold, for Christ's sake, what are you *doing* here?" Sweeny's voice lowered, softened. "What are you doing with *them*?"

Benno raised his hands in a gesture of bewilderment. "I'm just doing my job, Wilf. Conducting a funeral. It's peculiar, yes, but we get all sorts of odd requests. You wouldn't believe some of the things we've been asked to do. Last year, I remember, there was a woman . . ."

Sweeny waved him silent with the pistol. "Okay, I don't want to hear about it. I'm sick and tired of listening." His eyes darted from face to face, from the bowed heads of the tall chanting men to the arched, withered back of the black man hurling invocations to the heavens, then down to Harriman and his companion. They were both stirring, little moans sneaking from their lips like the roaches that used to scuttle out from under the refrigerator and across the cracked linoleum floor of the kitchen in New York. Sweeny nodded. His anger had passed and he was glad he hadn't killed Harriman. He'd never killed anyone, had managed to get through the war without killing or even hurting anyone, as far as he knew, without even firing a shot. He frowned at the pistol. Truth was, he didn't really know how to use it. The people he'd hurt in his life, it hadn't been with guns or even his hands.

There was a clattering behind him, the sounds furniture makes as it's toppled over by burglars in a hurry to flee, and Sweeny spun around as two men emerged from the entrance of the pit, vigorously brushing at their clothes. One of them wore a white lab jacket and an authoritative air; the other, in the chequered sports coat and hat he wore every day to the office, a cigarette sending up a curl of smoke from his stretched lips, was De Lisso.

"They oughta be more careful where they leave things," the police reporter said, gazing blindly into the daylight's glare.

"The lantern was there so you could see not to bump into other things," his companion said. He was lumpy, with hair growing in tufts from his ears, and was clearly irritated by the dirt on his white jacket. He grabbed De Lisso's sleeve and they stopped, staring at the naked black man, who had fallen to his knees, arms outstretched in supplication to the waterfall, an animal wail pulsing from his throat.

"Good God."

"Jesus," De Lisso echoed. "I told you these was a bunch of nuts." He let his gaze wander away from the black man to the knot of people standing by the hearse. "Hey, Sweeny, I been looking for you." His eyes were as round and dark as olives.

"Hey, Jim," Sweeny said coolly. His eyes darted self-consciously to the pistol in his hand when he saw the other man glance at it. "What brings you out here?" De Lisso had already delivered himself of more than Sweeny had ever heard him say.

"Eh? Well, don't get sore, but Callan said you was maybe onto something real big and I should sort of, you know, keep an eye on you, backup like."

Sweeny began to laugh, slapping his thigh with the pistol. "Oh, yeah, I'm onto something big, all right."

De Lisso and the other man strolled up cautiously. The man in the white jacket was as dark-bearded as Sweeny and his cheeks glistened with a blue haze. He looked with astonishment at Harriman, who was now sitting up, moaning, and the sandy-haired man, who had rolled onto his back, bubbles of bloody saliva popping from his mouth.

"Well, you know," De Lisso said awkwardly. "I hitched a ride up here with Doc Kramer, you know, the coroner?" He indicated the other man with his thumb. "He was coming anyway, so . . . say, Doc, there's a coupla patients for you, looks like."

The coroner shot a glance at the pistol in Sweeny's hand, then brushed past him and knelt beside Harriman. "Jesus," he whispered.

Sweeny stuffed the pistol into his belt. It had grown heavy in his hand. "Be my guest, doctor. I think they look worse than they are, though. I'm not skilful enough to do any real damage."

"You do that, Sweeny?" De Lisso said with wonder.

Sweeny ignored him and watched Kramer dabbing at Harriman's face with a handkerchief. "What brings *you* out here, doctor?"

Kramer looked up sharply and fixed Sweeny with a gaze dry as a cotton swab. "I came to sign a death certificate. Mr. Harriman here asked me if I'd . . ."

"Wait a minute," Sweeny cut him off. "For Limousine? I thought you'd already done that." Sweeny turned to De Lisso. "And how did you two get here, anyway? You came with him, you said? How?"

De Lisso took off his hat and mopped his forehead with a chequered arm. His slick black hair glistened with dandruff. Before he could answer, there was a shout and a splash behind them and they spun around as the black man, his arms flung high above his head, thrashed through the pond toward the waterfall, shouting, repeating a word Sweeny couldn't make out.

De Lisso's lips puckered in distaste. "Hey, seriously, Sweeny, Callan said you was maybe onto something big. I can't make heads or tails of it."

"This is it," Sweeny said. He was watching the black man shivering beneath the waterfall. There was something funny about him. "How'd you get here, Jim?"

"Who, us? We came the back way, Sweeny." The police reporter patted Sweeny gently on the arm. "Geez, I hate these lousy features. Creeps and kooks. Used to be, you wrote stories about people doing worthwhile things, things to help people, stuff like that, inneresting stuff. Nowadays, it's all weird stuff, that's all people wanna read about. Hell, just a buncha creeps and weirdos."

"There is no fucking back way," Sweeny said sharply. He was starting to move slowly toward the pond, his eyes fixed on the man under the water-fall. He wasn't black any more; the cascading water was melting away the makeup and, except for a deep streak running down from his chest to his belly and smudges under his eyes and around his nostrils, he was pallid as the underside of a dying fish.

"Yeah, well I'm just here because Callan said, you know, you was onto something big maybe. I hope you ain't sore."

Sweeny laughed. "No, I ain't sore."

"Good, that's good. What is this big story, though, Sween?"

"This is it." Sweeny was laughing hard, his side aching with it, his shoulders shaking, laughter rattling through his throat. He closed his eyes and dark night spun around him, punctuated by stars bright as matches crackling in the cold. The back of his head ached, as if it were resting against a hard floor, and dizziness swept over him, like a breath of cold air gusting into a room through a crack in the window. "This is it," Sweeny sputtered, and he snapped his eyes open, expecting to see night frosted with stars. Instead, the dizzying blue sky swum above him, laced with flimsy bands of cloud and, further to the west, a solid mass of dark cloud slouched toward them. As he watched, a thorn of electricity arced through the dark clouds, followed by a rumble of distant thunder. A moment later, he heard another sound bending itself into shape, then it was his name and the voice was July's.

"Sweeny."

She was standing beside him, her hand on his arm, and he turned so suddenly he banged into her. "Hey," she said.

Kramer and Benno were helping Harriman into the hearse, and the sandy-haired man, holding his broken wrist against his chest and wincing in pain, was right behind them. The two tall men had tossed off their robes and joined their friend in the pond, the three of them frolicking under the waterfall. Squinting into the sun, Sweeny could see their pale thin arms flashing, the thin trails of soaked, colourless hair running along their bloated bellies. De Lisso stood beside the pond, hip cocked, shaking his hatless head. He was writing on a folded pad of paper.

"Feel like getting wet?" Sweeny asked.

"Sure. Looks like we're going to anyway." She nodded in the direction of the dark cloud now racing their way. "Sounds like fun."

"Just a second."

He strode over to the hearse. The sun was behind his back and he had to squint through his reflection in the window to see Harriman lying small and crumpled on a bench, his face a red smudge. The lithe dancer's body was utterly without grace now, the immaculate suit jacket filthy and torn. The penetrating grey eyes were closed, the skin around them puffy and red. One spasmodically jerking hand was thrown up over his face; Sweeny could see brown mottles above the knuckles.

"You lose, Harriman," Sweeny shouted at the hearse door, shaking his fist at the crumpled man on the other side. "You fucking thief, you lose. You hear me, Harriman? You lose, you bastard, you lose."

Harriman made no movement and Sweeny reached for the door handle, but he was arrested by the reflection in the glass: an old, used-up man with tangled white hair, staring in surprise at something he hadn't expected. The man was over six feet, with broad shoulders and a sagging middle. Although the man was dressed, Sweeny could see him as if he were naked, the once-powerful chest caving in like the roof of an abandoned mine. The seamed belly protruded over the genitals, and the flesh on the arms hung like laundry from a line on a windless day, damp and heavy. But it was the face that was most striking—a curving, hairless forehead; thinning, almost colourless brows; shallow, watery eyes floating above deeply etched bruise-dark pouches; creased cheeks held in place by oversized ears and a plow-handle nose; a small, puckered mouth with cracked lips jutting over a chin long overtaken by folds of skin. It was a turtle's face, not a man's, the face of a turtle too long inside its shell. But there was nothing sheltered about this face: it was both callused and vulnerable, like the life behind it—it had been kicked, sat on, spat on, walked on, ignored, used, watched to bloody death, scraped to death, soaped silly, the life shaved off it. Watched to death, that was what was wrong with it.

Sweeny stepped back, stung, pulling the pistol from his belt. He pointed it at the glass, the muscles in his hand and arm tensing as he squeezed the trigger, but there was only a thin snapping sound and a sour smell, familiar but elusive.

"What the hell?" He fired again and there was another puny crack, another burst of stinging odour. He pulled the trigger rapidly but there was only the useless clicking of the iron hammer. And with each click, the rage and fear ebbed out of him, leaving him drained, calm, bewildered.

"Caps," De Lisso said beside him. "Sure make those guns look real these days. You should see the arsenal my kids got." Smoke wafted across his face from the cigarette and he squinted with disinterest at the pistol. A door slammed and Kramer came around the hearse, his eyes taking command.

"Haven't you done enough damage?" he asked, gesturing toward the pistol that hung uselessly from Sweeny's hand. "I'm afraid Mr. Harriman may be seriously injured. What did you hit him with, I'd like to know?"

"Jesus," Sweeny said. "God only knows."

"What's that?" the coroner asked sharply, peering at him.

"That's just an expression, Doc, just an expression. I *haven't* done enough damage. I ain't even begun." He wheeled around and threw the pistol with force into the pond, almost hitting the bald man, who was on his knees, the water up to his chin, singing what might have been a hymn in a language that might have been Greek.

"This is it, eh?" De Lisso said. He took the cigarette from his mouth and picked a speck of tobacco from his tongue.

"Yup," Sweeny said.

"Callan said it was something big, that's the only reason I'm here."

Sweeny shrugged. "Sure." He noticed the axe beside the hearse where he'd dropped it and bent for it.

He took July's outstretched hand and they went to the edge of the pond. The three tall men were sitting in a circle, their hands joined, eyes turned sightlessly to the sun. The muddy water came midway up their withered chests, to just below their sagging, hairy nipples. There were white hairs growing on the shrunken shoulders of the man with the drooping nose, and the russet mane receding along the back of his head was streaked with them, creating an illusion of sand on a sloping, deserted beach. The whites of the bald man's eyes were laid over with a delicate pattern of red cobweb lines. The man who had been black smiled toothlessly at him, his mouth hanging open like the sagging door of an abandoned cabin in a ghost town. "Hey, man," Sweeny called to him, but there was no response. Instead, there was a sharp burst of thunder, and the sky above them darkened.

Sweeny and July took off their shoes and socks and rolled up their pants, then waded into the water. Sweeny stepped on something sharp and bent over to retrieve it, pushing up his sleeve. It was the pistol. He handed it to July, dripping and glistening in the sun. "Here, hold onto this."

"Makes sense. You never can tell what's gonna happen in the parks these days. Maybe we'll even see a bear."

At its deepest, in the pond's centre, the water was no more than waist high and it was considerably shallower along the edges. With his pants legs rolled up above the knee, Sweeny managed to get to the waterfall without getting them wet, but July sloshed through the water after him with abandon.

"Here's where we get wet," he said. "Can't get around it."

"I *am* wet."

They took deep breaths and ducked through the flashing cascade, the water a cold shock on their heads and necks, and scrambled dripping and cold onto the ledge at the cave's mouth. Sweeny took July into his slippery arms, holding her till her teeth stopped chattering. Light filtered in softly through the steaming curtain of water behind them and they were able to dimly make out the contours of the low cavern. It was dome-shaped, with stalactites hanging perilously from its low, oppressive ceiling. The mouths of tunnels leading off the main cavern yawned black and forbidding at them. There was a strong smell, rank in their nostrils, of the earth's juices.

"Somebody's been eating eggs in here," July said. "Rotten eggs."

"Sulfur. Like matches." Sweeny ran a finger along the wet stone above his head and extended it toward her nose.

"The better to burn with," she said, wrinkling her nose and turning away.

There was a kerosene lantern sitting on a natural rock ledge. Sweeny's heart sunk when he touched it—it was still warm. "They've been in here." He leaned the axe against the ledge and struck a match; the greasy wick accepted it immediately. Shadows sprung up on the sloping cavern walls and a yellow glow ebbed from the lantern's streaked glass.

"Sweeny, oh God, what's that?"

July was pointing across the cavern at a long narrow box surrounded by rocks. Someone had been attempting to wedge it in, perhaps cover it entirely, but had given up, or been interrupted. Sweeny shook his head, dispelling a new wave of dizziness. In the lantern's pale light, July seemed thin, sexless. Her wet hair was pressed tightly against her cheeks.

"It's a coffin." He took her hand and led her across the cavern, picking their way over stones and debris. Over the years, many people had been in the cave. They'd left beer cans, yellowed cardboard boxes, the printing from their labels evaporated away, refuse of food, sex, and the smaller pleasures. A chill ran along Sweeny's spine like a child's hand on a banister. *It wasn't safe after all.*

The coffin was a simple grey laminated box, without marking, but there wasn't any question in his mind that it was the one from the funeral, the one he'd assumed Limousine had been in.

Had been. The stench of the sulfur swarmed over him and he had to reach for July's arm to keep from falling over. He would have to find out.

"You okay?"

"Sure." He kicked at a rock. "This is where the ashes were, under here."

"They were trying to bury the coffin there, weren't they? Cover it with rocks?" She made a face. "Ugh."

He felt her tremble, and his own strength and sureness returned. He took her into a tent of his arms, her face pressing wet and cool against his shoulder. She had put the pistol in her belt, and it loomed hard and cold between them, pressing against his groin. He held her tightly and a shudder passed between them like a spark of electricity, arcing from his arms into her shoulders, from her belly to his, from his face to her hair, from her breasts to his chest, along the tight passageway between their legs. For a moment, they were one creature, one lonely beast holding onto itself in its cave, hidden from the world, hiding its face in its hands.

The sound of an engine coming to life broke them apart. The smooth purr of the hearse was barely audible above the *swoosh* of the waterfall. Sweeny went to the cave's mouth and stood sideways, watching through a crevice in the rock where the fall's spray couldn't soak him. The sleek grey car was backing up, sunbursts dancing along the windshield hiding the faces of the occupants. Sweeny squinted, but it was useless, and his lips slowly curled into a small smile. Whoever had pointed out the pun to him— Benno? Or was it Delancy?—had been right: the hearse *was* a limousine, that's all, just a vehicle for getting from one place to another. Nothing more than that. The car stopped, a window was rolled down, and Harriman stuck his head through it. Even from his distance, Sweeny could see the elegant man's face was clean and shining, all trace of blood washed away, the bruises not yet turning black and puffy, and there was a silver whistle, the kind scoutmasters carry on plastic lanyards around their necks, in his thin lips. A clear, sharp stream of sound burst from the whistle with astonishing clarity and the three tall men rose noisily and splashed their way out of the pond. They talked and laughed as they dried themselves with their robes. The bald man with the bulging eyes looked back over his shoulder toward the waterfall as they walked to the hearse, but Sweeny didn't think he saw him. Doors swung open, the tall men stuffed their angular legs inside, doors slammed shut, Harriman gave one final, triumphant toot on the whistle. The engine revved and, in a moment, the car disappeared behind the ruin of the cabin and the waterworks. There was no sign of Benno or Kramer or De Lisso, but the idiot with the nostrils like mine pits stood in the clearing watching after his guests' departure, nodding his head. When the sound of the engine had receded, he walked slowly to the sagging door of the cabin, hesitated for a moment to look up at the darkening sky, then went in. The waterfall masked the sound but Sweeny imagined he could hear the door creak as it swung closed, a circular kind of music like that his grandfather's rocker used to make on the loose boards of the porch. A bird fluttered low over the clearing, its *caw* sounding sharply through the waterfall's humming curtain. There was a flash of lightning, another clap of thunder.

"So long, Harold," Sweeny said, so quietly the words barely registered in his own ears. He lit a cigarette, sucking the smoke in greedily, as if there were some life-giving substance amid the particles of ash and tar and gas that seared through his lungs. He coughed, first mildly, to ease the tickle, then violently, his lungs rebelling, and he had to grasp hold of a sta-lactite to steady himself. He tossed the cigarette into the waterfall, spit-ting after it and wiping his eyes. His ribs ached from the effort of his coughing fit but his head was clear. There was something beautiful about it all, the final gestures so perfect in their execution, the subtleties so well blended, that appealed to his sense of the dramatic, to the romantic that still lived within him, and his mouth formed the small smile again. If he sat down and thought about it, he was certain, it would all make sense finally, except for the pieces that, after all, didn't *have* to fit. But it didn't really matter, did it?

"You okay, Sweeny?" July stood where he'd left her, within the small cir-cle of light cast by the flickering lantern.

"Sure, never better." He wondered where she fit in, but blinked the thought away. He didn't want to know. "You sit over there." He gestured to a flat rock at the cave's mouth from which she'd be able to watch him and still, at any sound, swing around and gaze out unobstructed through the ceaseless flow of the waterfall, its colours rippling like an electric spark. "Bring your cannon with you and stand guard."

"Sit guard, you mean."

Sweeny didn't reply. He guided her onto the rock with his hands on her shoulders and leaned over to kiss her. Even here, the air thick with the odour of sulfur and ashes, she smelled clean and pure as a baby's breath. Her mouth was soft, sweet, and warm, like a handful of raspberries just picked in the sun.

"Grist for your mill," Sweeny said. He tapped her nose with his finger.

"Yeah." She didn't smile.

"Like your father used to say."

"Yeah." They gazed at each other in silence for a moment. Sweeny's body hummed with the purity of a wire in the wind, producing enough light and heat to carry him for a lifetime.

"About my father . . ." July let her eyes fall behind a curtain of lashes.

"Forget it. You know, I once did a story about a guy who had an eye transplant. Cornea, actually. This was a few years ago. It was in New Jersey. Trenton. There's a big state prison there, and there was a guy on death row who, you know, left his body to a hospital. The day they electrocuted him, they did the transplant on this other guy, a baker, I think he was, a Cuban refugee. He'd been blind for I don't know how long."

July shivered. "And it worked?"

"Sure. A couple of weeks later, he could see good as you or me. Through dead man's eyes. That's what the headline said on the story I did. Dead man's eyes." He shrugged. "I just thought of that."

The coffin was sealed and he was glad he'd brought the axe. It took several whacks to break it open. He knelt beside it, holding the lantern high with one shaky hand, raising the lid with the other. Except for the rushing of the waterfall behind him, it was silent in the cave and he could hear his heart rattling against his ribs. Then he heard another sound and he realized it was raining, the chime of rain falling into the pond blending with the silver rush of the waterfall. "We're gonna get soaked walking back," July said.

Something small scurried across his foot and Sweeny looked up, disoriented. The low ceiling of the cave was as black as sooty night, frosted with limestone tears glistening like stars, myriad specks of light travelling from great distances across the reaches of heaven. He bent over and peered into the casket.

There was a body inside all right, that of a big man—that much, at least, wasn't illusion—but there were shadows on the face. He reminded himself that he had never seen Limousine, the man who had checked into the Queen's Hotel and died in the middle of the night, alone in a room so far in time and distance from anything that mattered. Except that he wasn't far at all, he'd come home. He'd fallen out of bed—Charlie Cook said some-one heard a *thump*—and he must have lain there for a moment, jarred awake, surprised to find himself on the floor, surprised to find himself dying, feeling the buckled linoleum beneath him and some little thing skit-tering across one bare foot. Perhaps, from where he lay, he could see the window, staring down at him like the vacant eye of a lunatic. One pane was cracked, a jagged black cartoon lightning bolt, and behind it was clear black night, clear black winter night, frosted with stars, fireflies beating against a screen door. He could feel the hardness of the floor beneath him, the cold nostril breath of night snorting in through the cracks in the win-dow. He could feel his blood, its rhythm slowing, his skin beginning to dry, his bones starting to go brittle.

Sweeny shook his head, scattering the dizziness that was settling around him like fog. "Sweeny?" July called from her guard station on the rock, her voice echoing softly against the walls of the cave, but he didn't answer. He reached his hand slowly into the coffin, his fingers prepared for the soft touch of whiskers, pulling them back abruptly from the dark face as if snapped at by a bare electric wire. The face was smooth shaven—and still warm.

He raised the lantern higher, the way he used to do when he would sit on the porch with his grandfather in late evening, reading to him, when darkness had overcome them, and the shadows skittered away like mice in a kitchen. "Sweeny?" July called again, her voice soft as light from distant stars penetrating the indifferent night. He glanced in her direction but his vision was obscured by a blizzard of shooting stars bright as matches crackling in cold winter night, the sulfurous walls of the cavern luminous with them, sparking in the empty darkness. A new wave of dizziness swept over him, the blood in his temples roaring. His shoulder ached. It took all his strength for him to lift himself off one knee, bending forward, his heart noisy as a lion in its cage. *Dear God*, he said, but the words froze in his mouth. The eyes were closed on the face below him, but recognition was easy enough.

DAVE MARGOSHES is a journalist and writer of fiction and poetry. His recent books include the novel *I'm Frankie Sterne* (NeWest Press), and the poetry collection *Purity of Absence* (Beach Holme). His published work includes dozens of short stories and poems in magazines and anthologies, as well as several other books, including: *We Who Seek: A Love Story*; the short story collections *Fables of Creation* and *Long Distance Calls*; two other volumes of poetry, *Northwest Passages*, and *Walking at Brighton*; and a popular biography of the socialist premier of Saskatchewan, *Tommy Douglas: Building the New Society*.

Margoshes is the winner of a number of awards for his writing, including the Stephen Leacock Poetry Prize (1996) and the John V. Hicks Award for fiction (2001).

Margoshes lives in Regina, Saskatchewan.